Exceptional

Circumstances

Also by James Bartleman

The Redemption of Oscar Wolf (2013)
As Long as the Rivers Flow (2011)
Raisin Wine: A Boyhood in a Different Muskoka (2008)
*Rollercoaster: My Hectic Years as Jean Chrétien's Diplomatic
Advisor 1994–1998* (2005)
*On Six Continents: A Life in Canada's Foreign Service,
1966–2002* (2004)
Out of Muskoka (2004)

Exceptional

Circumstances

a novel

James Bartleman

DUNDURN
A J. PATRICK BOYER BOOK
TORONTO

Copy Editor: Michael Melgaard
Design: Laura Boyle
Printer: Webcom
Cover Design: Laura Boyle

Image credits: RYGER/Shutterstock.com

Library and Archives Canada Cataloguing in Publication

Bartleman, James, 1939-, author
        Exceptional circumstances / James Bartleman.
Issued in print and electronic formats.

ISBN 978-1-4597-2910-0 (pbk.).--ISBN 978-1-4597-2911-7 (pdf).--
ISBN 978-1-4597-2912-4 (epub)
        I. Title.
PS8603.A783E94 2015   C813'.6   C2014-905054-2
                                                      C2014-905055-0

1   2   3   4   5   19   18   17   16   15

Conseil des Arts
du Canada

Canada Council
for the Arts

Canada

ONTARIO ARTS COUNCIL
CONSEIL DES ARTS DE L'ONTARIO
an Ontario government agency
un organisme du gouvernement de l'Ontario

We acknowledge the support of the **Canada Council for the Arts** and the **Ontario Arts Council** for our publishing program. We also acknowledge the financial support of the **Government of Canada** through the **Canada Book Fund** and **Livres Canada Books**, and the **Government of Ontario** through the **Ontario Book Publishing Tax Credit** and the **Ontario Media Development Corporation**.

Care has been taken to trace the ownership of copyright material used in this book. The author and the publisher welcome any information enabling them to rectify any references or credits in subsequent editions.

J. Kirk Howard, President

Printed and bound in Canada.

Visit us at
Dundurn.com | @dundurnpress | Facebook.com/dundurnpress | Pinterest.com/dundurnpress

Dundurn
3 Church Street, Suite 500
Toronto, Ontario, Canada
M5E 1M2

For Marie-Jeanne

"Acts of torture can be committed by almost everyone — not just by psychopaths."

— *New Scientist*, November 2004

Contents

Contents

Foreword

In quiet moments — and I have many of those now at my retirement home in sleepy Penetang — I often think back to my tumultuous beginnings as a junior diplomat more than three decades ago. I ask myself whatever possessed me to go from being an idealistic twenty-three-year-old hoping to make the world a better place to becoming an amateurish secret agent in war against international terror — and later on, an even more hapless spy subcontracted out by my superiors in the Department of Foreign Affairs to work for the CIA. I suppose I went wrong in part because I was young, naïve, and impressionable, and had little experience of the world outside small-town Ontario. But I also thought I had something to prove — wanting to demonstrate that a Métis in the 1960s, when my people were looked down upon as outsiders, could be just as good as anyone else in Canadian society in anything we set out to do. I did nothing illegal, and my accomplishments — if that is what they could be called — led to praise and early promotion. This book, more a confession than a memoir, is my attempt to come to terms with my reckless behaviour in those early years.

Luc Cadotte,
Penetang, June 2002

Part One

Canada

July 1943 to November 1968

1: Love and Ambition

I come from a Métis working-class background. Every year from May to October, my dad helped load and unload freighters on the docks of Penetang, a small town on the southeasterly tip of Georgian Bay. He drew unemployment insurance and fished and hunted the rest of the year. When I was a kid, I got along well with everybody — Métis, white, and Indian. We all went to the same elementary school and my friends came home with me to eat Mama's *tarte au sucre* and to listen to Grandpapa's stories of his days first as a fur trader and later as a soldier in the trenches during the Great War — as he still called World War I. We played cowboys and Indians late into the evenings. Everybody wanted to be cowboys, even the Indian kids — nobody read any racist meaning into it — at least not when we were really young.

My friends made me welcome in their places — the Métis and Indian mothers fed me hot bannock topped with brown sugar and the white ones gave me peanut butter cookies. But as the years went by, and as we grew older and started high school, our relationships changed. The white kids found excuses to avoid coming to my place. A couple of Métis friends made ugly racist remarks about the guys from the reserve when they weren't around and stopped inviting them home. Then, one by one, the

Indians dropped out of school until there were only a handful left, and when the white and Métis kids ran into them on the streets, they pretended they didn't know each other. When white kids from families moving into town to take jobs at the ship-yard showed up at school, I overheard some of my Métis buddies tell them they weren't really Métis. They were pure French they claimed — *pure laine* as they say in Quebec. But they were as brown-skinned as me or any Indian, and I could tell the white kids didn't believe them.

It was around then that I began to understand the complex-ities of racial identity in our small town. The Indians, I saw, were at the bottom of the social scale. The Métis, because of the white blood of our fur-trader forbearers, ranked higher than Indians but still lower than whites because of our Indian ances-try. To be white was to be at the top. It was simple enough. Then one day I went with my parents on a shopping trip to Toronto. A group of Franco-Ontarians from somewhere up north were laughing and joking among themselves in French as they waited for a movie theatre to open on Yonge Street. "Speak white, you French bastards," someone shouted from out of the shadows. That's when I found out that white people dis-criminated among themselves as well.

I'm proud of the fact I never pretended I was a dark-skinned white — an Italian or Greek, for example — even though I might have been able to get away with it. I loved my brown-skinned parents and my dark brown-skinned grandpapa, and wouldn't hurt their feelings for anything in the world. As a child in ele-mentary school, I had worn my identity lightly. As a teenager in my last years of high school, exposed to the atmosphere of prejudice permeating the halls, I asserted my pride in my herit-age. Although basically shy, I began telling anyone who would listen that Louis Riel, who led the Métis nation in two disastrous rebellions against Canada out west in the nineteenth century, was my hero. I put a Métis flag on my bedroom wall and took to wearing a Métis sash on the anniversary of his death. I may have overdone it, but for the rest of my life, I have bristled whenever anybody spoke ill of my people.

Life was otherwise good. I did well in school — not surprising since I was one of those lucky people blessed with an exceptional memory. It wasn't photographic, but it was as close as you could get. I could store away and recall almost everything I read or heard. "It's a gift from God," the parish priest told me. "But don't let it go to your head. You're no smarter than anyone else, but it's an aptitude that'll help get you through school and when you look for a job."

By high school, I had earned enough money from working alongside my dad on the docks in the summers to buy myself a 1950 Ford hardtop sedan. It was rusted and sometimes wouldn't start without a push, but it had a manual shift and I could beat any of the other guys who drove Chevs or Pontiacs in street races. I also had a girlfriend, Corinne Lalande, an Indian girl from the nearby Christian Island reserve who lived with relatives in town. We had known each other since we were kids in the same grade in elementary school, but we hadn't paid much attention to each other until high school when we defied the unwritten convention and started to hang out together.

She took me to pow wows and I took her to Métis fiddling contests. She took me canoeing in the waters around Christian Island and I took her horseback riding, my favourite weekend sport throughout high school. Her folks invited me to their house for meals and my family made her welcome at my place. Eventually, she started coming home with me every day after school and we'd do our homework together. She'd join us for mass and share our big lunches on Sundays. At these times, Grandpapa made her laugh, telling her his grandmother had been a good Catholic Indian from the Cat Lake Indian reserve in northwestern Ontario, winking at me and saying that Indian girls made the best wives.

But Corinne and I didn't need any encouragement from Grandpapa to take our relationship further. In those days, most young people in Penetang — and across Canada for that matter — married young, sometimes when they were still teenagers. We were madly in love, walking around hand-in-hand, causing a stir because she was so beautiful with her long straight black hair, clear skin, and classical Indian features. I wasn't bad looking in those days either, being tall with European features and light brown skin like so many of the Métis guys. We talked endlessly about sharing our lives together and decided that after high school, we'd enrol in one of those one-year business schools that taught typing, shorthand, office management, and bookkeeping. She'd focus on typing and dictation with the goal of becoming somebody's private secretary. I'd concentrate on typing, file management, and accounting, and look for a job as a payroll clerk in the shipyards after graduation.

We decided that as soon as we got jobs, we'd have a wedding service in my family's parish church followed by a reception and dinner at the community hall over at the reserve. By that time, we'd have picked out an inexpensive apartment to rent — something over a hardware store or Chinese restaurant. We'd save every penny to buy a vacant lot close to my parents and eventually we'd have the money to put into building on it. I was good at working with my hands and would do the work myself, with help from my dad, grandpapa, and my cousins and uncles — all the members of the Cadotte clan.

Like a lot of other couples just starting out in life in Penetang, we'd spend the first few years living in the basement. We'd layer tarpaper on the top of the capped ceiling to keep out the rain and snow and partition the open space below into a bedroom, living/dining room, bathroom, and kitchen. After a year or two

— depending on how much money we'd put away, and whether any babies had come along — I'd begin work framing in the first floor. Eventually, in ten years or so, the house would be finished and paid for, complete with a screen porch where Corinne and I could spend the summer evenings with our children. Both families supported our plans and we couldn't have been happier. Then on January 12, 1962, in my last year of high school, the course of our lives changed.

My day had started as it always did at that time of the year. I loaded up the furnace with coal to last the day, shovelled out the driveway and path to the road, drove to Corinne's to pick her up, navigated my way to school through a tunnel of ten-foot-high snow banks, parked my car as usual behind the school, and went in to attend classes. Everything went well until our three o'clock class on the history of New France. The teacher, Angus Fairbanks, came in and sat on the edge of his desk, smiling and swinging his leg as he always did when he thought he had something interesting to tell us.

"As you know," he said, "I've always believed it important in the teaching of history, even at the high-school level, to use original sources to supplement textbooks. I have here in my hand," he said, holding up a book of documents, "English translations of the *Jesuit Relations*, sent to the Paris headquarters of the Jesuits by their missionaries in the field. The one I'll read from describes the martyrdom of St. Jean de Brébeuf and Gabriel Lalemant, tortured to death by the Iroquois during their attack on the Huron town of St. Ignace, a few miles from here, on March 16, 1649."

After introductory remarks on the Jesuit attempts to convert the Indians, Fairbanks started to read. It was a subject we all knew. We'd studied it in elementary school and had been listening for years to our parents and grandparents talk about the seventeenth-century battles between the Hurons and the Iroquois in old Huronia, the homeland of the Hurons. We knew that the Iroquois, provided with weapons by Dutch traders, had fought a vicious war for the control of the fur trade against the Hurons, who were backed by the French. Without Fairbanks having to tell us, we knew that the Hurons had lost and fled to make new homes elsewhere. We knew several of the French priests had been had been killed and canonized as saints. We knew they'd been buried not far away, in Midland at a church called Martyr's Shrine which brought a lot of tourist dollars into the region.

But the people around Penetang, at least the ones I knew, had always been uncomfortable with the subject. Terrible things had happened in those far-off days that weren't fit to mention, certainly not around the dinner table. And nobody, especially the veterans, including my own dad and grandpapa, who had seen and maybe done awful things overseas, wanted to be reminded of the things people sometimes did to each other. And with so many Indians living in the reserves around Penetang, nobody wanted to embarrass them by bringing up past massacres by Indian warriors, even if those warriors were from different tribes and came from somewhere else. We had enough problems getting along with each other as it was. All of us wanted Fairbanks to stop reading and put away his book, but nobody dared interrupt him — he was, after all, the teacher, and teachers were more respected in those days.

And so we all sat there, not daring to look at anyone else as Fairbanks, a newcomer to the community, unaware of our local taboos and oblivious to the damage he could cause, carried on reading. And by the time he finished, my so-called extraordinary memory was a gift I regretted having. For the text I stored away against my will, and which would return periodically throughout my life to trouble me, began with a flourish and ended in horror. The following is an excerpt from what he read with the gruesome parts cut out to spare the feelings of the reader:

> Father Jean de Brébeuf and Father Gabriel Lalemant had set to go to a small village, called St. Ignace, distant from our cabin by about a short quarter of a League, to instruct the savages and the new Christians of the village. It was on the 16th day of March in the morning, that we perceived a great fire at the place these two good Fathers had gone. This fire made us very uneasy; we did not know whether it was enemies or if the fire had caught in some of the huts of the village.
>
> The Reverend Father Paul Ragueneau, our superior, immediately resolved to send someone to learn what might be the cause. But no sooner had we formed the design of going there to see, than we perceived several savages on the road, coming straight toward us. We all thought it was the Iroquois who were coming to attack us; but having considered them more closely, we perceived that they were Hurons who were fleeing from the fight, and who had escaped from the combat.
>
> The savages told us the Iroquois came to the number of twelve hundred men, took their village and seized Father Brébeuf and his companion and set fire to all the huts. They proceeded to vent their rage on those two fathers, for they took them both and stripped them entirely naked and fastened each to a post. They tied both their hands together. They tore the nails from their fingers. They beat them with a shower of blows

from cudgels, on the shoulders, the loins, the belly, and the face — there being no part of the body that did not endure this torment. Although Father Brébeuf was overwhelmed by the weight of these blows, he did not cease to encourage all the new Christians who were captives like himself to suffer as well, that they might die well, in order to go with him to Paradise.

Those butchers, seeing that the good Father began to grow weak, made him sit down on the ground, and one of them, taking a knife, cut off.... Another tore out.... Others came to drink his blood ... saying that Father Brébeuf had been very courageous to endure so much pain as they had given him and that by drinking his blood, they would become courageous like him....

When Fairbanks described the torture and deaths of the priests, we all bowed our heads, not in prayer but in embarrassment, not wanting to look around and catch the eyes of our fellow students. About half the class were Métis and the others were mainly the sons and daughters of white British and French settler families, with three Indian girls, including Corinne, in the mix. I felt sorry for Corinne and the other girls from the reserve. Their ancestors had played no part in the events the teacher was describing but I was certain they were feeling humiliated and ashamed just for being Indian. I felt that way as well, even though I was only part Indian. Grandpapa had told me there were many Indians in my family tree, in addition to his grandmother, and it just made sense that one or more of those distant relations were alive in those days. For all I knew, they might well have participated in the massacre.

I stole a look at Fairbanks who remained perched on the edge of his desk, still swinging his leg nervously, his face flushed with excitement, a small smile on his face, and his eyes glued to the text he was reading. *He's enjoying doing this to the Indian and Métis kids,* I thought. I glanced at one of my classmates who came from an old settler family — Hilda Greene it was. We'd been in the same class since Grade 1 and I'd never like her. Her face was twisted into a humourless grin and the freckles on her face were glowing like Christmas tree lights. I imagined her worst stereotypical views of Indians and Métis were being confirmed. I wanted to stand up and tell Fairbanks to stop reading. "The material's grotesque," I wanted to shout. "You're embarrassing everyone," I wanted to scream ... but I didn't.

Fairbanks finally completed reading the worst parts and moved on to the peaceful finish — like a pianist playing a piece of classical music who ends a thunderous passage with calm reconciliation. But there was no feeling of understanding in the classroom, just a deep, uneasy silence. Nobody spoke, nobody looked up from their desks. I heard Fairbanks say, "Well, what do you think? That brought history alive didn't it? If that doesn't raise your awareness of the inhumanity of man to man, nothing will." It was a truism that grated on my ears; he'd probably picked it up at university.

Still, nobody said anything. Finally I heard him call out my name. I don't want to boast — that's not my style — but I was the top student in history and could always be counted on to offer my opinion on any subject under discussion. "Luc," he said, almost imploring me to break the sullen silence in the room, "what do you think? Help me get a discussion going."

I said nothing, and then looked up to see the others looking at me, expecting me to take the lead. "What do you think?" Fairbanks asked. "A little hard to digest, but you must admit that really brings local history alive."

"I'm sorry, sir, but you wouldn't want to hear what I really think."

"No, go ahead, Luc. Get your concerns off your chest. We need honest debate."

"I think it was a big mistake to read the document that way. It wasn't put in context."

"It seemed pretty straightforward to me."

"Not to excuse the Iroquois," I said. "But their actions were no worse than what the so-called civilized Europeans were doing at that time in history. Dominican priests were acting as agents of the Inquisition in Spain and Portugal and torturing and burning people by the thousand at the stake to save their souls. Innocent people throughout Europe and in the American colonies were being put to death for witchcraft. Anyone suspected of breaking the law was routinely tortured in those days to get confessions before being put to death. The Inquisition threatened Galileo with torture if he didn't deny that the earth moved around the sun. You got to consider context," I said. "The behaviour of the Iroquois has to be seen in context. Indians today shouldn't be judged by the actions of some warriors in the heat of battle centuries ago. Reading that old report like that hurts the feelings of Indians today. Context is everything."

"I'm sorry if I've upset you," was all he could say.

That just got me even more worked up and I carried with my angry rebuttal. "And what makes today's white people think they're more humane than the seventeenth-century Iroquois. Most, if not all, of the so-called advanced countries in the world, including Britain, France, Spain, Portugal, and the United States, hauled millions of Africans across the ocean to lives of slavery in the Americas throughout the eighteenth century and most of the nineteenth century. The United States and most Latin American countries treated Indians like vermin fit only to be exterminated. In this century, the Germans murdered civilian non-combatants by the million during World War II. Even in Canada, as we meet here today, the government is dragging Indian children from their homes to be sent to be brainwashed in residential schools."

Fairbanks let me go on until I calmed down and said my response was exactly what he had hoped to stimulate. "I want you to feel deeply about history. I don't want you to take my word for anything. I don't want you to take the word of a priest writing about a slaughter that took place a few miles from here without making up your own minds on who was in the right."

But nobody else said anything. Corinne began to cry, which made me feel awful. I think Fairbanks realised he had made a mistake but didn't know what it was. "It wasn't my intent to demonize the Indians, if that's what's bothering you. I just wanted you to think for yourselves."

He then asked a number of questions to stimulate debate, but nobody spoke up and the rest of the period was spent in an embarrassing silence. When we filed out the door at the end of class, however, I overheard Hilda Greene, her lips curled in derision, whisper to one of her friends, "Indians were savages back in them old days and they're savages today. My dad says it's in their nature and they'll never change."

When we went back to history class the next day, an unhappy Fairbanks said he had received calls from parents to say he had gone too far in reading the *Jesuit Relation*. Someone had told him he was a sadist, out to titillate and not educate their children. Looking my way, he said someone else said his presentation lacked context. The chairman of the school board, who hinted his contract might not be renewed for the next year, had called to complain.

"The people of Penetang obviously want their history be portrayed as it is in movies, with all the bad things happening off screen and all endings happy ones," he said. "But I can't teach that way, and I'm going to take a job somewhere else next year where the locals are more open-minded. In the meantime, I have no intention of saying anything more in this class about Indians or Huronia."

The incident made a lasting impression. Grandpapa used to say the Métis had inherited the best of what our white and Indian ancestors had to offer. We were better singers and fiddlers than the French, better tap and square dancers than the Scotch, better trappers and canoe men than the Indians, and braver and better looking than the whites and Indians. He said these things to make me laugh, but I believed there was a grain of truth to them. But the remark of the girl about the inherent savagery of Indians planted a tiny seed of doubt in my mind. Did my Indian blood condemn me to come to no good, no matter what I did in life? Was I genetically predestined to failure? Was the real reason I always made a big show of expressing pride in my Métis identity an attempt to mask internal doubts?

I hoped not, but wasn't sure. But suddenly, I no longer wanted to become a payroll clerk, or to live in a basement after I got married, find fulfillment helping raise a family, and spend my time sitting in a screened porch. I wasn't sure what I wanted to do, but I wanted to prove to myself that a Métis was just as good as a *pure laine* Franco-Ontarian or the son or daughter of settlers from the old country. To do that, I'd have to set my sights on becoming something different for the rest of my life. I'd have to go to university and become an engineer or a school teacher, something to prove myself to people like Hilda Brown.

The next day, after classes were over, I went to see Fairbanks in his classroom before he left for the day. If he was mad at me for taking him on in history class, he didn't show it. In fact, he was delighted when I told him I was thinking of going to university and wanted his advice. He probably thought his reading of the *Jesuit Relation* had led to my decision to rethink my ambitions in life.

"If you don't go to university, what would you do?" he asked, smiling broadly.

"I'd go to Business College and study to become a payroll clerk. Then Corinne and I'd get married and settle down here in Penetang."

"You'd be making a big mistake," he said, no longer smiling. "Not the part about marrying Corinne. She's a fine girl, but you have the ability to go far in life and you'd soon be bored in a clerical job. In my opinion, you should take a four-year honours history program and apply to join the Department of External Affairs as a Foreign Service officer. You love history, especially diplomatic relations, and have an extraordinary grasp of the subject. In fact, in twenty years of teaching, I've never come across a student with your abilities. You would have to study hard and pass some tough exams, but you'd get in."

"But I'm not sure I'd want to spend a good part of my life outside Canada. And Corinne probably wouldn't want to leave the Georgian Bay area."

"Why don't you ask her? Her answer might surprise you. But if you don't want to become a diplomat, why not become a high school history teacher and get a job in this part of the province when you graduate? "

Although I didn't let it show, I was by then excited at the prospect of going to university. But I still needed some reassurance. "But none of the guys around here go to university," I said. "Everybody'll think I'm a snob."

"No they won't. They'd be proud to see one of their own getting ahead — and you'd be a role model for the Métis and Indian youngsters. And don't be intimated by the cost. Your dad can speak to some of his contacts on the freighters and get you a job as a deck hand for the summer. You can take out a student loan to pay the difference. You have no excuse not to do it. Don't waste your life in a dead-end job."

My parents were supportive when I told them my plans to go to university. At last the Cadotte family would be able to count a white collar professional in its ranks! Corinne said she was pleased when I told her I now wanted to go to university to become a high school teacher, but didn't look at all happy when I said the wedding would have to be postponed. Afraid she'd be really upset if I told her Fairbanks had recommended I apply to join External Affairs on graduation, I didn't even raise the possibility. In retrospect, I think she guessed I was holding something back because she then said — a little too fast for my liking — that she'd now drop her plans to be a private secretary. "I'll take the three year program offered at the Soldiers Memorial Hospital in Orillia to become a registered nurse. That way both of us will be professional people, and have the money to buy a proper house and not have to start our lives together living in a dark damp basement."

When I told her that I wouldn't be able to see much of her when I was on the freighters and at university, she said, again a little too eagerly, "That's no problem. We'll keep in touch by letter and see each other when you come home for Christmas."

I had no trouble gaining admittance to the University of Ottawa, which gave its courses in English and French, perfect for a bilingual guy like me. I also found work as a deckhand in the summers on the freighters after my dad put in a good word to a friend. During the first six months of our separation, Corinne and I wrote every day and she obtained leave from the hospital to make the fifty-mile trip from Orillia to Penetang to attend church and eat Sunday lunch with my parents, even though I wasn't around. The following six months, we exchanged letters every week, and she cut back on her visits to my place. After that, we wrote once a month until our correspondence slowly came to an end, and she stopped visiting my family altogether. Eventually she wrote telling me she had known since the moment I told her I was going off to university that we would grow apart. Perhaps it was for the best, she said.

My parents and grandpapa were shocked at the collapse of the relationship. They were fond of her and had come to look at her as a member of the family. But Grandpapa was the only one who became visibly upset, rebuking me when I came home for the Christmas holidays. I didn't try to defend myself. "We just grew apart," I said.

"No," said Grandpapa, "You think you're too good for her now that you're going to university."

Perhaps it was inevitable that Corinne and I would drift apart. A new world, one I hadn't known in my hometown, had opened up. I took advantage of everything a university could offer, the subjects on the curriculum, and the library books on French existentialism, nineteenth-century French novels, and the latest in Biblical revisionism. I read a dozen volumes of the *Jesuit Relations*. I was a member of ten or so clubs including the United Nations Student Association, the History Club, the International Affairs club, and the Spanish club. We discussed issues Corinne and, for that matter, my own family, would never understand — or so I was convinced in my arrogance.

I didn't even answer her letter, telling myself I would look her up during a visit home and say goodbye in person — but I never did, another example of my growing conceit. But I agreed our breakup was for the best — all the more so since Grandpapa had been right — becoming a teacher was no longer good enough for me. I decided to follow Fairbank's suggestion to join the Department of External Affairs and become a diplomat.

2: When Values Differ

In January 1966, my last year at the University of Ottawa, I applied to join the Department of External Affairs. To be honest, despite my bravado, I really didn't think I'd get in. After all, thousands of university candidates, many with advanced degrees in law, economics, and history, applied for the dozen or more openings that came available each year. It was the home department of Lester Pearson, Canada's only Nobel Peace Prize winner. Dozens of the top bureaucrats in Ottawa had emerged from its ranks. In those days, before its decline set in, it had a reputation for excellence among foreign ministries around the world and at the United Nations.

True, I had done well in my time at university, but the University of Ottawa wasn't Oxford, Cambridge, Queens, Laval or the University of Toronto — the institutions of higher learning favoured by generations of aspiring Canadian diplomats. I wasn't a Rhodes Scholar like a disproportionate number of the Department's members. Moreover, I didn't fit the mould of the typical Foreign Service officer. Most were the offspring of what was then called the two founding nations: middle-class British settler stock and French Canadians who could afford to give their children classical college educations. Today, people say the Natives are the third founding people, but they're just trying to be politically correct.

However, I had one secret weapon — my memory. In preparing for the written examinations held in early March, I spent months in the library reading back copies of the *Economist, Time Magazine, Le Monde,* the *New York Times,* the *Globe and Mail,* and *Le Devoir.* Incredible as it may seem, I remembered almost everything I read. And when they handed out the test papers, I saw that the questions were presented in multiple choice, which made my job easier. I was able to dredge up accurate answers to each and every one of them. The people who marked my paper must have thought I was a genius.

But passing the written exam was only the first step. I next had to face a panel of senior officials, the so-called oral board, who would grill me on all manner of issues and decide whether I should be taken on. Early one Friday morning in late May, I put on the dark blue suit I had bought at a reduced price at Tip Top Tailors, straightened the tie the salesman had thrown in free of charge, and set out through streets lined with budding maple, oak, and black ash trees for the East Block of the Parliament Buildings. As I walked, I wondered what I'd do if I got a job offer. Would I be smart enough to survive among all those super intelligent and sophisticated people? Would I be up to the challenge of living in strange countries with exotic cultures? But would I ever forgive myself if I turned down a job that might lead me to do great things with my life?

Arriving at my destination, I walked up the steps of the imposing stone High Gothic–style building which housed the offices of senators and the minister of External Affairs, and made my way to the conference room where the oral board was conducting its interviews. The chairman, Theodore Longshaft, I knew by reputation. He was the highly respected and feared director general of Security and Intelligence. After a cordial welcome, he pointed me to a seat with his pipe and invited the other five board members to ask questions. There was a shuffling of papers as they searched for my file among the overflowing ashtrays and papers piled in front of them. I heard someone say in an irritated voice, "Let's get this over with as soon as possible...."

An older, florid-faced, white-haired board member, sweat dripping from his chin, his tie askew, peered at a picture in front of him, looked at me to confirm I was really Luc Cadotte, smiled, and introduced himself.

"My name is Milton Burump, director general of the bureau of United Nations and Global Affairs. Appearances to the contrary, I don't eat junior Foreign Service officers or individuals hoping to become one." After waiting for a second to see if his sally would elicit a chuckle — it didn't — he asked the first question.

"Dear Boy, I hope you don't mind me calling you 'Dear Boy.' I call everyone under the age of forty, Dear Boy. No offense meant. Please relax. Speaking for the others — if the others don't mind — all our questions are going to be as easy ones. Now I see from your file you have the distinction of being the first candidate for the position of Foreign Service officer since the establishment of the Department to have registered a perfect score on the written examination. Did you cheat? If so, tell us now, Dear Boy, for we don't want cheats in the Department."

"No I didn't cheat," I said, too surprised to be insulted, and left it at that.

Burump looked at me and shook his head as if he didn't believe me. He then made a great show of removing his glasses and polishing them with his tie, like an eccentric university professor. "I'm going to give you another chance to answer, Dear Boy. In the Department, we always take the word of a gentleman. Are you a gentleman, Dear Boy?"

I've never been afraid to speak my mind and let my irritation show. "Probably not," I said, "but I have a special memory and can remember most things I read or hear. That accounts for my score."

"Oh I see. That must mean you're an *idiot savant*," he said, smiling condescendingly, "like the people who perform in circus sideshows. But isn't using those powers a form of cheating?"

"I'm neither an idiot nor a cheat," I said, somewhat defensively. "I'm no more intelligent than anyone else but I have an ability to remember things."

I wasn't sure if he was some sort of malicious jokester who liked to humiliate people he had just met, or whether he had put his questions in good faith. Whatever it was, I didn't like it. To make it worse, the others had laughed when he asked me if I was an *idiot savant*. I felt they were all putting me down. They probably knew I was a Métis — my name would have given me away —and wanted to have some fun at my expense before dismissing me out of hand. I've always had a problem with my temper and I now wanted to tell Burump to go to hell, to tell him to "Dear Boy" somebody else, to tell him he was a snob with his talk of what constituted gentlemanly behavior. I wanted to get to my feet and tell everyone in the room that they could take their job and stuff it, and then stalk to the door, shove it open with one great push, step out, and slam it as hard as I could behind me.

But something told me that was exactly what Burump and the others wanted me to do, to provoke me into abandoning my attempt to join the Department. So I forced myself to smile and made a superhuman effort to laugh and pretend Burump had just been joking. And when I came out with my feeble little laugh, more a humourless chuckle, everyone in the room burst out with great guffawing and hooting. It had just been a harmless joke after all — I had almost let my temper disqualify me.

One after the other, the now-friendly board members threw questions at me, asking me to comment on issues as diverse as growing tensions between Israel and its neighbours, the Unilateral Declaration of Independence of the white regime in Rhodesia, border clashes between Indian and Pakistani troops, race relations in the United States after the Harlem and Watts riots, and the changing face of the United Nations in a decolonizing world. I did my best to provide good answers but couldn't help noticing that nobody other than Longshaft appeared to be paying attention. Two of the members were reading newspapers, someone was scribbling notes on what looked like a draft memorandum, and others were staring out the window. Burump was the greatest offender, smiling with great animation and encouragement most of the time but falling asleep periodically, letting his head drop on to his chest, and snoring noisily for a moment before waking up with a snort and turning his attention back to me.

The first time that happened, I stopped speaking and looked to Longshaft for direction.

"He has a sleep disorder that makes him drop off like that. He means no disrespect."

It was then the turn of a board member in his mid-fifties named Jonathon Hunter, a senior officer sitting beside me, who I later learned was on sick leave, to pose his questions. Long and gaunt with thinning brown hair, he turned his weary blue eyes toward me, fixed his gaze at a point just over my head, and asked me for my views on the American involvement in Vietnam. "The tragic war in that country keeps me awake at night," he explained in a low gentle voice. "I was one of the longest serving members of the International Control Commission in Hanoi in the 1950s and still have friends there. I can't imagine what it must be like to live under the constant American bombardment."

The stench of Hunter's breath, more sewer than medicinal, reached me at the same time as his words and almost made me gag. I suddenly felt ill at ease and on high alert. I knew very well that almost nobody in Canada supported the American position on the war. Demonstrations were taking place every day outside the American embassy in downtown Ottawa, not two hundred yards from where we were meeting, and in front of American consulates across the country. The Canadian public was enthusiastically welcoming thousands of American draft dodgers and deserters pouring over the border each year. The Canadian prime minister had just delivered a speech in Philadelphia in which he urged the United States to withdraw its troops from Vietnam — to applause in Canada but provoking the outrage of the American president.

I assumed the board members would share those views and question my judgement if I went against the consensus. However, in those days I accepted the domino theory, the argument that a communist victory in Vietnam would lead to a communist takeover of Southeast Asia, and then to gains elsewhere in Asia. I couldn't and wouldn't say something I didn't believe even if it ruined my chances of joining the Department, and so I said, "I watch the news on television like everyone else and am well aware that thousands of American soldiers and tens of thousands of Vietnamese civilians have been killed in the war to date and that many more will die before victory is won. But that's the cost of freedom." And to make it worse, in words that embarrass me today for their ignorance, I said the Americans should continue the war to defend the security of the free world against communist aggression.

Hunter reacted by gasping and clutching at his heart. I thought he was playing a prank on me as had Burump, and smiled at him in appreciation. But it was not a joke. Someone got up and offered him a glass of water, but he waved it away saying he was fine. I waited for the others to challenge my position, but other than looking deeply concerned, nobody said anything, or even glanced my way for that matter. It was as if they had just discovered I was so hopelessly pro-American and reactionary, there was no point in spending more time with me.

Longshaft, who had not participated in the discussion to that point, addressed his colleagues, "Everyone who appears before this board is entitled to his opinion, and it's refreshing to hear someone speak so candidly on such a controversial a topic."

Turning to me, he asked if I knew the writings of Albert Camus, the great French humanist winner of the Nobel Prize for literature.

"I do." I said. "I've read most of his books."

"And so you're familiar with what he said about the struggle of the Algerian people for their independence from France — the struggle in which France used torture as an instrument to fight the National Liberation Front?"

"He was torn between his support for the Arabs and Berbers who were native to the region and his own people — the *Pieds-Noirs* — the European settlers who had lived in Algeria for generations."

"Camus once told a journalist that if he had to make a decision between Justice and his mother, he would choose his mother. What did he mean?"

"Camus was saying that whatever the merits of the Arab and Berber cause, he would support his mother's people — the *Pieds-Noirs* — in the conflict. Blood and family came before Justice."

"Do you agree with Camus?"

"I do. When two values conflict you should support your family."

"You would have opposed the struggle for the independence of Algeria?"

"If I had been Camus I would have. If I had been an Arab or Berber I would have supported the fight to end French rule."

"Your file says you're a Métis. If you had lived a hundred years ago, would you have supported Louis Riel in his fight against Canada?"

"Yes, of course … unreservedly and blindly if need be. He was family."

"Oh my God! Stop playing with the mind of the candidate!" Burump said. "Let him think for himself!"

"I'm just exploring his views on some fundamental issues," Longshaft said to Burump. Turning to me, he said, "I'd now like to discuss the foreign policy priorities of the Canadian government. As any properly prepared candidate knows, national security, national unity, and human rights are key components along with others such as economic well-being and environmental protection. For the sake of our discussion today, however, I want to focus only on the first three. Do you think that any one of them should take precedence over the others? " He leaned back in his chair, stared at me impassively, and puffed on his pipe, waiting to hear what I would say.

I looked back at him wondering why he had asked that particular question so soon after questioning me on the wars in Vietnam and Algeria. Was there some sort of link between the three priorities he selected? Was he trying to help me or to trip me up?

"Please answer the question. We don't have time to waste."

"National security trumps human rights."

"And why do you say that?"

"Because the first priority of any government is to safeguard the national territory of the state against foreign aggression and to defend its citizens against terrorism. Without national security, there couldn't be human rights — or anything else for that matter."

"Is that why you say the United States is right to intervene militarily in Vietnam, to safeguard its national security and those of its allies in the free world?"

"I suppose so, yes."

"Even if the United States violates the human rights of the Vietnamese people?"

"Yes, that follows logically. I suppose so."

"You didn't deal with national unity. Where would it fit in your order of foreign policy priorities? Ahead? Behind? In-between national security and human rights?"

"When you say national unity I assume you mean the need to keep Quebec from declaring independence from Canada?"

"That's what I mean."

"Then I'd put national security ahead of national unity."

"Does that mean you would favour using force to keep Quebec a part of Canada?"

"No I wouldn't. If the people of Quebec want to create their own country, they should be allowed to do so as long as it was done in a democratic and peaceful way."

"Then what do you mean when say you would put national security ahead of national unity?"

"I mean that national security as defined as the defence of Canada against external threats and domestic terrorism should trump national unity. And that's because the Quebec is an internal and not an external problem. Quebec's place in Confederation is something Canadians and Quebeckers have to sort out peacefully among themselves."

"Would you put human rights ahead of national unity?"

"No I wouldn't because the suspension of human rights might be needed someday to safeguard national unity. National security, national unity, and human rights should constitute the proper order of priority."

"Now let's take another tack. Assume the Department accepted you as one of its Foreign Service officers, and posted you abroad to a country overseas. Let's call it country X. Let's say country X is in the Third World, maybe in one of those former colonies which are just now joining the United Nations as independent countries. What if you received instructions from the Department to do something your conscience told you was wrong? What would you do?"

"Could you be more specific?"

"Ah the specifics. The devil is always in the details. Now let's say you were instructed to accept information from a security institution in country X that a security institution of the Canadian government needed. For the sake of argument, let's say it was the RCMP but you knew the information had been obtained through torture. They do a lot of torturing in those countries,

Mr. Cadotte. It's hard to do business with certain countries without getting your hands dirty, Mr. Cadotte."

"No I wouldn't accept it. That would be contrary to everything I was brought up to believe."

"You mean you would refuse to carry out instructions that would violate your moral compass? Even if all that was involved was going down to headquarters of a foreign security institution to pick up a sealed package of information and making sure it was delivered to the Canadian agency that wanted it? Even if was to help the RCMP whose mandate includes protecting Canada and Canadians against terrorism, espionage, and issues of a similar nature?"

"I wouldn't do it if I had reasonable grounds to believe the information had been extracted through mistreatment or torture. The RCMP can do its own dirty work."

"It's not that easy. The RCMP doesn't have liaison officers in every country of the world. It relies on members of the Department to do a lot of its messenger work."

"I still wouldn't do it."

"But what if the Department, in its wisdom, told you that the information you were to pick up was from a foreign security agency that routinely tortured its prisoners. And what if the information was needed to protect Canadian property and lives? Would you do it?"

"With respect sir, there's no morally acceptable answer to your question."

"But we live in the real world, Mr. Cadotte. Anyone wanting to work in the Department sooner or later will be faced with issues like the one I raised. Please answer my question."

From the tone of Longshaft's voice, I was sure I would fail the oral exam if I didn't at least make an effort to answer and tried to temporize. "Not just to protect Canadian property and lives," I said. "The bar wouldn't be high enough."

"But what if you were told it was to safeguard Canada's national security, which you have just argued trumped national unity and human rights as foreign policy priorities?"

"In exceptional circumstances like those, maybe I would," I said, aware that I was now wading into deep dirty waters. "But I would need to know more."

"What if I told you the information could stop terrorists from exploding a miniature nuclear bomb in downtown Toronto and killing tens of thousands of people?"

"That's a far-fetched example but I'd definitely be on side. Everybody would be on side."

"But what if it wasn't to prevent a disaster like that, but to save one Canadian life?"

"I wouldn't do it. The moral cost of torturing someone to save one life, even if Canadians weren't he ones doing the torturing, would be too high."

"Ah! Now we are getting into moral costs. What do you understand by that term?"

"I mean the corruption of character."

"Personal or national?"

"Both."

"Now, what if the information could save ten Canadian lives?"

"Still too high."

"How many lives would you need to save to accept the information?"

"The circumstances would have to be exceptional."

"There you go again, Mr. Cadotte, invoking exceptional circumstances. According to your file, you are Roman Catholic and were once an altar boy. Now despite your Christian upbringing, you claim everything depends on the circumstances. Are you a relativist? Don't you believe in absolute values? Your church expects its members to accept absolute moral values. I think you are stalling, Mr. Cadotte. How many lives saved would make the use of torture exceptional, Mr. Cadotte?"

"Maybe one hundred lives?"

"Why not fifty?"

"My moral compass would allow me to accept one hundred lives saved but not fifty."

"But the moral compass of someone else, another Canadian Foreign Service officer for example, might allow him to accept fifty?"

"Maybe."

"Ten?"

"Maybe ten for some people. Maybe a thousand for someone else. It would depend on their definition of exceptional circumstances and the moral compass of the person concerned."

"What if the Department expected you to do things not involving torture that were in Canada's national interest but were of doubtful morality?"

I had no idea where Longshaft was going with this line of questioning and looked around the room at the other board members gauge their reactions. Hunter was slouched forward in his chair, a faint smile on his lips, concentrating his gaze on his clasped hands stretched out on the table in front of him. The others had been watching me intently ever since Longshaft had started asking me questions, like so many hungry cats observing a mouse caught in a trap.

"Could you be more specific?"

"We live in the real world, Mr. Cadotte. Have you heard the old expression? I imagine you have, 'A diplomat is an honest man sent to lie abroad for his country.' That's an exaggeration of course. After all, diplomacy relies on honest dealing to accomplish its ends, but not always. Sometimes we are expected to lie a little or a lot to advance and protect Canada's national interests. We live in an imperfect world, Mr. Cadotte. Are you aware, that in many countries of the Third World, Canadian diplomats help Canadian companies bribe local officials to award them contracts even though the costs of the bribes are passed on to the people of those countries? And that in many of those countries the mass of the people live in grinding poverty and can ill afford to pay the added costs? The diplomats do it because the contracts make money for the Canadian companies and provide jobs to Canadian workers. And when they make Canadian businessmen happy in this way, the businessmen tell the Department that their representative in country X is doing superb work and the officer concerned is rewarded by being promoted. Would your moral compass allow you to help a Canadian company obtain a contract through bribery?"

"I would never do such a thing."

"Even if Canadian jobs were at stake?"

"No, I still wouldn't."

"Are you aware that the Canadian government, at this moment, is helping Canadian asbestos companies market their product overseas when they and the companies know asbestos causes hundreds of thousands of lung cancer deaths each year? What would you do if you received instructions to promote asbestos in the country of your accreditation?"

"I wouldn't do it."

"What if you were told you would be fired for insubordination if you didn't do as you were told?"

"I still wouldn't do it."

"Are you saying the exceptional circumstance argument doesn't apply to asbestos sales but does when it comes to accepting information derived from torture?"

"That's right, torture is acceptable in exceptional circumstances but selling asbestos is an absolute abomination, and always inexcusable; lung cancer is a horrible disease."

"I think we've gone as far as we can in dealing with these issues," Longshaft said. "Unless there's a member of the board has something else to ask Mr. Cadotte on this topic."

Without looking up from the table, Hunter mumbled something nobody understood. "Please speak up, Jonathan," Longshaft said. "We would all benefit from your views."

"With the indulgence of the board, I'd like to repeat a little joke attributed to Winston Churchill, which has some relevance to this discussion. Churchill said to a socialite: 'Madame, would you sleep with me for five million pounds?' To which the socialite responded, 'My goodness, Mr. Churchill ... Well, I suppose ... we would have to discuss terms of course....' Churchill asked, 'Would you sleep with me for five pounds?' and the socialite responded, 'Mr. Churchill, what sort of woman do you think I am?' To which Churchill said, 'Madam, we've already established that. Now we are haggling about the price.'"

Nobody laughed, and I could tell from the angry looks the others directed at Longshaft that he had violated some sort of understanding. Maybe they didn't think the topic was fit to be discussed with someone who wasn't yet a member of the Department? Maybe they didn't want to be reminded about the disagreeable things Foreign Service officers were sometimes required to do?

Whatever it was, Burump, his jowls quivering, reacted badly, telling Longshaft, "I don't have anything else to raise with the candidate, but there is something I must say to you, Theodore. In more than three decades of service at Ottawa and abroad, I never once came across a case where a Foreign Service officer was asked to pass to headquarters information derived from torture by an institution of a foreign government. I have never heard of a case where one of our officers helped a Canadian company bribe a local official to obtain a contract. I admit that we are all instructed to promote the sales of products like asbestos and tobacco, which are not good for anyone's health, and we sell automatic weapons and light armoured vehicles to governments that will use them against their own peoples, against oppressed minorities, or in wars against neighbouring states. We obey because we realize we live in an imperfect world and if we didn't win those contracts, then someone else would. But the Department I know and love is staffed by decent, law-abiding and loyal officers, not by a gang of goons."

"Maybe if you had to deal with the sorts of things that come across my desk every day, you wouldn't feel that way." Longshaft responded. "I deal with the underside of life and you work on the sunny side. Now back to business. Mr. Cadotte, as my last question, please discuss the issue most likely to trouble domestic peace in Canada in the years ahead — take all the time you want. Then you'll be free to go and we'll break for the day."

I knew the board expected me to talk about the Quiet Revolution in Quebec — the struggle of Quebeckers to carve out a new place for themselves in Canada after centuries of corrupt priest-ridden governments and two hundred years of domination by English-speaking business elites. It had been the issue that occupied the headlines, the editorial pages, and the debates in Parliament for years. Royal commissions had been struck, and a new national flag thought to be more in tune with the times adopted. English-speaking Quebeckers, unwilling to make an effort to learn French, and afraid they would have no place in the political order, were abandoning their Montreal enclaves of privilege to make new lives for themselves in Toronto. At the same time, a terrorist group, the *Front de libération du Québec,* the FLQ, emerged from the shadows to try to turn the quiet revolution into a violent one. They were bombing the symbols of the old order such as armouries and post offices, and robbing banks and liquor stores to finance their operations. Nobody, however, took them seriously. After all, Canada, Quebec included, was a liberal parliamentary democracy. The FLQ was an anomaly which would eventually just fade away.

I was confident I knew the issues thoroughly and would have had no problem laying them out to the board and fielding any questions they might have. But I didn't want to do it. I wanted to talk about the condition of Aboriginal people in Canada, especially the Métis, but I didn't think the board would be interested. I was also still under the shock of Longshaft's relentless Jesuitical examination of my moral compass. He had opened up my soul in the company of strangers and found it wanting. With his little joke, Hunter had insinuated that I was no better than an intellectual whore, ready to trade lives if the price was right. I didn't know why I had allowed myself to be drawn into a repulsive debate on the costs and benefits of torture in the first place.

Glancing around, I saw the board members looking at me as if I was some country hick, too naïve to understand the complex nature of the world and the moral compromises officers of the Department had to make to save Canadian lives and sell Canadian goods. Suddenly, I felt out of place in this room of sophisticated, cynical senior officers and didn't want to subject myself to another cross examination on an issue closer to my heart than to theirs. Perhaps I would go to teacher's college after all and go home to Penetang to teach at my old high school.

"I think I'll withdraw my application to join the Department," I said, and got up and left the room.

3: Unreasonable Expectations

The next evening, to my surprise, Burump called me at my rooming house. "I wasn't at all happy with the way the interview went yesterday, Dear Boy," he said. "I'd like you to come see me before you make up your mind about a career in the Department."

By that time, I was having second thoughts about leaving the conference room in a huff. By giving way to a fit of childish pique, I had turned my back on the career of my dreams and I hated the idea of becoming a teacher like Angus Fairbanks in small-town Ontario. I was thus delighted that such a senior officer had taken the trouble to call me and hoped he wanted to give me another chance.

"I didn't know I was getting an offer."

"Don't be impertinent with me. I'm on your side. Come see me in my office in the Daley Building on Rideau Street first thing Monday morning. There are a few things you should know."

I was standing outside his door when Burump arrived for work and he told me to accompany him to get a cup of coffee. A few minutes later we emerged from the elevator into a windowless basement snack bar.

"This is our gourmet restaurant," he said. "The specialties are always the same — fried-egg sandwiches smeared with ketchup, baked beans, and buttered toast; french fries with salt and vinegar; hamburgers with the works; hotdogs with mustard; apple and raisin pie; muffins; and awful, tepid coffee. The odour of boiling grease and burnt toast adds to the charm. "

As we waited in line to buy our coffee, a steady flow of people passed by carrying food back to their offices. Without exception, they took the time to greet Burump — some nodding their heads in recognition, others stopping a minute to comment on the weather, and others to share a joke. Burump laughed at all the jokes good or bad, delighting in the human contact, addressing everyone, man or woman, indiscriminately as "Dear Boy," and in some cases introducing me as a future member of the Department.

"This may be a greasy spoon," he said when the parade of admirers trailed off momentarily, "but the greatest people in the world come here every day for coffee — people whose first love is the Department, people who aren't afraid to pack their bags, gather up their wives and their children, and leave to spend the best years of their lives in the hottest, most unhealthy and crime-ridden parts of the world. In this place, former ambassadors mix as equals with secretaries and clerks and communicators. Sometimes the minister comes over from the East Block to shake hands and say hello."

Just then I spotted Longshaft coming our way, a cup of coffee in his hand. "I hope your presence here means you haven't given up on us," he said.

"Mr. Burump wanted to see me."

"Oh, did he now?" he said, nodding to Burump who nodded back. "Well, don't believe everything he tells you. And now that you're here, you might as well see me as well. My offices are on the ninth floor. Tell the guard at the door I told you to drop by."

On our way back to his office with coffee and muffins, Burump continued greeting friends and acquaintances. "This is one of my oldest friends" he said, introducing me to a middle-aged woman who stopped to ask him if he had opened his cottage for the season. When the friend departed, Burump told me he had served with the woman in New Delhi after partition. "It was a dreadful time, the Hindus were slaughtering the Muslims and the Muslims were doing the same to the Hindus. Millions were killed. Trains would pull into the railway station in New Delhi filled with the corpses of men, women, and children slaughtered by their communal enemies."

Another person, a registry clerk, had been with him in South Africa. "Do you remember," Burump said to his former employee, more for my benefit than for his, "the Afrikaners were introducing Apartheid. The African National Congress was fighting back under Nelson Mandela, the greatest man who ever lived. They caught him and jailed him on Robben Island where he remains to this day. It was heartbreaking to witness the black people being rounded up and transported like so many cattle to far-off townships, out of sight of the whites, and there was nothing we could do about it."

"Now come in and make yourself at home, Dear Boy," Burump said, when we reached his office. I took a seat in front of his desk but he sat down on a sofa, took a sip of his coffee, and waved me over to join him. "This is where I receive my special guests," he said. "And you are more special than most. Do you know why?"

I was put off by the overly intimate tone, and so I fixed my gaze on a half dozen framed photographs on the opposite wall and waited for him to answer his own question. The pictures were impressive. In one, a much younger Burump, in the World War II battle dress of an officer of the Canadian armoured corps, was poking his head and shoulders out of the turret of a tank somewhere in Western Europe. In another, in formal diplomatic attire, he was shaking hands with Jawaharlal Nehru, India's first prime minister. In still another, he was having coffee with a smiling Nelson Mandala.

"I'll tell you why, Dear Boy," Burump said, after giving me time to admire the pictures. "I'll tell you why you're special, and I think you'll be pleased. It's because you're a Métis, that's why."

"What's so special about being a Métis?" I asked, afraid of the direction the discussion would now go.

"I don't want to sound patronizing, but a lot of us here in the Department have long believed that Canada will never live up to its potential as a force for good in the world if the voice of its Aboriginal people isn't heard."

"That's not the fault the Aboriginal people."

"I know ... I know the history," he said, cutting me off before I could get launched on Louis Riel, the Indian Act, and residential schools. "Your people were treated badly by settler society and are still subject to discrimination. But in a perverse way, as a result of your history, you're in a better position than someone like me, who comes from a long line of Scottish-English lawyers, to understand and show compassion to the downtrodden people of the Third World. At the moment, many of them feel compelled to take up arms against their governments to obtain equal treatment. Even in Quebec, that same sense of historic injustice is what drives the FLQ to violence — although everybody says it's just a fringe group and nothing to worry about."

I had never heard anyone say being oppressed could turn you into a better, more compassionate person. "How can understanding the misery of the Third World people serve Canada's national interest," I asked.

"Don't be obtuse, Dear Boy. Look at it this way. In my opinion, the championing of Canadian values abroad is a national interest as valid as national unity, trade promotion, peacekeeping, protection of the Arctic, or any other interest you can think of. That's why we need Aboriginal officers in positions of influence in the Department. But that will never happen unless they are recruited just after they graduate from university, and, like everyone else, are given every opportunity to become ambassadors and deputy ministers. Now after years of waiting for it to happen, you come along — a first-class Métis university graduate who has applied to become a Foreign Service officer. The results of your written exam were outstanding and you did an excellent job on the oral exam. I called you here to be sure you kept an open mind on the subject should you get a job offer."

I wasn't at all convinced that Aboriginal values were any different from Canadian ones. Or that Canadian ethics were any different than the beliefs held by people anywhere else in the world. Or that it should be the business of the Canadian government to push moral principles down the throats of foreigners. But I didn't want to say that to Burump. I didn't want to hurt his feelings when he had taken the trouble to call me at home and to receive me in his office. So I fixed my eyes on the floor and muttered, "Thank you sir … very nice of you to take time out of your busy schedule to tell me that."

I then looked at him — asking myself what further nonsense he was about to tell me — to see him vigorously rubbing his glasses with his tie. His face was lit up with a huge smile and tears glistened in the corners of his eyes. It was as if I had given a treat to a large affectionate puppy. After looking at me tenderly, he reached over and patted my knee. "I always get choked up in moments like this," he said. "I've spent my life helping others … nothing gives me greater satisfaction.

"Dear Boy," he said, smiling and speaking at the same time, "I knew you were a Métis as soon as I saw your name and hometown in the file. For generations, my family has vacationed on an island on Georgian Bay, close to Penetang. Our cottage is my real home, not the house I own in Ottawa. There's something wonderfully primeval and Canadian about the place. It's Tom Thomson country — wind-swept bent pine trees on rocky islets, magnificent sunsets, tremendous summer storms, moonlit nights, the call of the loon, fresh-picked blueberries, pan-fried fresh pickerel, windswept cliffs, noble Indians paddling by to sell beadwork and deerskin moccasins."

"Yes I like it too," I said, hoping to bring this part of the conversation to an end. But Burump was unstoppable. "Above all, it's the land of the Métis. I know the history of your people, how French *courier de bois* in the upper Great Lakes took Indian women as wives in the eighteenth century, how they fought with the British against the Americans in the War of 1812, how they left their community at the north end of Lake Huron to make new homes at Penetang when the peace settlement handed their lands over to the Americans. When I was a child, Métis people with names like Langlade, Bottineault, Comptois, and yes, Cadotte, used to come to our cottage to have coffee and a piece of pie with my grandparents. I love your people, Dear Boy."

By that time I was staring once again at the floor. I then heard him say, "I'd give anything to have been born a Métis."

Without looking up, I said, "I don't believe you."

"What's that, Dear Boy? What did you say?"

With my eyes still locked on the floor, I repeated, "I don't believe you … you wouldn't have wanted to be born a Métis."

"You're probably right, Dear Boy. You must forgive my presumption and tendency to use stereotypes. Only a Métis can understand what it means to be a Métis. I get carried away with my own eloquence and venture into areas where I have no right to go."

Nothing else came out my discussion with Burump that morning other than his warning about Longshaft. "I am light and Longshaft is darkness," he said. "He came out of the war convinced that man was intrinsically evil, whereas I emerged believing in the inherent goodness of people. He believes in original sin and need for redemption, and I don't. He sees evidence of communist conspiracies all over the world, and I don't. He believes it's acceptable to work with dictators and repressive governments, and I don't. He was a junior officer in Prague in 1948 when the communists staged their coup and murdered the democratically elected prime minister — that turned him into a cold warrior. He was ambassador in Cuba during the missile crisis and thinks Canada could have done more to support the Americans. He thinks the Cubans sent Lee Harvey Oswald to kill President Kennedy in Dallas. He's more comfortable working with the RCMP, the CIA, and the SIS than with colleagues like me in the Department. I'm a great supporter of the United Nations and all it stands for, and he's not. He trusts few people, and I trust everybody and hope they trust me. Now what else can I tell you?"

I have never liked it when people spoke about friends or acquaintances behind their backs. There's something hypocritical about it. Once again I shifted my attention to the framed photographs.

"I could go on and on all day," Burump said, poking me to make me pay attention. "I'm sorry, Dear Boy, but you absolutely must listen to what I'm saying. I'm telling you these things about Longshaft to warn you. He and his staff carry out hush-hush and not always pretty things out of his suite of offices on the ninth floor. Even though he's a fanatic, he has the ear of the prime minister, and most members of the Department are afraid of him. If you're offered a position in the Department, he'll try to recruit you and draw you into his web of intrigues. So be careful and come work for me. Together we'll do great things."

Soon afterwards, I was on the ninth floor trying to convince a suspicious guard, sitting at a desk in front of a closed steel door, that the Director General of Security and Intelligence, just thirty minutes before, had asked me to drop by to see him.

"Mr. Longshaft doesn't invite people to just drop by to see him," he said. "His visitors always need appointments."

"Why don't you call his office and find out," I said, handing him my driver's licence as proof of identity.

After taking a telephone from its place on the wall, he kept his eyes on me as he talked to someone inside Longshaft's sanctuary. He then smiled, handed back my license and resumed reading the morning newspaper. A few minutes later, the door opened to reveal a woman of uncertain age who looked me over carefully and beckoned me to follow her. She then scuttled ahead through a warren of deserted corridors lined with closed doors, like a mother superior leading a novice through a convent of nuns, until we reached a large door covered with deep green felt. After pushing it open, she told me not to take up too much of the boss's time, and motioned for me to go in.

Longshaft, who was reading a file on a desk otherwise devoid of papers and documents, looked up and said, "Oh, it's you, Cadotte. You took your time. Come take a seat at my desk. I liked the way you handled yourself Friday afternoon," he said, not waiting for me to sit down. "Especially the way you dealt with the issues of moral costs, exceptional circumstances, and the national interest."

"I don't think Mr. Hunter was impressed with my views on Vietnam," I said after sitting down.

"He's worn out, waiting to die. His opinion doesn't matter."

"Mr. Burump didn't seem to appreciate them either."

"You've just come from his office and I'm sure he gave you an earful about the Department's mission to spread Canadian values around the world. He probably didn't say we have never practiced at home what we preach abroad. We make speeches at the United Nations condemning colonialism but never mention the way we treat the Indians."

"Or the Métis."

"Or the Métis. Nobody remembers their contribution in the war." He then smiled and said, "There were a handful of Indian and Métis soldiers in the battalion I commanded in Normandy in 1944. They were mean, ruthless sons-of-bitches. Not afraid of spilling blood, but absolutely dependable and fearless. Whenever there was a tough job to be done, I always picked them."

"I take it you'd like Canada to follow a more hard-headed approach to the world in its foreign policy."

"If it was up to me, I'd pull Canada out the United Nations. It's just a talk shop for Third World lovers anyway. I'd kill the aid program — it sends our hard-earned money abroad to be wasted. I'd put more money into the military — it's ridiculously weak. I'd spend more on trade promotion, and strengthen our ties with the United States, NATO, and the governments of South America."

"Anything else?"

"A lot of people in the Department, led by your friend Burump, think I'm a cold-war warrior who sees communists under every bed, but I know what I'm talking about."

"Is Canada the target of any sort of communist conspiracy?"

"We Canadians are confronted with two levels of threat. The first is existential. The West, led by the United States, is fighting to hold the line against the Soviets and its friends around the world, including Cuba, in this hemisphere. The second isn't existential but worrying just the same. I'm talking here about the FLQ and its escalating campaign of bombings, bank robberies, and murders in Quebec."

"Are the two linked?"

"They are. As we talk, the Cubans are supporting terrorist groups trying to seize power in almost every country of Latin America. If they succeed, the Soviets will obtain bases in our backyard to threaten us with its nuclear weapons. And the FLQ will gain supporters to help it in its campaign to seize power in Quebec."

In my naïveté, I agreed with Longshaft's explanation, and told him so before asking what Canada could do to counter the threat.

"I'm convinced our first priority must be to help the United States combat the terrorists in Latin America. The free world must meet force with force. When pro-Cuban guerrilla groups pop up in the cities and countryside, we should stamp them out."

"Why don't we try pumping development assistance into these places to create jobs, deliver health care, and build roads and schools and the like to deal with the roots of unrest? Wouldn't that be that be more effective?"

"That's been tried but it's never worked — takes too long and there's too much corruption."

"What about the morality of it all?"

"Just last Friday you agreed that, in exceptional circumstances, the usual rules of ethical conduct could be changed, didn't you?"

"I did, but I came to that conclusion on logical grounds, not on moral ones."

"I don't see the difference."

I didn't press the point. Instead, I asked him how fighting terrorism in Latin America would help us combat the FLQ in Canada.

"The Americans know a lot about Cuban support for revolution in Latin America. They share that information with us. But they don't know much about FLQ ties to the terrorist groups themselves. Or if they do, they're not giving it to us."

The subject interested me and I asked him what Canada was doing to find out more.

"At the moment, we're getting ourselves organized. We've set up an Interdepartmental Task Force on International Terrorism to monitor developments and handle crises as they come along. One of the things I'm doing is posting hand-picked Foreign Service officer recruits to our embassies in the region to be our eyes and ears and report back on their findings. In your case, after a couple of years training at headquarters, you're going to Colombia."

"Does that mean I'm getting a job offer?"

Longshaft ignored my question and said, "I want you to find out what is going under the surface in that country, get a feel for the political climate, and find out how the security forces are doing in their counter insurgency campaigns. I want you to make an effort to get to know people in the barrios — that's what they call slums in Colombia — and get out into the interior to see if there's any truth to press reports that the terrorists are growing in strength. I want you to send your reports directly back to me at headquarters. The Task Force has its own communication centre here on the ninth floor. I'll see that the right people get to see your product."

"Why me?" I said. "Surely there are plenty of more capable recruits who'd do a better job."

"I don't like it when junior officers fish for compliments. I picked you because in the interview last Friday, you said the use of torture was acceptable in exceptional circumstances. I liked that. It shows intellectual courage. Ruthlessness if you will — something the average Canadian diplomat, who thinks compromise and reconciliation are virtues rather than signs of weakness, doesn't possess. Ruthlessness in my line of work is good. And ruthlessness will be needed in your new assignment. You're also a brown-skinned Métis — no offense intended. Terrorists love Aboriginal people. Your identity will give you a level of entree into a milieu not normally open to a white diplomat."

I was offended and a little confused. Burump wanted me in the Department because Aboriginal Foreign Service officers could help Canada live up to what he claimed was its potential for good in the world. When he said that, I thought he had read too many stories in his boyhood comic book collection about noble Indians and half-breeds. And now Longshaft had just told me he wanted me in the Department because I had demonstrated a ruthless streak in the interview, like the Indian and Métis sons-of-bitches in his battalion.

But should I wish to take it, a position as a Foreign Service officer was now mine — but for the wrong reasons. I persuaded myself that if I hadn't turned my back on the interview board, I would have been offered a job anyway, based on my merits rather than on my race. I reminded myself that I had done well academically — actually better than well — I had been an A student, was widely read, and had learned to speak Spanish quickly and fluently. I took refuge in the thought that I hadn't asked the board to give me a job because I was a Métis — something I would never do. I told myself it wasn't my fault that Burump and Longshaft wanted me to work for them because I stood for something that fulfilled their deepest fantasies.

In due course, a registered letter arrived from the Department with the offer and I accepted it, rejoicing at my good luck. But my joy was tempered by a sense of doubt, a feeling that I hadn't earned entry to the Department on my merits.

4: Courting Charlotte

I threw in my lot with Longshaft and spent the summer on the ninth floor as I prepared myself for my posting to Colombia, set to begin in November 1969. The security guard greeted me with a pleasant "good morning, Mr. Cadotte," as he unlocked the steel door when I came to work in the mornings. Longshaft's private secretary, Mary Somerville, now brought me coffee when I called on her boss. My new colleagues included two other recruits, Dan O'Shea and Gregoire Harding, who had joined the Department early in the year and would leave on their first postings in the late fall. I shared an office with them and they initiated me into the arcane world of the Canadian Security and Intelligence community.

More than four decades later, the security oath I swore on joining the Department still prevents me from saying exactly what we did. Let's just say we began each day pawing through bags filled with intercepted diplomatic, military, and security communications, from friends and presumed enemies alike, looking for nuggets of information on the great international developments of the day not available anywhere else. We then spent the rest of our mornings reading assessments sent to us by other intelligence organizations, economic and political reports from Canada's embassies, scholarly articles by academic experts, and scraps of information from anywhere, secret or unclassified, to put the intercepted information in context. The afternoons we pulled this information together and wrote reports for the most senior decision-makers of government, which, Dan and Gregoire told me, nobody read.

And the reason nobody read our reports, they said, was because our Intelligence partners didn't share with us the really juicy information they got from their spy agencies. They kept that for themselves, to make their reports exclusive, and thus more interesting, for their leaders. Longshaft had been trying for years to persuade the government to establish Canada's own spy service to collect the information the Brits and Americans wouldn't give us, but had always been turned down. But when the FLQ began waging its war of terror in Quebec, the government changed its mind. The prime minister told Longstaff he could run a modest network of spies to collect information on terrorist organizations in Latin America to see if they supported the FLQ. But since there was no money in the budget, he said Foreign Service officers on their first postings would have to do the job.

"Just the same," I said, "he must have a lot of influence to be able to persuade the prime minister to take a step of that nature."

"The Guardians were on side and prepared the ground with the prime minister," Dan said, assuming I knew what he was talking about. But I didn't and said so, prompting Gregoire to explain who they were.

"It's an informal group that's been around for decades in one form or another," he said. "There's no entrance requirement other than being unattached politically and a member of the Public Service. In fact, you can't apply to join. But if someone demonstrates the right stuff — being a progressive thinker seems to be the quality they look for — someone will take note and an invitation to join will be forthcoming."

"What about excellence, industriousness, high personal ethics, and the like? Where do they fit in?"

"I suppose those qualities are taken into account but being a progressive thinker is more important."

"And what does being a progressive thinker mean?"

"I suspect it means sharing the world view of the Guardians, but I really have no idea."

"How do you know those things?" I said. "Do you belong?"

"No I don't, but its existence has been an open secret in Ottawa for years. Most people in Ottawa think it's just another Old Boys' network, similar to other networks of influential people in towns and cities across Canada."

"Its members come mainly from the Privy Council Office and departments like External Affairs, Finance, Public Safety, Justice, National Defence, and agencies like the RCMP and the CSEC," Dan added. "They hold no formal meetings, and they don't circulate agendas or records of decisions taken. Instead, they join the same fishing and luncheon clubs where they mix business with pleasure, reaching informal agreements on the advice to give to ministers and prime ministers in times of crisis. Their influence comes from the fact they're based in and around the national capital and the political class is dependent on them for guidance. Longshaft may well ask you to join sooner or later ... he seems to like you."

I didn't tell them I had no interest in joining such murky outfit and would say no if approached. Neither did I mention I was destined to become one Longshaft's spies, afraid my new friends might laugh at me. Being so well informed, they probably knew that anyway but, being discreet, never mentioned the matter to me. They likewise said nothing when other junior officers of the class of 1966, recruited like me to do some part-time espionage work in Latin America, joined us on the ninth floor.

Dan and Gregoire had rented a cottage at Lake Kingsmere in the Gatineau Hills, across the Ottawa River from Ottawa, and were looking for someone to share the costs, so I agreed to be the third. After buying a car and moving in, I discovered the cottage was the unofficial hangout for new Foreign Service officers. Every Saturday afternoon, twenty or so classmates, together with their wives, girlfriends, and friends, would come with their bathing suits and supplies of food, beer, and wine to swim, dance, and talk until late in the evening.

Those who had joined up early in the year briefed the newcomers on their headquarters assignments. The new recruits listened with deference to the words of our experienced colleagues hoping to pick up some pointers. Everyone was proud to be a member of the Department and we talked about the things we would do to make the world a better place. Some said they wanted to help stop the spread of nuclear weapons. Others wanted to end Third World hunger. Still others wanted to save the planet from environmental ruin. Nobody said they wanted to be an intelligence analyst reading the private mail of other countries or a secret agent spying on Latin American revolutionaries.

It was at one of those parties toward the end of the summer that I met Charlotte Lefidèle. She wasn't a Foreign Service officer and I don't know who brought her, but as we sat around a campfire on the beach, I saw her looking at me. I smiled and she smiled in return. I got up and joined her, asking her in English if she was alone. She answered in French saying she was. When I answered in French, she said she'd been looking at the Foreign Service officers to see if she could identify the Quebeckers by their appearance. "And you," she said, "are a Quebecker."

When I asked her why she would waste her time that way, she said it was just for something to do. "I don't know anyone here, and the person I came with left without me."

"Well you're wrong ... I'm a francophone Métis from Ontario."

"Then I guess Quebeckers look like francophone Métis," she said, laughing. "I'm not a Quebecker either. I'm Franco-Ontarian from Ottawa, although my mother comes from Quebec City. But let's drop the subject. Tell me, what do you do? Are you a Foreign Service officer?"

The light wasn't good and it was hard to read her expression, but I had the impression I had just passed some sort of test when I said yes. "Could you give me a ride back to the city," she said. "I've no way to get home."

A few days later, we had lunch together in a small restaurant in the market area of the city, and I saw her in the light of day. She was older than I had initially thought, but made up in sophistication what she lacked in good looks. She ordered escargots for her first course and I did the same, even though I wasn't enthusiastic about eating the slimy little things. She ordered steak tatare with a raw egg yolk on top, but I couldn't stomach the idea of eating raw hamburger and ordered a well-done steak and french fries. She told me a Beaujolais would go well with escargots, steak tatare, and steak. I ordered a bottle and she drank most of it.

I told her I had gone to the University of Ottawa before joining the Department. She said she had attended the same university "a few years earlier," had written the Foreign Service officer exams, but had not received a job offer, and had settled for a job as a nursery school teacher. I told her I had lived in Penetang before Ottawa, and she said she had once visited Martyr's Shrine to pray at the Stations of the Cross, but hadn't had time to visit my hometown. She told me she had lived in Ottawa all her life but her passion was travel, especially to Mexico and Cuba, which she had visited many times, learning Spanish in the process.

I told her my dad was a stevedore on the docks and my grandpapa had traded in furs with the Indians in the early days. She said her father was a judge, her grandfather and great grandfather had been judges. I told her I was an only child, and she told me she had a brother who was a lawyer married to a former teacher who had given up her career to raise a family. She also had a sister who had wed her childhood sweetheart who was now a superintendent in the RCMP. In reply to her question, I told her I was a practicing Catholic, and she said she went to mass every Sunday and didn't believe in taking the pill because the pope was opposed to birth control. I told her I was working as an analyst in the Department and was scheduled to be posted to Colombia in the fall of 1968. She told me she had always wanted to live in Colombia.

In the weeks that followed, we saw a lot of each other. Most days after work, we met for drinks at a neighbourhood pub, sometimes going back to her apartment to spend more time together. She made it clear from the outset, however, that she didn't believe in premarital sex and told me to keep my hands to myself. About a month into the relationship, she invited me to meet her family at Sunday dinner. The evening was a great success. Everybody went out of their way to make me feel welcome. The judge, it turned out, had many friends in the Department, many of them ambassadors, several of whom I had even heard of. The RCMP superintendent, corpulent and red-faced, who had married the oldest daughter, knew Longshaft professionally and said he was a "know-it-all snob." The lawyer son said he had considered applying to join the Department after he had been called to the bar, but Foreign Service salaries were low, his then fiancée was afraid of bugs and poisonous snakes and foreigners, and wanted to live in Ottawa, close to her mother.

It turned out that Charlotte had told everyone that I was a Métis, and to make me feel comfortable, Madame Lefidèle said her great-great grandmother had been a Huron from Loretteville, the Indian reserve near Quebec City. Not to look pedantic, I didn't tell her the Hurons originally came from the Penetang area and some of them had sought refuge with the French colonial government at Quebec City after their wars with the Iroquois in the mid-seventeenth century. The meal was served by a uniformed maid on porcelain dishes and eaten with sterling silver cutlery. The judge opened bottles of fine imported French wines and took the time to explain to me the differences between a Chateau Angelus grand cru classé and a Vosné Romanée. I went home with the distinct impression that the family approved of me. I was francophone, Catholic, a Foreign Service officer, and unmarried — a perfect catch for the youngest daughter who was no longer young. My Métis identity was irrelevant.

In the months following the dinner, the Lefidèle family welcomed me into their circle. Every Sunday, dressed in a well-cut navy blue suit, a freshly pressed white shirt, and an elegant silk tie — purchased from the Timothy Eaton Company with my first paycheque — I accompanied the family, grandchildren and all, to Sunday services at the Basilique Notre Dame. Afterward, I went back for Sunday lunches and tried to look interested as the family complained about the absence of Latin in the mass, the use of guitars during the hymn singing, and the unseemly familiarity displayed by the priest to the congregation — all unnecessary reforms imposed by Pope John XXIII. After lunch, we took coffee in the parlour and as the others meandered on about family affairs, I nodded and listened as if I was already married to Charlotte.

When the family left on weekends for their ski chalet in the Gatineau Hills that winter, I accompanied them. I bought a pair of skis, ski boots, and poles, and Charlotte gave me calf-skin gloves, a stylish ski jacket, and a white sweater for *après-ski*. I gave her a Métis sash, which she wore for the rest of the winter. She introduced me to classical music, taking me to performances of Handel's *Messiah* at the Basilique, to string quartets from visiting groups at churches throughout the city, and to performances of the Ottawa Symphony Orchestra. I didn't enjoy myself but pretended I did. She included me in the small dinners and cocktails held by the members of her close circle of friends. She enjoyed herself but I didn't. The highlight of the summer was a visit we made to Ile Sainte-Helene in Montreal to take in

Expo '67, the world's fair hosted by Canada to mark Canada's centennial year. We visited the La Ronde amusement park, Buckminster Fuller's geodesic dome, as many national pavilions as we could, and an open-air Ed Sullivan show featuring the Supremes and Petula Clark. We had a ball.

As the summer of 1967 turned into fall and then into winter, Charlotte and her mother made clear that it was time I proposed. But I was in no hurry. I enjoyed Charlotte's company, but recognized there was no spark, no passion, no love in our relationship. If we went ahead and got married, it would be a marriage of convenience. She was bored with teaching nursery school children and wanted to experience the life of a diplomat's wife abroad. I was more attracted to Charlotte's family and their lifestyle than to their daughter and hers. On the other hand, she understood the art of making up seating plans, arranging flowers, preparing menus, giving orders to servants, receiving guests, and knew which wine went well with fish and which one with game or steak. She could provide the social graces I lacked, build up my self-esteem, and help me deal with the nagging sense that I had been hired only because I was a Métis.

So it wasn't until the early spring of 1968 that I took out a bank loan and bought a diamond engagement ring — a long-term career investment so to speak — and asked her to marry me. There were hugs and kisses all around at the family Sunday dinner when we announced the good news and she showed off her ring. The judge went down to the cellar and brought up the bottles of Dom Pérignon he had put away years earlier for the occasion. After the obligatory toasts, everyone wanted to know if we had set the date. Although she hadn't discussed the subject with me, Charlotte said the wedding would take place before the fall so we could travel together to Colombia. And since the fall was only a few short months away, there was a lot to do: speaking to the archbishop to ask him to conduct the ceremony, reserving a time at the cathedral, organizing a high mass and full choir, importing a soloist to sing "Ava Maria," reserving the ballroom of the Chateau Laurier Hotel for the reception and dinner, preparing her trousseau, going to Montreal to be fitted for a bridal dress, and preparing the guest list, among other things.

"And then we must prepare ourselves for life in Colombia," she said. "I've already read up on what to expect and spoken to a few people I know who used to work at the Canadian embassy in Bogota. The *Bogotános* dress very conservatively and I'll need four or five classic *tailleurs* for dinners and receptions. I'll also need the right clothes to wear casually during the day and a different set to use when we visit the coast and another for our travels to Cali and Medellin in the valleys. I'm so excited. And Luc is excited too, aren't you, Luc?"

I did my best to smile and said that I was indeed excited.

"We will need china, silverware, tablecloths, candelabras — everything to entertain in style. The government will ship all this to Bogota, won't they, Luc?"

"Yes, of course anything at all, as long as they're needed."

"Then you might as well take the mahogany furniture I inherited from my grandmother which has been gathering dust for years in storage," Madam Lefidèle said, addressing her daughter. "I was going to give it to you when you got married anyway."

"Oh thank you, Mama! I'm so excited. And you're excited too, aren't you, Luc?"

I said I was still excited and Charlotte and her mother carried on in this vein for the next hour, paying no attention to the others who shook hands with me, mouthed their congratulations, and slipped away. I tried to look happy but was beginning to feel that marrying Charlotte would be a mistake. Seeing my look of despair, Charlotte's father smiled indulgently and told me to have another glass of champagne and cheer up. "It's always this way. The best thing to do in these circumstances is to leave everything in the hands of the women and accept everything they decide."

Eventually, Charlotte ran out of things to say and came over to join me on the sofa. Holding my hand, she told her parents we were now going to Penetang to see my family. "We need to announce our engagement and obtain their blessing, don't we, dear?"

"Yes, of course, dear," I said, doing my best to hide the sudden pain in my stomach that hit me when Charlotte addressed me as "dear."

"Let's go this weekend and surprise them," Charlotte said. "That'll be so much fun."

"Yes, why don't you," said the judge. "And take the Buick; we'll make do with the Studebaker for a few days. You should travel in style to bring the good news."

Penetang is a long way from Ottawa and I hadn't been home all that often since I joined the Department, but my family couldn't have been more welcoming — at least initially. Everyone crowded around to admire the Buick and Charlotte's engagement ring. Charlotte, however, didn't reply when Grandpapa asked her how much a judge earned and how much the ring had cost. She pretended not to understand when she asked where the washroom was and was told it was in the backyard. When she returned from outside and someone asked her if she had trouble finding it, she did not laugh along with the others. She seemed unimpressed by the framed pictures of Pope Pius IX and Louis Riel, which hung on the parlour wall beside a mounted moose head and an array of 303 rifles and shotguns. She sat uncomprehending through dinner as Grandpapa, wearing a reversed baseball cap and old clothes at the table, put on a show, spitting food and waving his arms as he babbled on in a mixture of French, English, Michif, and Ojibwa about his youthful fur-trading exploits in the bush of northern Ontario.

Charlotte looked alarmed when Mama summoned Stella, our old Labrador collie mongrel, from her usual place on a blanket near the stove in the kitchen and fed her food scraps from the table. A look of disgust crept across Charlotte's face when Mama placed her plate on the floor to be licked. Grandpapa compounded the damage by winking at Charlotte and saying the Cadottes always let their dogs clean their dinner plates with their tongues. "That way there's no need to wash them." Charlotte didn't get the joke.

It was right about then that I understood Grandpapa and Mama didn't like Charlotte and would do anything to sabotage our marriage plans. Grandpapa had never behaved in such a boorish way before when guests were invited for dinner. And Stella, as loved as she was in the Cadotte household, had never been fed from the table and certainly had never licked a dinner plate. Later, over coffee and dessert in the parlour, I went on at great length about the warm welcome Charlotte's family had accorded me over the past year, including me in family meals, excursions, and visits to their summer cottage. Grandpapa wasn't impressed, and rendered the coup de grace to the evening when he smiled wickedly at Charlotte and told her she wasn't the first girl I'd brought home. He went on to her about Corinne and what a wonderful person she was — even though I did my best to change the subject. After the others had gone to bed, I started to apologize to Charlotte for the behaviour of my family but she cut me off in mid-sentence and left the room.

The next morning I wasn't surprised when she said she wasn't feeling well and wanted to return home immediately. I was relieved when she handed back her engagement ring and said the marriage off when we reached Ottawa — although I felt bad about wasting her time and that of her family in a courtship that never had a chance of success.

Just before my departure for Bogota, in November 1968, Long-shaft called me in for a final briefing, this time on Ambassador

Joseph O'Connor, Canada's head of post in Colombia. "There are three types of ambassadors in the Department," he said. "Pragmatists who are in the majority; idealists like Burump, who are almost as numerous; and a handful of do-nothings like O'Connor. It's a shame because O'Connor was once a competent officer who joined the Department after serving honorably in the navy during the war. He rose steadily through the ranks, making no mistakes but doing nothing extraordinary. Most people believed he would end his career as a deputy ambassador at a small embassy but nothing more. And then to the surprise of everybody, the government plucked him out of the ranks and sent him abroad as ambassador to Colombia. It turned out that O'Connor and the prime minister had been classmates at the Collège Jean-de-Brébeuf in Montreal before the war, and the prime minister wanted to do him a favour. He's only been in Bogota a few months and he's done nothing but complain about the weather and play bridge with members of the social elite. He won't like it if he finds out you're reporting directly to me."

"But aren't you going to let him know what my real mission is?"

"Eventually. But for the time being let's keep the special relationship between you and me. You know what's expected of you. Send in your reports ... he'll never find out."

Part Two

Colombia

November 1968 to February 1969

5: Why Me?

I first heard the sound of an enraged mob chasing a gamine along the sidewalk in downtown Bogota late on the afternoon of November 18, 1969. I had just arrived to take up my appointment and was in the office the office of Ambassador O'Connor, introducing myself.

"The good people of Bogota are just chasing a pickpocket," O'Connor said, seeing my startled expression. "Happens all the time — it's our daily entertainment," he got up and went to the window to look out. "Nobody can walk more than a hundred yards without some snotty-nosed street kid — they call them gamines down here — trying to rip off your watch or steal your wallet. The crowd will administer some rough justice when they catch it — maybe even kill it. I don't blame them."

"They'd kill a child?" I asked.

"It's easy to see you've just arrived," O'Connor said, turning and looking at me more carefully. "Come over here and take a look. You've got a lot to learn. That little delinquent isn't a cuddly little boy or girl, much less a child like we're used to back home. It's a gamine, an outcast that survives by eating garbage when it can, selling itself on street corners, and picking pockets when all else fails. One of them even ran off with my briefcase when I was entering the embassy when I got here in the summer. They live in packs like stray dogs. They think like dogs — are no better than dogs. Decent people have to protect themselves by treating them like dogs."

"See," he said, after I joined him at the window, pointing up the street to where a dozen men were kicking a motionless child.

"Why don't they leave it to the police?"

"The police have better things to do with their time. And so do I," he said, pointing me back to my seat. "Now, what led you to request a posting to this godforsaken place? When your staffing officer put forward your name for the job, he said you were one of the top officers in your class. Said you could've gone to Washington, London, or Paris — anywhere you wanted. Said I was lucky someone like you wanted to come here. I should've been flattered but I was left wondering what's wrong with you, whether you had something to hide."

It was the first time I had heard I could have had one of the big posts, but I had no intention of admitting that to O'Connor.

"I didn't want to be one of a dozen or more junior officers at the bottom of the food chain, working for a first secretary, who was working for a deputy ambassador, who was working for an ambassador. I studied Spanish at university and wanted to be responsible for managing a program of my own in a Latin America country in turmoil like Colombia. The Department told me there was an opening here for a second secretary to run the aid program, manage the consular section, and carry out general political and economic reporting. I put my name forward and here I am."

"And so you are. But I still don't understand. There's only a few dollars in the aid program, and other than a handful of businessmen and a few pot-smoking CUSO volunteers — that's the Canadian University Service Overseas, in case you didn't know — handing out used clothes to the poor, there's no expatriate community to speak of. Crime is so bad, tourists stay away. Trade is minimal. Nobody back home cares what happens here. I don't know why they keep this place open."

"I know what CUSO stands for," I said, and shifted uneasily in my seat.

"What's the matter? Need a jolt of caffeine? If so, the coffee's over there," he said. After I lapsed into silence he gestured at a tray of coffee on a nearby credenza, "Don't expect me to serve you."

Glad to have an opportunity to collect my thoughts, I took my time pouring my coffee. The meeting wasn't going well.

"Now tell me something about yourself," O'Connor said after I returned to my seat. "Where you're from, the university you went to, and why you really wanted to come here."

"I'm from a town on Georgian Bay called Penetang. I went on to the University of Ottawa where I graduated with a four-year arts degree in history and romance languages, learning to speak Spanish in the process. I wrote the Foreign Service officer examinations and was lucky because I got a job offer. After that, with my academic background and interest in Latin American affairs, I asked for a posting to Bogota."

"I'm glad you already speak Spanish. I don't, and am too old to learn. I also know something about your hometown, although I've never been there. I served on a minesweeper that was built in the shipyard there. Come and see me whenever you want to talk," he said, dismissing me.

I was on my way to the door when he called me back. "Take a seat," he said, and I had scarcely sat down when the words burst from his mouth like water from a broken dam. "Sorry I was rude to you. I never asked for this post. One day last spring without warning I got a phone call from the prime minister. I'd met him at boarding school before the war but didn't know him well. He told me he thought of me when he was looking at a list of ambassadorial openings. Said he saw that Bogota was available. Said he wanted to do a favour for an old classmate and was sending me there. Didn't even ask me if I wanted to go. Just assumed I'd accept because it was an ambassadorial appointment and I was just a middle-ranking officer. But I wasn't cut out to be an ambassador and never should have accepted. Didn't speak Spanish ... didn't know the history or culture of the place ... was too old to learn."

He looked at me as if he was seeking my permission to continue. I nodded back and he carried on. "But you can't say no to the prime minister, especially when he thinks he's doing you a favour. My wife and I are still getting used to this place and it shows. Spent my entire career in Western Europe and United States. Safe and familiar ... just like home. Here, there are earthquakes, kidnappings, traffic jams, honking horns, garbage, parasites, amoebas, dysentery, pickpockets, endless rain, pollution, people never smile, it's so far above sea level it's hard to breathe. One minute I'm overwhelmed by the misery of the people ... can't control my emotions and start to weep like a baby. Next minute, I say the most heartless things about those poor wretches who live in a misery not of their making. Don't take what I said about the gamines as my real feelings. It's just that I get so frustrated at sitting here day after day and have to listen to the terrible cries of the crowds chasing those kids, and there's nothing I can do about it. There's nothing anyone can do about it."

Not knowing how to deal with his appeal for help, I muttered something reassuring and got up to leave, afraid he might lose control of himself again. "No, no, Luc," he said, "stay a moment longer. I'm really glad you're here. Really, really glad. You're young and resilient and will get along fine. I won't be able to give you much guidance and help, but you're coming from headquarters and know what they want. Just go ahead and do your job."

On leaving the ambassador's office, I sought out Alfonso, the driver who'd picked me up in the embassy car at the airport earlier in the day. "I need you," I said, and he understood from the tone of my voice not to ask questions. He put down the newspaper he was reading, pulled on his suit jacket, and followed me out the door to the sidewalk.

"I saw a crowd of people kicking a gamine out here," I told him as I led him towards a figure lying on the sidewalk. But instead of a child, I saw what looked like a barefoot old man with a bloodied face, naked from the waist down and dressed in a filthy cast-off suit jacket many sizes too big for him.

"I thought I'd find a gamine," I said, turning to Alfonso. "The ambassador said the people were chasing a gamine."

"But it is a gamine, señor. It's a child. A gamine child."

I got down on my knees to take a closer look, wiped some of the blood away from his face and saw that the person was no more than six.

"Go get the car, Alfonso. We'll take him to a hospital."

"Si, señor, whatever you say, señor. But no hospital will take a gamine."

"Why not?"

"They say they're dirty and they steal. And they have no money to pay."

"But I'll cover the costs."

"And then what, señor? If you persuade the hospital to take him, what will happen to this gamine after he's released? He'll just go back to the streets and start picking pockets again. It's a bad idea to take a gamine to a hospital."

I bent over the gamine who appeared lifeless. "He's just a child, Alfonso. Where can we take him if the hospitals won't accept him?"

"Señor, excuse me for saying so, but there are thousands of these gamines in the streets. He looks innocent and harmless lying there quietly on the sidewalk, but these children are dangerous. They roam the city in big groups, and if he learns where you live, he might come with his friends to rob or kill you. Even if he doesn't cause you any harm, if you care for one, you'll feel obliged to look after them all. Where do you draw the line? Take my advice, señor, forget this gamine. This is only your first day in Colombia."

Suddenly, the gamine opened his eyes, stared at me in terror, and tried to hit me in the face with his little fist. "Don't be afraid, I'm going to help you," I said. But the gamine struggled to his feet, and sobbing uncontrollably, limped off to lose himself in the crowd. And to my shame, I let him go.

That night, settled into the comfortably furnished fifth-floor apartment rented for me by the embassy in an upscale neighbourhood, I couldn't fall sleep, unable to forget the pitiless howls of the enraged rabble chasing the gamine along the sidewalk. Nor could I forget the sight of the terrorized little boy attempting to defend himself against what he must have believed was another big person trying to do him harm before getting up and fleeing, injured and wailing in fear, to seek a refuge wherever he could find it. *I must be suffering from cultural shock,* I told myself. *Law-abiding citizens here apparently deal with petty thieves in ways we would never tolerate in Canada. They must have their reasons. Who am I to judge? I'm a foreigner, a diplomat, and visitor in their country.*

But I knew nothing could justify the beating and killing of children, whatever their offense. I was just making excuses for my cowardly behaviour when confronted with absolute evil. I had lacked the compassion and courage to help the gamine and had allowed Alfonso to convince me that brutality against gamines was an acceptable way to deal with homeless children. Eventually, I grew drowsy, fell asleep, and began to dream. I was a boy of six again, swinging on a rope attached to a high branch of an apple tree in the front yard of my home back in Penetang.

A soft warm spring breeze was blowing out of the West off Georgian Bay, filling the air with the perfume of apple and lilac blossoms. Robins, gulls, crows, and red-wing blackbirds were calling to each other in their secret languages, and in the distance I could hear the familiar sounds of a locomotive shunting boxcars in a railway yard, the hammering of steel on steel somewhere, mothers calling to their children, and further away a tugboat blowing its horn as it shepherded a freighter into its berth in the harbour. I swung higher and higher, crying out in pure animal pleasure at the joy of existence. I had never felt so alive, never been so happy, never so secure in the love of my parents, my uncles, aunts, and cousins, and of my devoted grandpapa, especially my devoted grandpapa, who had attached the rope to the branch of the apple tree.

Suddenly, within my dream, I heard the roar of the mob and saw the gamine staring at me again with frightened eyes. "Why you and not me?" the gamine was whispering. "Why you and not me?" Still within my dream, I realized the gamine's question had only one terrible answer. Life was a game of chance. I could have been born as that gamine. Even worse, the gamine was warning me that my life, with all its bourgeois comforts and petty First World concerns, could change in an instant, and I could become him. I woke up in a start, filled with the most profound pity for the gamine and all the people like him in Colombia and full of fear for myself.

I had taken a first-year course in psychology at university and was aware that social scientists thought dreams were often attempts by the unconscious mind to come to terms with problems encountered by people in their waking hours — no more than that. But I had always believed in the power of dreams to let you see into your soul, to unearth secret truths about your being, to provide glimpses into the future and to provide insight into the human condition. Throughout my life, things I had seen in dreams had come to pass — the death of a dog I had loved to distraction, the visit of a distant cousin who had moved out west with his family years ago when he was small, a banal injury suffered by my dad in an accident on the docks.

Consumed with dread that something was about to happen that would drag me down into the depths, I spent the rest of the night sitting up in bed on high alert, staring out the window into the dark until pitch black gave way to faint light. When the first rays of sunlight came creeping over the mountain, I heard Hortensia, the silent maid hired by the embassy to look after my daily needs, come out of the kitchen to set a place for me at the dining room table. A few minutes later, she padded to my bedroom door, knocked, and in a soft voice— she knew I was awake — told me it was time to get up and have breakfast. To avoid giving offense, I thanked her profusely for the toast, scrambled eggs, and coffee she served me, but ate little. After getting dressed and picking up my briefcase, I went out the door and down the stairs to the driveway where Alfonso was waiting for me.

I said good morning, got into the back seat and he eased his way into the heavy traffic. At each red light, crowds of gamines awaited, thrusting in my face newspapers, shoelaces, shoe polish, bars of soap, religious icons, firecrackers, cheap plastic dishes and cutlery, cigarettes, matches, and tourist maps of Bogota, imploring me to buy them. Each wore a filthy suit jacket hanging down to his knees, and each seemed to me to be the gamine beaten the day before outside the embassy. Each locked his eyes on mine and whispered in a voice only I could hear, "Why you and not me? Why you and not me?" From time to time I heard Alfonso say, "Señor, señor, I have something important to tell you," but I was incapable of responding.

At the embassy, I went directly to my office, closed the door and sat down, only to hear once again the howl of the enraged mob chasing another gamine along the sidewalk. But this time, I didn't dare get up to look, afraid I would break down in tears. A few minutes later, Alfonso knocked timidly on my door and came in to see me leaning forward, my elbows on my desk and holding my head in my hands in despair.

"*Con permisso,* Señor, I didn't mean to disturb you."

"That's alright, Alfonso," I said looking up. "I was just resting"

"I was trying to tell you on the way to the office that I know a woman, a former nun, who runs a small shelter for gamines near a barrio. She receives no money from the government but keeps it going with handouts from people like me. Could I take you to see her, señor? She's an educated person and would do a better job in telling you about the gamines than I could. "

"I don't understand," I said. "Yesterday you warned me about the dangers of helping gamines, but today you want to take me to meet someone who does just that."

"Dealing with gamines in the street is one thing, señor," Alfonso replied, "Visiting a shelter to see happy children is less risky."

I accepted the offer, but didn't do it because such a visit would provide fodder for a report back to Longshaft or because it might lead to other contacts and be good for my career. No, I accepted it because I needed to talk to someone like a former nun who spent her days working with children in need, someone who might be able to help me come to terms with the question raised in my dream — "Why you, and not me?" I sensed the reason O'Connor remained paralyzed by cultural shock was because he had asked himself the same question when he arrived in Bogota, and hadn't been able to answer it. I didn't want that happening to me.

Busy settling into my new position, it wasn't until the next week that I was able to take Alfonso up on his offer. "I'm going to show you a part of Bogota that tourists never see," he said as we started our journey. "Hundreds of thousands of people come to Bogota every year to escape the fighting in the countryside," he said. "There's nowhere for them to live. The government doesn't have the money to help them and so they scrounge building materials from building sites and garbage heaps, find ways of hooking themselves up to the city electrical grid without killing themselves to get free power, and walk miles to get water from wherever they can. The men work for next to nothing as gardeners, cleaners, carpenters — anything to earn a little money. Some join criminal gangs and steal cars and sell drugs — others are recruited into paramilitary groups and are sent into the countryside to protect the big landowners and fight the guerrillas. The women look for jobs as maids and cooks. When there's no money coming in, they work in the brothels and streets to feed their families. The children are left to fend for themselves and often leave the barrios for good to beg and steal — anything to survive."

Before long, we left the business and residential sections with their well-paved roads and elegantly uniformed traffic police and took our place in a slow moving procession of trucks and buses, spewing black smoke from their exhausts as they proceeded over a series of ridges towards the southern outskirts of the city. I saw and smelled the barrios of Bogota. They were packed with hovels made of scraps of lumber for walls and rusty sheets of galvanized tin for roofs, open sewers for sanitation, and snarls of dirt alleys for passageways. Worn-out women and pot-bellied children carrying plastic canisters of water stopped and stared at us with blank eyes as we went by. Burning garbage and the rotting corpses of dead dogs and cats littered the road.

Men ran toward us when they saw our car approaching with its diplomatic licence plates. Alfonso shook his head and shrugged his shoulders at them. He told me they were desperate, hoping to be offered a day's work by a rich gringo visiting their neighbourhood. Others stared at us with undisguised hostility, as if to say they didn't want outsiders coming to gawk.

Alfonso parked in front of a partially completed house on the edge of the barrio and turned to me with a nervous smile. "Excuse me for being so bold, Señor Cadotte, but do you think the embassy could find some money to put an addition on the shelter? It wouldn't cost much. It's only got two bedrooms to house a dozen gamines. If we added two more bedrooms, we could take another dozen children off the streets. I ask you because Señora Lopez would be too shy to do so."

"Now I know why you invited me here," I said as we got out of the car, laughing at how easily I had been taken in. Suddenly a group of children burst out of the door, ran up and threw their arms around his waist, crying out his name and hugging him.

"As you can see," he said, "I'm known here."

"You certainly are, Don Alfonso," said a soberly dressed woman in her mid-thirties wearing a small silver cross, who pushed her way through the throng to embrace him. "And who have you brought to see me today," she said looking at me.

"This is a Canadian diplomat, Señor Cadotte," Alfonso said. "He's new to Colombia and wants to know about the *gamines*. And this is my friend, Señora Lopez, the person in charge of the shelter," he said to me.

"Come sit with me and tell why you're interested in our gamines," Señora Lopez said, leading the way into her office and taking her seat behind her desk.

While anxious to talk to her, I wondered what had made me think I could appear on her doorstep — someone she didn't know — to seek her guidance on how to handle the biggest moral issue I had ever faced. When I hesitated, she went out and came back with two cups of black coffee, handed me one, and joined me on my side of the desk.

"I wouldn't have disturbed you if it hadn't been important," I said and fell silent again, thinking about how best to express my need. "I just arrived and am having some problems adjusting to a place so different from Canada," I finally said.

"Take all the time you want," she said. "Getting used to a new country is never easy."

"It's not just that," I said. "Last week, on the sidewalk outside the Canadian embassy, I saw a mob beat senseless a child no more than six years old. I thought at first it was a gang of criminals, but it was a crowd of people taking out their anger on a gamine who had picked somebody's pocket. My ambassador said these things go on all the time. The people in the mobs are always different, the gamines are always different, but the results are always the same — ordinary, presumably good people do appalling things to children doing bad things to survive. You're a Colombian. You work with the gamines. Alfonso told me you were once a nun. Can you help me understand what's going on?"

"Only a saint could answer such a question. Mobs chasing gamines aren't the worst of it. Death squads of off-duty policemen, paid by store-owners who think the presence of gamines on the streets is bad for business, kill dozens of them every week and dump their bodies in the gutters. The authorities do nothing about it."

"How can people deal with the sight of so much suffering? How can they sleep knowing what's happening on the streets?"

"Frankly, I think the Devil has taken up residence in Colombia. He's the one who makes good people do evil things. And when good people like you come to Colombia, you place yourself at his mercy."

"You must be joking."

"I don't joke about things like that."

"Isn't that contrary to church doctrine?"

"No. The church believes in the existence of the Devil, and is certain he's always searching for ways to tempt and corrupt mankind. He's just more active in Colombia than elsewhere."

"I don't want to be rude," I said, suddenly afraid she might be right, "but isn't that sort of thinking just an excuse for doing nothing? For justifying the behaviour of mobs and policemen who beat and kill gamines?"

"No, I don't," she said. "And I'd like to ask if Canada is a country the Devil has never visited? Is it a country where good people never do evil things?"

She was smiling and I thought she was just making the point that I was being sanctimonious and wasn't expecting a serious answer.

"In Canada," I said, smiling back to show her I got the joke, "people don't believe in the Devil any more. In the old days they did. The French Jesuits, for example, who came to convert the Indians in the seventeenth century, thought they had come to a land controlled by the Devil. They sent reports back to Paris saying the Indians who tortured and killed their fellow missionaries were agents of the Devil. But nobody I know believes that sort of thing today. Many don't even believe in God. I'm in the group that believes in God but not in the Devil. Maybe because I find the Devil so frightening. But we have never been short of evil in Canada. Plenty of evil down through the centuries."

"Excuse me for asking, but you are brown-skinned and have the eyes of an Indian. Are you an Indian — a Canadian Indian?"

"No, I'm a Métis — a French-speaking Métis — a descendant of an Indian mother and white father sometime in the past."

"Like the *mestizos*?"

"Something like that."

"And how are your people treated by the other Canadians and the government?"

"The Métis have the same rights as other Canadians."

"And how about the Indians?"

"You knew the answer to that question before you asked it. Yes, the Indians are Canada's gamines, the people whose children are taken away from their parents at the age of six and sent to residential schools where more often than not they are harshly treated and indoctrinated in the ways of the white man. But are you saying that injustice to Indians in Canada means I shouldn't be shocked at the treatment of the gamines in Colombia — that there should be some sort of moral equivalence?"

"I'm just one person doing my best to look after a few of the little ones. But I'm also a Colombian and don't want you to judge us without putting matters into context, without recognizing that things are not ideal in other countries as well."

"I accept your point, but how did you become so involved?"

"I've always been concerned about the poor. After I finished my university studies, I joined a religious order that worked with the poor in the barrios. But the government was convinced we were somehow involved in promoting revolution and put pressure on the archbishop who shut us down. I did as I was told, but I was so angry I left the order and began working here on my own."

"Are there many nuns who feel the way you do and leave their orders?"

"Many, and not just nuns. Priests do the same thing. Have you ever heard of Liberation Theology?"

"I have, but don't fully understand it."

"If you want to understand Colombia, you have to study its teachings. Better yet, maybe I could introduce you to Diego Rojas, the person who knows more about the subject than anyone else. He was chaplain at the National University, but angered the oligarchy for telling the students they should dedicate their lives to promoting social justice. The archbishop excommunicated him and drove him from the church and told the secret police he wouldn't object if they arrested Rojas. He left Bogota to join the ELN — that's the National Liberation Army — one of the guerrilla groups fighting government troops in the countryside. I would have done the same if I hadn't been looking after gamines."

"You would really do that?" I said. "Introduce Diego Rojas to a stranger?"

"I can't commit Rojas to meeting you, but he's often told me that the outside world gets its information on the revolutionary struggle from the government and the big oligarch-controlled newspapers. He's even mentioned he would like an opportunity to give his side of the story to objective observers. Maybe he'd like to start with you. You're not a stranger. We've drunk coffee together and exchanged confidences on great moral issues. You're a good man with a sensitive soul, a rare person that Diego would want to know. Besides, diplomats from countries like Canada are honourable people, not like American diplomats who are in league with the CIA and the secret police. Diego comes back on recruiting missions, and always comes to see me. If you want, I'll ask him, and if he agrees — and I can't guarantee that he will — I'll call you."

"Aren't you afraid the secret police will listen in?" I said, trying not to be melodramatic but concerned just the same.

"There's ways around that. If I say 'the package has arrived' when I call, that means you should come that same night to meet him at the shelter at eleven o'clock. But come alone, and wait in your car until we come to join you. But if I say 'the package hasn't arrived,' that means Diego doesn't want to see you."

I left the shelter to return to embassy well aware the meeting with Rojas might well not take place. I had also come to the conclusion that the questions I had been asking had no answers. My choices were limited. I could give up, overwhelmed by culture shock, and go home. I could stumble on ineffectively like Ambassador O'Connor, besieged by the scenes of misery around me, putting in time until my posting was up. Or I could get a grip, harden my heart, and get on with the job Longshaft sent me to do.

I chose the last option — or at least I made the effort — deciding to let nobody, whether a figure in a dream, an ambassador in the midst of a breakdown, or a good-hearted former nun, stand in way of my mission in Colombia. To salve my conscience, I would give 10 percent of my salary to Señora Lopez for her shelter. I would also exercise my discretion as head of the aid section to allocate Canadian government aid money to pay for the addition to the shelter.

As soon as I reached my office, I sent the following message to Longshaft:

> I have the honour to inform you that I arrived in Bogota on November 18 and reported for duty at the embassy. Ambassador O'Connor welcomed me to the mission and gave me a free hand to prepare political and economic reports on Colombia as I saw fit. A week later, I followed up a lead and called on Rosario Lopez, a former nun who is the director of a shelter for street children, located on the fringes of a large barrio in the southern outskirts of the city.
>
> We established excellent personal relations although I was surprised to learn she blamed the Devil for the atrocious behaviour of so many Colombians in recent years. She also provided her views on the roots of discontent in the country and, significantly, she proposed exploring the possibility of arranging a meeting with the revolutionary leader Diego Rojas the next time he visits Bogota from his camp in the countryside. Apparently he is interested in establishing contacts with diplomats to provide the world with his perspective of the "revolutionary struggle." Although the chance of a get-together is not high, I accepted her offer since an opportunity of this nature might never happen again. I am well aware, however, that the Colombian authorities might object on the grounds such a meeting would constitute *prima face*, interference in their internal affairs. Should he find out, Ambassador O'Connor would

likewise not be pleased and seek to cancel my posting and send me home.

I should be grateful for your guidance on how to proceed. Should you prefer I not follow up, I would find an acceptable reason not to meet Rojas. I repeat, however, that such an opportunity is unlikely to happen again.

That night I slept fitfully until seven. The next morning, looking out the back window of the car on the way to the embassy, I pretended the gamines were only unfortunate children, no worse off than the homeless Canadian youth in downtown Ottawa who wash car windows in traffic jams to earn a little cash to top up their welfare cheques — but I knew I was lying to myself. And when later in my office I heard the howl of the mob, I blocked out the sound with loud music and felt terrible.

The return telegram read as follows:

I was gratified to receive the report on your visit to the barrio and on your meeting with Señora Lopez. There is considerable interest in the Task Force in the possibility you might meet Rojas. Should such a meeting take place, you should seek an invitation to make a fact-finding visit to him at his camp and report back. I appreciate that such action might be considered to exceed the normal limits of diplomatic conduct, but the Task Force would not want you to forgo the opportunity to obtain insight into the mindset of the ELN.

6: Saint and Devil

The following week I bought myself a new Volkswagen Beetle — something to blend inconspicuously into the traffic and not attract the attention of car thieves or the secret police. Henceforth, I would be able to travel wherever I wanted without relying on Alfonso and the embassy car. Although I knew the way to the shelter, I made practise runs late in the evenings to get a feel for how long the trip would take should the call come. The rest of the time, I remained close to my desk, worrying about whether I had embarked on something too big to handle. Whenever the telephone rang, I picked it up, hoping Señora Lopez was on the line, only to be disappointed. I tried to keep busy by reading the local newspapers and carrying out routine paperwork, but couldn't concentrate. To make matters worse, the ambassador started coming to my office in the mornings around nine-thirty (after he had scanned the overnight messages from headquarters), and until lunchtime told me story after story about his life in the navy during the war, the important people he had met in his postings, and to rant on about the stupidity of the people at headquarters. In the afternoons, he would reappear and monopolize my time doing the same thing. Apparently he had nothing better to do with his time.

The call, when it finally came late one mid-December after-noon, was anticlimactic. The telephone rang. I picked it up. Señora Lopez said "the package has arrived" and hung up. No hellos or goodbyes. Real spy stuff. The ambassador, who was set-tled into a chair on the other side of my desk, asked me who it was. I said it was a wrong number and found an excuse to leave the office early to prepare myself mentally for my meeting. My goal remained to extract an invitation to visit the ELN camp. If I succeeded, accelerated promotion, maybe even a cross-post-ing to another embassy with enhanced responsibilities, might result. But if I failed, and I spent the night holding inconclusive heart-felt discussions on Liberation Theology and the inequities of Colombia's class system, Longshaft would think I had squan-dered an opportunity, and I would have to find some other way to contact the ELN ... otherwise my career might suffer.

At the appointed time, I was sitting in front of the shelter in in my darkened car, its motor and headlights off, waiting for Señora Lopez and Rojas to join me. There were no streetlamps, but the light from the city reflecting off low lying clouds illumin-ated the neighbourhood. Off in the distance, drifting in from the nearby barrio, came the sounds of babies crying, children playing, music from transistor radios, people laughing, singing and calling to each other, and, from time to time, voices raised in anger. I opened the car door hoping to hear better and in the process lit up the interior with the dome light. Before I could step outside, Señora Lopez, accompanied by someone I assumed was Rojas, came out of the shadows, and hurried toward me.

"I wasn't certain it was you, until you opened the door," Señora Lopez said. "This is my friend Diego. I won't be going with you — you'll want to speak privately to each other." Rojas joined me in the front seat and directed me to a nearby church shrouded in darkness. "I used to preach here," he said, as he pulled out a key and opened a side door. "The churches in Colombia are sanctuaries which the secret police don't violate. We can talk in peace in here for as long as we want."

After waiting a minute for our eyes to adjust to the murky interior, Rojas led me to a pew in the rear, asked me to sit down, and slid in beside me. For the first few minutes, we sat in silence, looking straight ahead, neither one of us wanting to begin. Finally, he turned and said, "This is the first time a diplomat has asked to meet me. Foreign representatives are terrified the Colombian government might object if it was to find out. But you, what's your reason? Is it curiosity? Is it personal? Did your government ask you to contact me?"

"Diplomats meet with leaders of opposition groups in countries all around the world, whether host governments like it or not. I wanted to see you since I'm new here and there're a lot of things about this country I don't understand."

"And so you wanted to consult a priest?"

"Not just any priest."

"You wanted a defrocked priest who's taken up arms against his government?"

"The most reliable source for what's going on, don't you think?"

"That depends what you want to know. And why did you pick me?"

"Because Señora Lopez suggested I meet you. I also wanted to ask the priest why ordinary people in this country chase and beat gamines to death in the streets. And I'd like to know what the revolutionary leader is fighting for."

"I think about those issues all the time. They're tied to others, such as why God permits suffering to happen in the first place. But before we get into such deep matters, let's first get to know each other. So why don't you start by saying where you're from and why you wanted to be a diplomat in Colombia."

I made the mistake of saying I was from Huronia.

"Huronia!" he said, becoming agitated. "You mean the Huronia of St. Jean de Brébeuf! The place where the Jesuits tried and failed to establish the Christian Kingdom of the Wendat! I've always wanted to visit Martyrs' Shrine to pray at the site where the priests were tortured and killed."

I was surprised that anyone in Colombia would know about this footnote to history. But before I could answer him, Rojas launched into a passionate speech on the Jesuits.

"They were revolutionaries before their time. They respected the dignity and culture of the Indians as they converted them. They established a Christian Indian state in Paraguay with its own army and social welfare system that lasted almost two hundred years. They were trying to do the same thing in your part of Canada when the Iroquois came and scattered the Hurons and their priests. I had the Jesuits in mind when I joined the ELN. I just hope our revolution doesn't end in failure like the one in New France."

"I thought Karl Marx was your hero, not Ignatius of Loyola." I said, thinking he might laugh at the comparison.

"They both are," he said, ignoring my attempt at a joke. "And so are Fidel Castro, Che Guevara, Ho Chi Minh, and Abraham Lincoln — all the great revolutionary leaders of history. But the Jesuits occupy a special place in my heart because I'm a Christian."

He then returned to the Jesuits, going on non-stop about his heroes and role models. From time to time, I interrupted him, trying to steer the conversation back to today, to the ELN struggle in the countryside. But he paid me no attention and carried on talking into the early morning hours. Then suddenly — it might even have been in mid-sentence — he asked me what was going on in Quebec.

Taken by surprise, I temporized, asking what he meant.

"Comrades from the FLQ came to see me not so long ago, They'd been to see the Cubans and came here to consult the ELN on how to turn Quebec into an independent communist country. They said they were planning something big, something spectacular that would shake the confidence of the English oppressors and change the political consciousness of the masses."

"Why are you telling me this?" I said. "You know I'll have to make a report."

"I'm telling you so that if the FLQ manages to pull off something dramatic in Quebec, Canada won't blame the ELN. We have enemies enough in the world without adding Canada to the list. Besides, I don't believe French Canadians are being oppressed by anyone. I know all about the Quiet Revolution."

Now that he had passed his message, Rojas wanted to drop the subject of Quebec and move on to other things. I asked him why he had become a priest and then a revolutionary.

"One day when I was a teenager, I was called by Christ to become a priest and was a seminarian in the 1950s, when Pope John XXIII was head of the church. He brought in the reforms of Vatican II allowing priests to celebrate the mass in the language of the people and to reach out to those of other faiths. Here, in Latin America, we had great hopes he would make the church an instrument of social justice, but by the time I was ordained, he was dead and the old guard was blocking change."

"Then why did you take your vows?"

"I would never have renounced my vocation and wanted to continue the fight. After the Vatican turned its back on reform, we launched the Liberation Theology movement to fight for the poor."

"How could that stop oligarchs from taking the lands of *campesinos* and killing Indians?"

"You asked me a little while ago why ordinary, otherwise law-abiding Colombians chase and beat gamines to death in the streets of Bogota. They do it because of sin — sin planted in their hearts by the Devil. The Devil is to blame when we Colombians never forget an insult and never forgive a wrong. The Devil is the reason why we always avenge an injury done to a member of our family even if the hurt was inflicted generations ago. The Devil is looking over the shoulders of the rich, making them want to monopolize the resources of our county, at the cost of exploiting and manipulating the poor."

"I'd like to ask the priest why God allows the Devil free reign to cause suffering in Colombia in the first place," I said, hoping to calm him down.

"Excuse me, Señor Cadotte," he said, stroking his beard, "I don't know the answer to that question. "But I do know," he said, speaking rapidly, "that almost three hundred thousand people have been massacred in this country in my lifetime alone. And I was born just thirty years ago. The people who carried out the killings, manipulated to slaughter others by competing political parties controlled by the oligarchy, were the neighbours of the murdered, friends who had lived in nearby villages for centuries. That is why so many millions of people fled to the barrios of Bogota. It wasn't just to find a better life. It was to escape the slaughter in the countryside. And when they came to Bogota, they infected others with the plague of evil they brought from the countryside. That's why there are more thieves, prostitutes, drug dealers, and killers-for-hire in Colombia than any other place in South America. That's why I rededicated myself to my life as priest, to be able to work with the poor and combat the Devil who is alive and thriving in the souls of our people."

"When you speak of the Devil being alive in the souls of the people, I assume you are speaking metaphorically?"

The words had barely left my mouth when Rojas leaped to his feet, shook his fist at me and cried out, "Get thee behind me Satan! Get thee behind me!"

I recoiled, wondering what I had done or said to enrage him, making ready to get away if he were to turn on me. But his passion spent, Rojas collapsed back onto the pew, bowed his head in prayer, and muttered what I took to be some sort of invocation.

"The Devil was with us in the church and took possession of your soul," Rojas quietly told me when he finished praying. "But I drove him away."

This man is insane, I thought. *Everyone in this country is crazy.* "I think we should be going," I said. "It's late."

"No, no, no, no," Rojas said, grasping me by the arm. "We can't leave yet. We have too much to talk about. I'm sorry if I frightened you, but it was for your own good. It won't happen again, I assure you."

When I made no reply but stayed put, Rojas told me about his efforts to introduce Liberation Theology to Colombia. "To help the poor and combat the Devil, I went into the churches and called on the oligarchs to share their wealth and their political power with the people. I called on the clergy to go into the barrios and work with the people."

"Like Jesus driving out money-changers from the Temple?"

"That's one way of looking at it."

"What was the reaction of the church hierarchy?"

"They were terrified the oligarchs would blame them for my actions, even though they were from the same class. They banned me from preaching in the churches but I went to university campuses, public parks — anywhere at all to call for a revolution in thinking among all sectors of the population. Whenever I spoke, huge crowds — not just the poor, but members of the middle class and students, professors, and artists — gathered to hear me. Then the archbishop called me in one day and formally ordered me to stop making speeches. I refused and he excommunicated me. I then left Bogota to join the ELN and to fight with an AK-47 in my hands. The ELN gave me command of one its units and we've been battling government troops for the past year."

"But how can you reconcile your role as a priest, even one expelled by the Church, with taking up arms. Did you lose your faith? Is that why you're able to kill policemen and soldiers?"

"My faith is strongest when I must kill. It is written in the Gospels that Christ said, 'I come not to bring peace, but to bring a sword.' In taking up arms on behalf of the poor, I am carrying out his will and fulfilling my ordination pledge to serve as intermediary between God and man."

"Does that mean you're prepared to kill *campesino* conscripts forced to join the army for the sake of the revolution?"

"That's right — God will forgive me for taking lives in a just cause."

"Don't the oligarchs and the church hierarchy claim God is on their side and you — not them — represent the forces of evil in Colombia?"

"They do, but they're wrong. God is always on the side of the weak. It's written in the gospels."

"But how can you expect a few hundred men scattered in a region as big as France to overthrow a country like Colombia with its tens of thousands of soldiers, helicopters, fighter planes, and American advisers?

"That's illusionary strength. We follow the teachings of Che, who said a few committed revolutionary fighters supported by the masses could overthrow a country whatever its size — provided the conditions were ripe.

"But look what happened to Che in Bolivia — hunted down and killed by a Ranger battalion trained by the Americans.

"But Che was not supported by the *campesinos* of Bolivia. Here we have their support."

"Are you supported by the Cubans?"

"Yes of course. Che Guevara and Fidel Castro are our heroes. I've been to see them in Havana. The Cubans help us as best they can, flying arms and equipment into remote airstrips — but Cuba is a poor country and its aid is limited."

"But Castro and his followers are communists. They're atheists. How can you accept aid from atheists?"

Taking me by the hand, Rojas led me to the front of the church and lit a candle to illuminate the sanctuary. "See," he said, pointing to a painting of Christ, a crown of thorns on his head, nailed to the cross, with blood oozing from his wounds. "The gamines beaten to death on the sidewalks, the Indians hunted and killed by paramilitary forces, the families starving in the barrios — all those who are ground down under the oppression of the oligarchy — are the suffering Christ. I'm worshiping Christ when I help them. The Cuban comrades are doing the same, even if they don't know it. I may call myself a Christian, and they may consider themselves communists and atheists, but we're all worshiping Christ in the suffering people."

"Would you call yourself a Christian Marxist?" I asked. "Like the worker priests of France a few years ago?"

Rojas may have thought I was showing off by displaying my knowledge of recent Church history and didn't answer. Instead, he led me back to the pew and asked me how he could best help me understand the revolutionary struggle. I quickly proposed he let me visit him in his camp in the hills. I could come on a fact-finding mission, I told him.

"Why not," said Rojas with the assurance of someone who trusts others easily. "Fidel welcomed journalists to his camp in the Sierra Maestra during his campaign to liberate Cuba. Their reports built support for his cause internationally."

"I remember them," I said. "The Toronto newspapers carried the same stories and the students in my high school were all hoping Castro would win."

"Yes, let me think about it. But before deciding, I'd like to ask a question."

"Go ahead," I said, "I'll give you an honest answer."

"What do you value more than anything else in the world?"

"Ambition and the love of family."

"I like that," he said. "You're not afraid to admit you're ambitious." He then punched me playfully on the shoulder, indicating I had passed some sort of test. "You're a decent person," he said, "someone I'd be proud to welcome to my camp. And don't feel you have to come on a fact-finding mission. Come as a friend of the revolution and to experience the hospitality of the ELN. I guarantee it would be something you'll never forget — something to tell your grandchildren someday. Even though we've just met, I feel I've known you forever."

"What's the next step?" I asked. "Do you have to clear your decision with your men?"

"I don't have to get anyone's permission," he said. "The others trust me just as I trust you. As long as you know how to ride a horse, it will happen."

I should have asked him why excellence in riding should be a condition for making a fact-finding mission, but I didn't, not wanting to give him a reason for changing his mind. Instead I told him horseback riding had been one of my favourite sports as a teenager, and he slapped me on the knee and said he thought that would be the case. "Now just be patient," he said, "I'll be back in touch with you through Rosario within the month."

The next morning, so early only the Colombian cleaning staff was around, I went to my office, closed the door, prepared a pot of coffee, and began writing the report I would send to Longshaft. By the time the other Canadian staff arrived for work, I had finished.

I have the honour to report that I met for six hours last night with Rojas in a secure location in the vicinity of the shelter for homeless children described in my recent message. Following are the highlights of our discussion:

1. We established an excellent personal rapport.
2. Rojas revealed an astonishing knowledge of Canada and its history ranging from the activities of the Jesuits in seventeenth-century New France to the Quiet Revolution in Quebec today.
3. His models for revolutionary action are Ignatius of Loyola, Pope John XXIII, Karl Marx, Fidel Castro, Che Guevara, Ho Chi Minh, and Abraham Lincoln.
4. Rojas is man of deep faith and political convictions who sees the face of Christ in the suffering people.
5. Rojas, like his friend, Rosario Lopez, blames the Devil for the evil committed by man in Colombia.
6. He recently received a visit from members of the FLQ seeking his advice on how to change Quebec from an oppressive capitalist province dominated by a racist English-speaking minority (as they characterized it) to an independent communist country run by and for the francophone majority. Most interestingly, they informed him they were planning to conduct a major terrorist operation in Quebec but provided no detail on target(s), timing(s), or location(s). The reason he provided such information to me, he said, was because he did not believe the people of

Quebec were oppressed, and was concerned Canadian authorities would learn of the FLQ visit to Colombia and blame the ELN for the upcoming actions of the FLQ in Quebec, setting back his plans to garner international support for the ELN cause.

7. Rojas was open to allowing me to make a fact-finding visit to his camp, but wanted time to think about it. The visit, if it were to occur, it would not happen before mid-January 1970.

I should be grateful for your instructions.

After reading the draft over for the last time, I added a final paragraph saying I was confident an invitation to visit Rojas at his camp would be forthcoming. I signed my name at the bottom, and delivered it by hand to the ninth floor communications centre. I was sure Longshaft would be pleased at my evening's work.

He was. The following is his answer, received three days later.

The Task Force read with great interest and not a little admiration your most recent report. You are to be commended for your initiative in arranging to meet Rojas and your skill in extracting pertinent information from him on matters affecting Canada's national security.

The information he provided on the elements that that led him to a life of terrorism will be shared with our American and British friends to augment data bases they maintain on roots of the phenomenon. His belief that the Devil lies behind unjust actions of Colombian oligarchs is of particular interest. On one hand, such a view reflects an irrational and gullible personality disorder that incorporates superstition into its worldview. On the other hand, if it is ascertained that other adherents of Liberation Theology are of same opinion as Rojas, our American and British friends could incorporate finding in their psychological and misinformation warfare strategies to discredit terrorists and their sympathizers among potential sympathizers.

The Task Force is, as you might expect, most interested and disturbed by report that FLQ representatives have been to see Rojas. We have long suspected they have contacts with terrorist organisations in Latin America like the ELN, in the Middle East like the PLO, and in South Africa like the ANC. Our concern is that FLQ will contact Cuba, if this hasn't already happened. Should Havana decide to provide material and training support to FLQ, the terrorist threat to Canada would increase immeasurably.

The Task Force would have preferred you to push your interlocutor to provide more information about the visit of the FLQ, for example by asking for names and descriptions of delegation members and pressing him to give you an indication of when and where terrorist operation would be carried out. It is important therefore that you continue the dialogue with Rojas, who apparently holds you in high regard. To this end, we authorize you to make a fact-finding visit to his camp in which your primary goal will be to obtain more information from him on FLQ intentions and plans.

7: Heather Sinclair

Time passed slowly as I waited for word from Rojas. To escape the daily visits from the ambassador, I sought out things to do outside the office. I called on Señora Lopez to tell her I had found the money in the embassy aid budget to pay for the expansion of the shelter, and handed over the first instalment of my own conscience money to use as she saw fit. I felt ill at ease when she thanked me, kissing me on the cheek, and telling me I was an angel sent by God to do his work in Colombia — when that was utter nonsense. I also paid a visit to a shop, not far from the embassy, distributing used clothing to the poor of downtown Bogota, managed by a CUSO volunteer. That was where I met Heather Sinclair.

She had the pouty lips and big, bold eyes of Brigitte Bardot and the voluptuous body of Marilyn Monroe — the sex symbols of that era. I waited until she finished serving a customer and introduced myself. She told me to sit down, closed the door, and came to join me. I asked her questions about the operations of her centre, but she answered in monosyllables. I tried to talk aid policy but she said she was tired of the subject. I invited her out to dinner at a nearby restaurant, and she accepted.

When the meal was over she said, "Let's get to know each other better." And for Heather, that meant coming back to my apartment, drinking Chilean Underraga Tinto wine, smoking cigarettes, discussing existentialism, and making love throughout the night. We met again the next evening after work for a meal and returned to my apartment for another night of conversation, love-making, and this time some sleep. She told me she was from Winnipeg, born just after the war when her father returned home after four years in the Canadian army in Europe to take up a position as branch manager for one of the big Canadian banks. She said that while vacationing at the family cottage, the summer before entering first year at the University of Manitoba, she was listening to an album of songs by Bob Dylan and suddenly realized her parents' life wasn't for her. She didn't want to marry young, raise two children, teach Sunday school, go to potluck suppers, drive a station wagon, join a service club, spend her summers at the lake, and take a holiday in Florida during March break. She didn't want to lead the usual comfortable life of the middle class, only to wake up when she was old to find she hadn't done anything in life she had really wanted.

She left home to attend the University of Toronto where she embraced Flower Power, the New Left, marches and rallies against the Vietnam War, Women's Liberation, and Third World causes. She went off as an exchange student at the Sorbonne in Paris for a year where she developed a taste for foul-smelling Gauloises cigarettes, cheap red wine, and onion soup. She said she was one of the groupies who hung out with Jean Paul Sartre and Simone de Beauvoir hoping to be chosen to share their bed. "For obvious reasons," she said, she was often the lucky one. Sartre and de Beauvoir concentrated on sex while she tried to discuss existentialism with him and women's rights with her. I didn't want to believe her.

She asked me if I was French Canadian, saying Frenchmen made the best lovers. I said, "Not exactly. I'm a French-speaking Métis." She asked me where I came from, and I said Penetang. I added that I had graduated from the University of Ottawa in the spring of 1966 and joined the Department a few months later. She said she really wasn't interested in my life story and was just making conversation and I told her nothing else. She told me her favourite authors were Allen Ginsberg and Jack Kerouac and quoted at length from *Howl* and *On the Road*.

I didn't like her taste in literature, but in an effort to appear interested, said I did. When she asked me to name my favourite book, I took my revenge by saying I didn't have one, but a series of favourites, written by priests in the seventeenth century, called the *Jesuit Relations*. I thought she'd laugh at such an outrageous choice, but after asking me to describe the plot, she said she'd borrow it from the library on her return to Canada, if only to read the torture scenes.

I went to the office that week as usual but walked around in a daze unable to think of anything but her. When she suggested I accompany her to a bring-your-own-booze party being thrown by a member of the American Peace Corps by the name of Charles Bullock on Friday night, I agreed. The evening got off to a bad start. We were making our way through the heavy evening traffic when Heather nonchalantly remarked she had been seeing a lot of Charles since her arrival in Colombia. "Something I thought I'd mention in case he acts jealous," she said, reaching over and stroking the inside of my thigh. "Just because he sleeps with me, he thinks he owns me."

It took a few seconds for her words to register, but when they did, I shoved her hand away and pulled over. "Are you still sleeping with this guy?"

"Not since I met you," she said. "But if he was to ask me to spend the night with him, and I was free, I probably would. I like him."

"Then being together this past week meant nothing to you?"

"Now you're behaving like Charles."

"Don't you think I have a right to be upset?"

"Look, Luc," she said. "Don't pull that male chauvinist bullshit on me. I already told you I'm a liberated woman. I like you, but I like other guys too. I'll sleep with anyone I want."

"Then get the hell out of my car. You can walk to your friend Charles's."

"I can't believe this. Do you know what would happen to a woman alone on the side of the road after dark in Bogota? I wouldn't last half an hour before I was mugged or worse. Just take me to Charles's. We can discuss our relationship some other time."

I put the car in gear and carried on, determined to see no more of her after the end of the evening. But she took my hand and told me she really liked me. "But you got to understand," she added, "I feel as strongly about my principles as you do about yours. Show a little flexibility. We can work this out."

By the time we reached Charles's, I had calmed down. Frankly, I couldn't have cared less about her views on Sartre and existentialism, Women's Liberation, the poetry of Allen Ginsberg and Jack Kerouac — or for the gaggle of draft-dodgers I was about to meet — but I didn't want to lose her. We might not have shared many interests, but I was lonely and she filled a void in my life at the time. After parking the car, but before going in to join the others, I took her by the hands, drew her to me, and told her I was sorry for my behaviour in the car. "It's just I've never met anyone like you before. I'm still a small-town guy at heart but I'm willing to learn."

"Oh, don't be silly," she said. "You're cute and funny — or at least you say funny things — and you're good in bed."

I put my head close to hers and whispered, "I thought back in the car you were telling me our relationship was over." She laughed, freed herself from my grip and looked at me sardonically. "Don't overdo it," she said before throwing her arms around me and thrusting her tongue deep into my ear with the consequences that can only be imagined. She then pushed me away and laughed again. "You're an animal just like me," she said. "We're going to get along just fine because we understand each other. Now let's go in and meet my friends."

The party was even worse than I had expected. With Heather leading the way, clutching our contribution to the evening's festivities — a bottle of Bacardi rum I had bought at a duty-free shop — we entered a dimly lit, rundown apartment building filled with the sounds of dogs barking and children laughing and calling to each other in the stairwell. The earthy smells of rice, beans, pork, yucca, and plantains, cooked for dinner earlier in the evening by the working-class residents, lingered in the air. Children appeared out of the shadows to run up to Heather, calling out her name and asking if she had brought them candies. To my surprise, she produced handfuls of them from her coat pockets, and distributed them to her young friends to squeals of delight.

We trudged up four flights of stairs to the rooftop apartment Charles shared with three other Peace Corps volunteers, went in without knocking, and stood just inside to get our bearings. Candles stuck in empty rum bottles provided a dim light and the air reeked with the skunky smell of marijuana and cheap cigarettes. A dozen or more people — men and women about my age or a little older — were clustered together in the centre of the room engaged in earnest conversation and smoking pot. Two oversize posters of Che Guevara covered the opposite wall. In one, he was the guerrilla warrior, wearing a black beret with a red star and pointing a pistol at an unseen enemy. In the other, he was the martyr, his eyes filled with pain and suffering and his body punctured with holes from the bullets of his executioners after they killed him in Bolivia a year or so before.

"Wait right here while I go to the kitchen to find some glasses and fix us some drinks," Heather said. Fascinated by the juxtaposed images on the posters, I walked over to examine them more closely.

Staring hard at Che the warrior, I saw him change into Rojas, the avenging angel, brandishing a bloody sword over a fallen enemy. When I switched my gaze to Che the martyr, he morphed into Rojas the Christ nailed to the cross crowned with thorns with blood dripping from his forehead and from the wounds to his hands and side. I looked away, aware that my imagination was playing tricks on me, but at the same time, filled with a premonition of what the future held in store for the defrocked priest.

I then heard the soft voice of Buffy Sainte-Marie singing "Universal Soldier" coming from a gramophone somewhere in the room. She was telling me, in the mood I was in, that Che Guevara, Diego Rojas, and every other revolutionary who took up arms to fight for justice were but pawns in the hands of divine providence and their efforts to bring about a better world were doomed to failure.

"Here's your drink." Heather was tugging on my sleeve to get my attention. "And snap out of it," she said. "You look like you've seen a ghost."

"I was listening to the Buffy Sainte-Marie. She's a favourite of mine."

"That's another thing we've got in common," she said as she led the way, her drink in one hand and the bottle in the other, to join the nearby guests.

"Why doesn't the upper class in this country share its wealth with the poor," a bearded volunteer, speaking with a heavy Swedish accent and smoking a joint, was asking. "Colombia is supposed to be a democracy, but the oligarchs get themselves elected promising reforms which never happen and simply share power among themselves. I know it's not part of their culture, but the Colombians should start volunteering to help the poor, like people do in our countries."

"But some do," I said, intervening in the conversation. I introduced myself, adding that I was Canadian. Heather did the same, saying she was a member of CUSO, but the others didn't acknowledge our presence. Apparently it ran contrary to conventional wisdom in aid circles to admit Colombians might have social consciences.

"As I was saying," the Swede said, continuing his monologue, "civil society as we know it in Sweden doesn't exist in this country or anywhere in Latin America for that matter."

I couldn't let that pass. "I know a former nun who runs a shelter for gamines," I said. "I've visited it and can attest to the good work she's doing."

"Are you some sort of volunteer?" the Swede said, making a show of looking doubtfully at my neatly pressed slacks, clean white shirt, and cashmere sweater as if I didn't belong in his company.

"No, I'm not," I said. "I'm a second secretary at the Canadian embassy, newly arrived in Colombia. The people who support the former nun's efforts are working class people — like one of the drivers at my embassy. I don't think you can generalize about anybody, including Colombians."

"Okay, Mr. Second Secretary," the Swede said. "Tell me how many gamines are being cared for at your friend's shelter."

"About a dozen, I guess, but I'm doing what I can to get funding from the Canadian embassy to double that number."

"And how many gamines are there in Bogota?"

"Who knows? I've seen some statistics — maybe thirty thousand?"

"You just made my case. Even with embassy help, your friend the nun's efforts are a drop in the bucket. It proves you can't rely on volunteers to do the job governments should be doing to meet the needs of their most deprived citizens. Even the work of foreign volunteers like the people in this room makes no difference in the overall scheme of things. "

"Then what's the answer?"

"The people in this country need a revolution to kick the parasites in charge of Colombia out on their asses and start fresh."

"You mean have a Cuban-style revolution?"

"Exactly," the Swede said, to murmurs of approval from the others in the group, including Heather. "Liberal democracy has been a failure here and in every one of these God-forsaken countries. Those on the top will never give up power until they're forced to."

"What about the people who'll die in the process."

"That'd be a one-time cost of bringing about social justice."

"How can you be so sure the costs would be one-time? Look what happened in the Soviet Union. After Lenin and Stalin took control, there were mass killings and the gulag. In China the killings go on decades after Mao seized control. And in Cuba, Castro's victory was followed by drumhead trials and mass executions."

"That's out-of-date thinking. Third World revolutionary movements put the people and not the party first. You diplomats really should get out of your cloisters and see what's going on in the real world."

From the way the others nodded their heads in agreement, I was the outsider whose views weren't welcome in their closed universe. I'd been treated the same way when invited to similar parties at university, where the lighting came from candles stuck in the necks of wine bottles, where the air was blue from marijuana smoke, and where the guests gathered in small groups to solve the problems of the world. They were parties where no quarter was given to anyone like me who went to mass on Sundays, who didn't do drugs, who spoke French with a Franco-Ontarian accent, and who didn't buy into the left-wing consensus in the room. In those days, I told myself I didn't care what others thought, but it hurt when the Anglophones called me a square and the Quebecers a *petit bourgeois*. The Swede's remarks were a put down and I didn't like it. My first reaction was to reply in kind, but I restrained myself. After all, I was the lucky one in the room, holding down a job as a diplomat in a well-respected embassy while the Swede and his friends were probably still wondering what they would do with their lives when they left Colombia.

A volunteer, whom I took to be British from his accent, spoke up to say insurgency groups had been fighting for years to overthrow the established order in Colombia and had gotten nowhere. Maybe armed revolution would never work in Colombia.

"I don't agree," the Swede said. "Out in the bush where I'm working, the ELN has the government forces on the run."

"What's the ELN?" Heather asked.

"ELN is short for *ejército de liberación nacional*, the pro-Cuban Army of National Liberation Army," the know-it-all Swede said. "It's been around for a few years and is made up of landless *campesinos* and students and intellectuals from the cities. Apparently, the famous defrocked priest, Diego Rojas, has joined its ranks and is in charge of one of its camps. A lot of people say he's Colombia's own Che Guevara, rallying the sons and daughters of the upper classes to the cause and even attracting members of the clergy who can't tolerate the efforts of the of the old guard bishops to maintain the status quo at all costs."

Others joined in to add scraps of information they'd picked from their sources about the ELN and Rojas. I knew things about him the others didn't, but my information was privileged, and I wasn't about to share it to score points at a party. Their views confirmed my impression that Rojas was someone extraordinary, someone who came along once every hundred years, with the potential to change the course of history. I truly hoped he'd send a message saying I was welcome to visit his camp. I wanted to discover the source of his charisma. I wanted to see for myself whether the taking up of arms in favour of a just cause was compatible with his role of priest, because even though excommunicated, he remained one under church law and doctrine.

Perhaps thinking I would once again start arguing with the Swede, Heather took me by the arm and led me away. "It's time you met Charles," she said. "His tour in Colombia is almost over and he's outside on the roof with his friends. He knows about you and says he has no hard feelings."

In those days, I was given to juvenile fits of pique and almost blurted out, "What about my feelings?" but thought better of it and mumbled, "Why not, he's the host isn't he?"

"The real hosts are the guys he's lives with, and this is a party to say goodbye."

I had been prepared to meet another hostile, heavily bearded, long-haired radical like the Swede when I followed Heather out onto the terrace to meet the man I now regarded as my rival. Instead, Charles greeted me warmly and asked us to join the group at his table.

"Cigarette?" he said, holding out a pack. I declined but Heather took one and poured drinks from our bottle for everyone before sitting down.

"Heather's told me about you," Charles said. "She says you're a nice guy. I hope she's right because I wouldn't want her to get hurt."

I didn't know what to say. His voice was soft. He was polite, clean shaven, and stylishly dressed in expensive slacks and shirt. He could have been one of my classmates at our Lake Kingsmere cottage. But, despite his nice words, I had the sense he was handing Heather over to me like a discarded mistress now that he was leaving. I didn't like him.

"So what are you going to do after Colombia," I said to make conversation.

"I'm trying to sort that out right now, like these other guys," he said, looking at the others who were listening to our conversation. "I joined the Peace Corps to avoid the draft and get sent to Vietnam. Back in 1966, the war had been going on for so long, I thought it'd be finished by the time my tour in Colombia was over. But here we are, two years later, and the fighting goes on with no end in sight."

"Are you going to report to your draft board?"

"You gotta be kidding," he said as the others laughed. "There's no way I'll go to Vietnam and kill a bunch of peasants fighting for their freedom. That's why I'm heading straight to Canada to make a new life for myself. It shouldn't be too hard to land a job. I graduated in engineering from Texas A&M and things are booming up there. Maybe I'll even find a Canadian girl to marry and live happily ever after."

He looked directly at Heather when made the last remark, and that made me mad. Charles and Heather had discussed getting together sometime in the future, maybe after she had finished her tour of duty with CUSO in two years' time! I would fill in until she saw him again! I was keeping myself under control, however, and if Heather and I were still talking when the party ended, I'd find out the truth.

It didn't take long, however, before I got into an argument with one of the other Americans. It started innocently enough, he asked me if I had attended any of the anti-war protests in New York and Washington in the past year. I said I hadn't. Raising his voice a little, he said, "Why not, don't you want the U.S.A. out of Vietnam?" From the way he was slurring his words, he was drunk and I answered him as nicely as I could.

"That's something for the American people and their government to sort out."

"That's a cop out. Tell us what you really think."

Losing patience, I told him that I didn't have to explain myself to him or anyone else.

"Oh yes you do," he said. "Everyone in this room is opposed to the war and in favour of social justice for the poor everywhere. Why did you come if don't share our views? "

"I'm here because Heather invited me. If I'm not welcome, I'll go."

"Relax, I was just having a bit of fun. Seriously though, what do you do think of the war?"

"If the communists win in Vietnam, it wouldn't be long before they take over all of Southeast Asia. The strategic balance in the region would change and Western security would be endangered," I said, parroting views I had accepted without question when espoused by Longshaft. But as the words left my mouth, I knew they were simplistic and naïve — a month in Colombia had changed my outlook on conflict in the Third World. Jonathan Hunter, the gentle member of my interview board, Rosario Lopez and Diego Rojas, and a handful of aid volunteers attending a party in Bogota had a greater understanding of the roots of the war than I had. But I wasn't ready to admit I was wrong.

"That's the official American line on the war — that's the sort of lying crap the Administration used to get Congressional support for the Tonkin Gulf Resolution, word for word. Surely you don't believe that bullshit," Charles said, injecting himself into the debate.

I lost my temper. I'd had a drink or two by then and, I must admit, I shared the notorious sense of inferiority about Americans that many Canadians possessed in that era. "Why don't you do your duty and go fight for your country in Vietnam," I said, letting him know he couldn't mess with a Canadian.

"Don't pay any attention," Heather said. "He's had too much to drink."

"No I haven't. I'm cold sober."

"Are all Canadians moralizing hypocrites like you?" Charles said. "Maybe I won't go to Canada after all."

"Stay home then. Nobody would care."

"Why don't you bugger off. You don't belong here."

"Are you coming," I asked Heather when I got up to go, expecting she would stay. But she left with me, neither looking back nor saying goodbye to anyone. And the next day, she moved into my apartment with all her possessions.

In the following weeks, we went together to the dinners, receptions, and parties held by the members of the Canadian and foreign community to celebrate the holiday season. Heather didn't behave herself anywhere. She made herself up to shock, with a platinum blond wig, bright red lipstick, accentuated cheekbones, black eyeliner, and blue, iridescent eye shadow. She drank too much, laughed too loudly, smoked her foul-smelling cigarettes, told off-colour jokes, and flirted openly and brazenly with the husbands. She wore to all events long black stockings, black leather boots almost to her knees, a short-short mini-skirt, and a close fitting blouse with a low-cut neckline exposing cleavage that left nothing to the imagination. During the singing of carols at the Christmas dinner at the official residence for the staff, she deliberately sang off-key, provoking laughter and upsetting the ambassador and his wife. And when Mrs. O'Connor made a point of asking her where she was living, Heather said she shared an apartment with two other CUSO volunteers, but everyone else knew she was living in sin with me. To my surprise, the other staff members, tired of going to the same old boring Christmas parties every year, loved her, laughing at her antics and manoeuvring to sit beside her. In retrospect, I should have known better than to bring her to the ambassador's Christmas dinner … or for that matter to any of the other events. But I was besotted with her and wasn't thinking straight.

But while my colleagues thought she was the life of the party, the O'Connors were not amused. Nor, it appeared, was the Papal Nuncio, the ultra-conservative envoy of the ultra-conservative Vatican to the ultra-conservative Catholic hierarchy of Colombia. That became clear when the embassy reopened its doors after the holiday season. I arrived for work around nine o'clock — later than usual since I had little to do at the office — and was met at the door by the ambassador's private secretary who looked concerned.

"The boss has been waiting for you and he's not in a good mood," she said. I went to his office door, knocked and entered as was my normal practice. The ambassador frowned, motioned for me to take a seat, and said he wanted to discuss a delicate matter. He pushed back his chair, went to the window and stared outside, and said nothing for some time.

"Mrs. O'Connor and I attended a reception to mark the New Year for heads of post at the presidential palace yesterday," he finally said, turning to face me.

"I hope everyone had a good time."

"No we didn't," he said. "Monsignor Ballacci, the nuncio, called me to one side and said he had heard from an impeccable source that you had been seen visiting an establishment run by a former nun, someone known to the police who harbours views hostile to the Church and the government of Colombia."

"She runs a shelter for gamines and is a good contact. I'm even planning to authorize some funding from our aid budget to let her expand her facilities."

"She may be doing good work but you must be careful. Baldacci has close ties to the church hierarchy and the secret police. They may be watching you."

"Anything else?" I said, hoping the interview was over.

The ambassador said that unfortunately there was — something that had badly upset his wife and disappointed him. "Monsignor Baldacci told me you were living in sin with a woman who wasn't your wife. I assume the woman is the young lady who disrupted the singing of carols at our Christmas dinner?"

"Her name is Heather and my living arrangements are none of his business."

"But it is his business. As nuncio, he's responsible for ensuring high ethical standards are maintained by all members of the diplomatic corps. It's my business too. The Department doesn't allow employees to live with women they're not married to."

"I understand it also has a veto over who we can marry," I said.

"As a man of the world, I don't care whom you sleep with, but rules are rules."

"Isn't the Department out of date with the times?"

"That's not for you or me to decide. Mrs. O'Connor is also aware Heather lied about where she's living. In the circumstances, Heather has to leave your apartment."

"And what if I don't agree?"

"Then I'll send you home and your career will be over." I must have looked worried because O'Connor, at heart a decent person added, "why don't you just marry her and make an honest woman out of her? That'll solve everybody's problem. She'll never be a proper Foreign Service wife, but I'll give you my approval just the same."

"I'll see what can be done," I said, not daring to tell him that Heather didn't believe in marriage and would probably say no. But I was actually happy — elated even. I wouldn't otherwise have had the nerve to propose marriage to her. And so that evening, I mentioned to her as nonchalantly as I could that the ambassador had told me that "for the sake of appearances" we either had to get married or she'd have to move out.

At first she laughed, but when she saw my face, she asked, "Is that what you want?" Relieved that she hadn't rejected the idea out of hand, I said, "I don't want you to move out."

With a tight smile, she said, "That's a strange way to make a proposal, but I don't want move out either. Let me think about it. I'll let you know in the morning."

That night, I couldn't sleep, and to avoid disturbing her, I took a pillow and a blanket and went to the living room to sit on a couch, drink a beer, and think over what I was getting myself into. What if she said she'd marry me? We hardly knew each other and I didn't love her, at least not in the usual sense of the term — like love portrayed in the movies. I had been down this road before with Charlotte — ready to marry someone I didn't love until we both realized it wouldn't work. But in contrast to my feelings for Charlotte, I was obsessed with Heather and would be desperately unhappy if I lost her. That was all that mattered.

Heather was sitting at the end of the couch the next morning when I opened my eyes. "The answer is yes," she said, on seeing I was awake. "I'll marry you, if that's what you really want. It doesn't matter one way or another to me." Her lack of enthusiasm confirmed my suspicion that she'd deceive me some day, but I didn't care. It was what I wanted. Afraid of her answer, I didn't dare ask if she had given up the idea of having an open marriage. Instead, I went into my bedroom and rummaged through my stuff until I found the engagement ring Charlotte had handed back to me when our relationship collapsed.

We both had trouble not laughing when I handed it to her. But she put it on and our engagement was official. Later on that day, we called on the ambassador and his wife at the official residence with the news. The ambassador offered us drinks but not congratulations, and Mrs. O'Connor cattily asked Heather if she'd be moving out of my apartment until after the wedding. "Of course," Heather told her. I don't think Mrs. O'Connor believed her ... but then, neither did I.

8: Raid on Sucio

On a cold, wet day in mid-January, Señora Lopez telephoned me at the embassy and asked me to call on her at the shelter. "I know a better place to talk," she said, after putting a finger to her lips when I went to see her. Equipped with an umbrella against the rain, she took me to the church where I had met with Rojas a month before, and led the way inside.

"I have excellent news," she said after checking to be sure we were alone. "Diego has sent word confirming his invitation. However, the comrades aren't happy — they're afraid the secret police might follow you and we've had to take precautions to make sure that won't happen."

"I'll do my part," I said. "I'll tell everyone that I'm leaving on a familiarization trip to the Llanos."

Two days later I travelled by communal taxi from Bogota to Villavicencio, some twelve hours down the mountain in the hot Colombian rainforest. Following the advice of Señora Lopez, I had crammed into a knapsack a hammock to string up between the trees for sleeping, mosquito repellant and netting, and a couple of bottles of rum to offer as gifts to Rojas. With a poncho covering my shoulders, my straight black hair, brown skin, and black eyes, I could easily have passed for a Colombian *mestizo* had I wanted to travel incognito.

But that was not part of my cover story. Señora Lopez told me to show my diplomatic passport if I was challenged by the police and explain I was on my way to spend a night with an American missionary at Cravo Norte, at the junction of the Casanare and Cravo Norte rivers in the southeastern part of the country. The missionary, I was to say, would take me up the Casanare River to spend a week or so at a settlement of Indians and learn about their way of life. That would be my excuse to make a side trip to see Rojas.

After a night in a cockroach-infested hotel at Villavicencio, I scrambled aboard an ancient DC-3 plane at the local airport and took my place among the passengers — soldiers returning from leave, cowboys, *campesinos*, chickens, and pigs — and flew to Cravo Norte where Jim Hetherington, the American missionary and underground supporter of the ELN, met me. Before leaving the airport, however, a policeman asked me to identify myself. When I produced my passport, he was suspicious, and demanded to know what a diplomat was doing travelling in a dangerous frontier area. He let me go when Jim stepped in to back up my story.

That night over dinner, Jim told me he was a member of a mid-West American fundamentalist church that had been working for decades to convert the Indians to Christianity. In recent years, paramilitary killers, hired by the big landowners, had begun raiding the Indian villages located on the jungle fringe along the along the Casanare River, killing the men and raping the women to drive off the people and open the area for large-scale cattle ranching. The government, he said, supported the landowners and the ELN did its best to protect the Indians. As a missionary, he was supposed to stay out of politics, but he supported the ELN in any way he could.

The next morning, Jim handed me over to his gardener, an Indian who spoke only his native language, to take me upriver by motorized canoe fifty miles to the settlement. "Somebody from the ELN will meet you there, and take you the rest of the way. He'll take you to Rojas."

The comrades scowled and turned their backs and Rojas didn't look at all happy when I arrived in the early evening at his camp a few days later. He greeted me stiffly, accepting my gift of rum without a thank you. "My men think your visit is a big mistake," he said.

"But we took every precaution to avoid being followed and I thought everyone approved my visit. Do you want me to leave?"

"No I don't. The comrades aren't strategists. They don't see the big picture. Just because the ELN controls part of the Llanos, they think victory over the oligarchs is within reach. They don't realize that as long as the outside world supports the government, we'll have no hope of winning. The balance of forces against us is just too great. They don't understand our need to bring outsiders like you to see our operations up close, and report back to your governments on the justice of our cause. I look upon your visit as being the first of many by objective diplomats and serious journalists. That's why I'm taking you along when we attack the town of Sucio, down on the Llanos. You'll be able to send a spectacular report."

"You can't be serious."

"Revolutionaries make revolutions," he said, "and the comrades get restive if they aren't in action. Besides, these operations are the way we popularize our cause, recruit new members, and replenish food and medical supplies. But I also want you to see true revolutionaries in action and be a witness to the love and esteem of the ordinary people of Colombia for the ELN. If the scouts make it back tonight as planned, and if their report is favourable, we'll leave tomorrow at dawn."

I listened to Rojas with growing unease. "But I'm here on a fact-finding mission," I said. "I'm a non-combatant and a diplomat. I can't participate in military operations."

"You won't be participating in a military action. You'll be observing a military action. The distinction is important. Besides, I've already told the comrades you'd show your support by accompanying us into action. If you don't, you'll undermine my authority. And if I lose control, I won't be able to guarantee your safety. They might insist on holding you for ransom or worse."

Rojas smiled when he made his last remark but he was implying I had to do as he said or suffer the consequences. The friendly Rojas I had met in the church was no more, and I didn't like the new one. "Now let me show you around," he said, taking me to a nearby high point and proudly showing me the view. "Those are the famous Llanos," he said, pointing down to the hot, low-lying plains I had just left. "They've been a zone of outlaws and cowboys for hundreds of years. Their horsemen are as famous in the history of Colombia as the Cossacks are in Russia's. Bolivar wouldn't have won the battles to gain Colombia's independence from Spain without the *Llaneros,* as we call them. The area is now a no-man's land with paramilitary forces, criminal gangs, the army, and the police fighting with the ELN for control."

I interrupted him to say I was hungry and Rojas quickly apologized for his lack of hospitality. He said he found it hard to stop preaching. "It's a *déformation professionnelle,*" he said, a habit he had picked up when he was a priest in good standing. He then took me to join the others who were gorging themselves on barbecued meat sliced from a side of beef suspended over a pit of red-hot coals. After serving ourselves, we sat with the others but they got up and left. Rojas shrugged his shoulders to indicate he either didn't want or couldn't force his men to eat with me. But before he could start lecturing me again, I asked where he had learned to speak French.

"I speak enough to get by," he said. "After my ordination, I spent a year in Belgium studying sociology at the Catholic University of Louvain. I wanted to get a solid theoretical foundation on the problem of poverty before I was given my own church back here in Colombia."

To be polite, I asked him if his studies had met his expectations. "More than just met," he said. "I learned more about Liberation Theology over there in twelve months than I did here in all my years at the seminary. And I wasn't the only one who felt that way. There were priests there from around the world, including Quebec. In fact, they were the ones who first told me about the FLQ and their future plans."

"I'd like to hear more about them."

"I was sure you'd be interested, and so will your authorities back in Ottawa. But let's do that later — after we come back from Sucio."

I crawled into my hammock as soon as we finished eating, aware that Rojas had trapped me. Despite my reservations, if the scouts came back with a positive report, I would have to accompany the guerrillas on their raid to get more information on the FLQ. Obtaining information on the FLQ was the principal purpose of my visit, and Rojas knew that.

Later that night, I woke to the sounds of loud voices welcoming visitors to the camp. The scouts had returned and were answering questions from Rojas and the others. I listened carefully, trying to make sense of their report, but was only able to pick out the words *el gringo* from time to time — indicating they were discussing my fate — amidst a cacophony of unintelligible words and what sounded like fierce arguments. When the guerrillas erupted in a great cheer followed by silence, I was sure the operation was on and that I would be going along.

The next morning, well before dawn, Rojas shook me awake and told me to get ready to leave. Within the hour I was riding down a mountain trail as part of a column of twenty men en route to take Sucio. The two scouts rode ahead to warn us if they ran into a military patrol on the trail. A half-dozen pack horses brought up the rear. No talking while riding was the rule. In the evenings, meals were eaten cold to dispense with the need for fires, and sentries were posted. By this time, although the comrades were not particularly friendly, they didn't move away when I joined them for meals. At the end of the third day, the scouts told us we were two hours away.

The following day, riding in the early morning toward the town with the guerrillas, I admired their carefree attitude, their ability to joke and laugh when facing danger. I became concerned that they paid no attention to Rojas when he ordered them to maintain operational silence. I didn't know until later that when the scouts had briefed Rojas and the guerrillas back at their camp, they had said Sucio was defended by only four policemen and a sergeant. I didn't know they had said the policemen spent their time drinking coffee and playing cards on the town square outside the jail and wouldn't be able to offer serious resistance. Not knowing what they knew, I was furious with the guerrillas, afraid their lack of discipline would warn the security forces we were coming and give them time to ready their defences.

As we drew closer, the column picked up speed and the guerrillas began to shout encouragement to each other and to sing old *Llanero* marching songs at the top of their voices. Rojas grew more frantic, shouting at his men to be quiet, but they paid him no attention. I became ever more anxious. My hands began to tremble and my stomach to ache. What if I gave way to fear and fled the scene of battle? What if I shit my pants? How would I explain myself to a furious Colombian government intent on sending me home in disgrace if they found out what I'd done? Was I breaking any sort of Canadian law? What would the ambassador say? Would he order me back to Canada? What would Longshaft say? Would he call me a blundering idiot and disown me? What would Heather say? Would she be proud of me? Was I having another nightmare? Yes that was it. I was having a nightmare and would soon wake up and draw Heather's body to mine ... and all would be good.

The column of horsemen raced through the outskirts of the town, drawing frightened looks from people going about their business. I glanced at the riders on my right and then at the ones on my left. They were no longer shouting or singing, but their flushed faces and broad smiles indicated they were looking forward to a fight. Their excitement was contagious, and I spurred on my horse. We were members of the British nobility Riding to the Hounds. We were Métis horsemen ignoring the withering fire from Gatling machine guns and attacking the line of Canadian troops advancing against them at the Battle of Batoche. We were the uniformed mounted troops of a defrocked priest, Colombia's own modern day Girolamo Savonarola, fighting for social justice on behalf of God and Che Guevara in the middle of the *Llanos*.

Afraid we were riding into an ambush, I crouched low as we thundered up with a great clatter of hooves on cobblestone to a plain cement block building marked in big letters CÁRCEL. If not proud, I was elated to be at the side of Latin America's most charismatic revolutionary leader — someone with the highest principles, someone who felt deeply about the welfare of the poor. No one else in the Department had done something like this. Four unarmed unshaven sleepy policemen, their jacket buttons undone, sat outside around a table drinking coffee, swatting flies, and gossiping. A dog was under the table. Chickens scratched in the dust. The policemen looked up in surprise. They lifted their arms in silent surrender, and the scouts shot them down with their Madsen sub-machine guns, knocking over the table, killing the dog, scattering the chickens, and blasting holes in the walls of the jail. A policeman with sergeant stripes emerged from the jail brandishing a pistol and the scouts shot him down.

Rojas leapt from his horse and went from dying policeman to dying policeman, absolving them of sin and blessing them as their souls departed for heaven. The guerrillas removed their hats and recited the Lord's Prayer. The sun was bright. A rooster crowed. Colombian cowboy music drifted in. A woman began to wail. The square was deserted. I remained on my horse looking at Rojas. He saw me and averted his eyes. Dogs barked and shutters slammed. I was hot and sweat trickled down my chest inside my shirt. My mouth and throat were parched, I reached for my canteen and drank my fill. Rojas looked at me. I was an extra in Sergio Leone's movie *The Good, the Bad and the Ugly,* in which the characters are all bad.

The guerrillas shot their weapons into the air and galloped away. A half dozen men entered the bank. There was gunfire. They re-emerged carrying bags of pesos and loaded them onto a pack horse. Others raided a pharmacy, a shop selling foodstuffs, and a dry goods store, and carried their booty to the pack horses. Rojas looked on, saying and doing nothing. The scouts kicked open the doors to a bar and were followed in by the others. Gunfire. Screams of women being raped. Laughter. It was humid, there was a smell of gunpowder and blood in the air. I puked. Rojas entered the bar. Voices were raised in argument. Women ran out crying. Rojas ordered his men to assemble the people on the square. They went from house to house kicking in doors and driving the people like cattle to their leader. Rojas pulled a crumpled piece of paper from his pocket and mechanically read out a prepared speech to the terrified crowd.

> Comrades, workers, brothers and sisters of Sucio. Greetings from the ELN, the one true revolutionary movement of Colombia. An epic struggle is being waged in our homeland between the forces of good and the forces of

evil. On the side of the good are the poor, the unemployed, the exploited, the hungry, the naked, the sick, the illiterate, , the parish priests and nuns, and those deprived of economic and political rights. They are the children of God and Fidel Castro is his disciple! On the side of evil are the big landowners, the private armies, the capitalists, the oligarchs, the television and radio stations, the newspapers, the armed forces, the secret police, and the church hierarchy. They are the offspring of the Devil and the president of Colombia is his acolyte! My comrades and I have come here today with love in our hearts as agents of the forces of good to seek your support in our struggle against the forces of evil. We thank you for your generous donations of money, food, and medical supplies. We invite you to send your young men to fight with us against the capitalist enemy. We assure you we will be back after the triumph of the revolution to help in the transformation of your community into a workers' paradise. Long live the town of Sucio. Long live the revolution. Long live the ELN.

Then unexpectedly, tears began to flow down Rojas's face, followed by enormous, heart-rending sobs. The assembled townspeople looked on nervously, perhaps sensing they were in the presence of a madman who might just as easily laugh as order his men to kill them. The guerrillas stared at their leader at first with incomprehension, and as his crying continued unabated, they stole surreptitious looks at each other with small complicit smiles, as if to indicate they had known all along he was a lunatic. Eventually, Rojas wheeled his horse around and galloped out of the square, followed by his men firing off their guns as if they were celebrating a great victory. I caught up to Rojas later in the day and asked him what had gone wrong, but he stared at me as if he was seeing me for the first time. It was at that moment that I regretted ever meeting Rojas. By insisting that I accompany his band of raiders, he had implicated me in murder and rape, leaving blood on my hands.

Rojas never spoke to me again. Despondent, I left for Bogota shortly after we reached the camp. I hadn't found out what the priests from Quebec had told him about the FLQ, but in the state I was in, it didn't matter. When back at our apartment Heather reacted badly, calling me sneaky and dishonest when she learned I had been to see Rojas, I made no effort to defend myself. When O'Connor sent a message to Ottawa demanding I be recalled, I didn't protest. When he told me he had withdrawn his permission for me to marry Heather, I said nothing. When Señora Lopez called to ask me what had happened, I hung up, unable to deal with her. I didn't care whether Longshaft would fire or promote me when I sent him a detailed report on the botched expedition. For what it was worth — and that would turn out to be not much — I marked my report "For Canadian Eyes Only" to keep it out of the hands of the CIA.

The following week, the Bogota newspapers carried stories with banner headlines on what they called "The Slaughter at Sucio." Rojas was identified and blamed for inciting his men to plunder the town. No mention was made of the presence of a foreign diplomat monitoring the engagement. A spokesman from the ministry of the interior said the raid would set back the efforts of the ELN to win over the Llaneros for decades — but that might have been self-serving propaganda. Then, several weeks later, the television stations of Bogota interrupted their regular programing to bring a special message to the people from the president announcing the death of the ELN leader.

The next day the newspapers carried photos of Rojas, lying dead on a stretcher as soldiers of an American-trained ranger counter-terrorism battalion posed for pictures around his body. His chest was pierced with bullet holes and it was evident he had been executed after being captured. By that time I had emerged from my funk, and was able to think more clearly. I knew I should have been upset by his death, but I wasn't — at least not initially. That would come with the passage of years whenever I thought back to the sight of Rojas weeping for his revolution in Sucio and to the nighttime conversation we had in the church. For the moment, the image that came to mind was of Rojas, completely out of touch with reality, rushing to perform the last rites to the policemen shot down without mercy after he lost control of his men. I couldn't help blaming him for their deaths.

I nevertheless called Señora Lopez, intending to express my condolences, but nobody answered the phone. I went to the shelter and hammered on the door until one of the employees let me in.

"The police took her away in the night, señor. I don't expect her back."

In the evening edition of *El Fuego*, the national newspaper, I read a small article reporting that an American missionary named Jim Hetherington had been arrested the day before for providing aid to the enemies of the state. It said the American embassy had intervened and he had been deported to the United States. In the back pages of the same issue, there was a small news report about an attack by paramilitary forces on an Indian settlement on the upper Casanare River. It said the Indians had been shot and their bodies thrown into the river to be eaten by alligators, but provided no further details.

Furious, Heather asked me if I said I had had anything to do with the death of Rojas and I told her I hadn't — something I thought was true at the time. She looked at me for maybe a minute — it could have been longer — and said," I don't believe you. The killing of Rojas coming just after your visit is too much of a coincidence."

Suddenly afraid she might be right, I hit back, saying the ELN had botched their attack and alienated the people of Sucio, who probably took their revenge by guiding the soldiers to the guerilla camp. "If I hadn't left when I did," I said, "I would have met the same end as Rojas."

"I guess I have no choice but to accept your word," she said, before going into the bedroom and slamming the door behind her. I went for a long walk to mull over Heather's accusations, returning late that night convinced that Longshaft must have handed over my report to the CIA, despite my request that is be treated as for Canadian Eyes Only.

Not long afterward, I received an invitation to dinner, specifying it was for one guest only, from the American ambassador in honour of three congressmen visiting from Washington. I had never met the ambassador, the most powerful foreign envoy in Colombia, and asked myself why he would include a junior officer from the Canadian embassy in his list of invitees. The evening of the event, when I presented my invitation and my diplomatic identity card, the marine on duty saluted, opened the front door and said, "Go right in, Mr. Cadotte, you're expected." Inside, an embassy protocol officer shook my hand and led me up a flight of stairs to a reception line and introduced me to the ambassador.

"Ah Mr. Cadotte, I've heard a lot of good things about you recently," he said before introducing me to his wife and the congressmen. After I shook the last of the proffered hands, another well-bred junior diplomat led me to a tuxedo-clad waiter for a glass of Californian sparkling wine and a canapé. He then hovered at my side, introducing me to the other guests — members of the Colombian national assembly and officials from the American embassy. I was the only non-American diplomat in the room. We made small talk until the butler announced that dinner was served.

The meal itself was an intimate affair — three tables of eight with one American congressman at each, flanked on each side by Colombian politicians. The other seats were filled with embassy staffers. I was not at the ambassador's table but was seated beside the next ranking American official, making me wonder why the Americans had invited me. I thought it had to be related in some way to Rojas. I then remembered that Longshaft, in his message back to me after my conversation with Rojas in the church, had said he intended to share that report with the CIA. *My hosts just want to know if I picked up any additional information in that encounter that could be useful in their anti-terrorist programs,* I told myself, unwilling to confront my responsibility for Rojas's death.

But my dinner companion didn't mention Rojas at all. Instead, he asked me polite questions — the sort strangers meeting at an official dinner could be expected to raise — about my home town, my family, my Métis roots, and my professional interests. He then smoothly turned the conversation toward the Vietnam War, the Cuban missile crisis, and national liberation movements in general before homing in on the ELN, asking thought-provoking and erudite questions on its philosophical, religious, and ethical underpinnings. He listened to my views with the utmost seriousness. When the dinner was over and I went home, I realized that while I had told him a lot about my background and provided my views on the major issues of the day, I had obtained nothing in return from him.

About that time, I noticed a car, a powerful, four-door sedan of the type used by police departments in the United States and

Canada — its windows tinted to conceal the identity of those inside — trailing behind me in the traffic. When I sped up, it sped up. When I slowed down, it slowed down. When I got up in the morning to go to work, it was waiting outside on the street. When I parked my Beetle on the street outside the embassy, it pulled in behind me and waited for me to come out. When I went shopping, two tough-looking, sun-glass wearing characters followed close behind as I made my purchases. When I asked them to leave me alone, they stared at me, their faces hidden behind their sunglasses, and continued to follow me.

Back at the office, when I described what was happening to Alfonso and asked him if he knew who they were, he turned pale, shrugged his shoulders, and said he didn't want to get involved. "I have a wife and children, Señor," was the reason he gave, as he raised his arms in a mute appeal for my understanding.

Two weeks later, Longshaft sent me a laconic message. "Pack everything and leave the country immediately," it said. "Your posting to Colombia is over."

Departure was a tense affair. Heather had not broken off our engagement but was still in a bad mood, and the ambassador made it clear he was happy we were leaving. A moving company came to the apartment to pack up and ship to Ottawa our few possessions, and a newly arrived member of the British embassy took the Beetle off my hands for a fair price. Alfonso was the only member of the embassy to see us off — and that was because he had no choice — his duties included driving departing staff to catch their flights back to Canada. As we waited in line to get our boarding passes, I saw one of the men who had been following me over the past several weeks standing near the counter as we checked in. And as the Avianca plane waited on the tarmac for permission to take off, I saw the sedan with the tinted windows parked on the side of the runway.

Part Three

Cuba

February 1969 to September 1970

9: The CIA

Longshaft greeted me warmly when I called on him the day after our arrival in Ottawa. "You did a brave thing down there in Colombia, accompanying Rojas on a raid," he said over coffee in his office. "It was exactly the sort of thing I wanted when I sent you to Colombia."

"Did you pass my message to you to the Americans?" I asked, hoping he would say no. "Was that how the Colombians found out where he was? Or did the people of Sucio lead the army to Rojas?"

"The CIA read your report — it provided them with the first detailed way through the maze of trails up the mountain to the ELN camp. They told the Colombians ... that's how they got him. But we didn't give it to them ... at least not right away. We didn't want Rojas killed any more than you did. He provided some good information on the FLQ when you met him in Bogota and we were hoping he'd be able to tell us more when they got him."

"Then how did the CIA get my report?"

"The Americans didn't need my help to get copy of your message. The CIA has been reading Canadian diplomatic mail for years, even though it's not supposed to. And we'd do the same with theirs if we knew how."

"Does that mean the killing of killing of Rojas, the massacre of the Indians, the disappearance of Señora Lopez, and the expulsion from Colombia of the American missionary happened because the Americans saw my message?"

"When I passed a copy after the fact to Harvey Lieberman, the local CIA Chief of Station, he didn't look surprised. That's because he'd already read it. By that time, the CIA had already briefed the Colombians. And he knew I knew. That's why I didn't answer your message. The Americans would have read it as well."

"I thought Canada and the United States had an agreement they wouldn't spy on each other."

"That just applies to the NSA and the CSEC. The NSA doesn't spy on Canada and the CSEC doesn't spy on the Americans. But that doesn't prevent the other American spy agencies from monitoring our mail should they want to."

Upset at receiving confirmation of what I already suspected, I lashed out. "Don't you find that humiliating to be treated that way, when we're supposed to be allies?"

"I suppose it is, but that's the way the game is played. The good news is the Americans are our closest friends and have our interests at heart. In fact, we're the lucky ones. They probably read everyone's mail, friends as well as enemies, only the others don't know it. And if I have information I really want to keep from the Americans, I never send it over the wires or by satellite transmission. I send it by diplomatic bag, or I discuss the matter directly with the officer concerned when he comes to Ottawa. Like I'm doing with you."

"I still find it humiliating."

"You've got to get rid of that attitude. They're our friends. As a matter of fact, the CIA probably saved your life in Bogota."

Unable to believe him, I answered curtly. "Tell me more."

"After the death of Rojas, the NSA intercepted a series of messages being exchanged among the members of the ELN hierarchy confirming it had sent a squad to kidnap you. If it couldn't kidnap you, it was supposed to kill you. They blamed you for betraying Rojas and rolling up his network, including Señora Lopez. By the way, Lopez was Rojas's wife, but I suppose you knew that already. As we speak, the Colombian secret police are questioning her to find out what she knows about the ELN."

"How can you be sure?" I said, not wanting to hear what he would say.

"The NSA reads the traffic of the Colombian secret police — and passes the messages to us. So far she hasn't said much, but they'll break her sooner or later."

"And then what?"

"Their normal practice is to fly terrorists after interrogation out over the Caribbean and dump them into the sea. And there's nothing anybody can do to help her," he said, anticipating my next question.

"Why do I owe the CIA any favours?" I said, still trying to absorb what he had said.

"Do you remember seeing a sedan with tinted glass, filled with tough-looking guys following you around in Bogota before you left? Those were CIA contractors. But they couldn't guarantee your safety. That's one of the reasons the CIA wanted you out. We agreed of course."

"What's the other reason?"

"The CIA wanted to keep you alive because it wants you to work for it."

"You must be joking."

"No I'm not. The CIA uses Canadians when it can't deploy its own in places where the United States doesn't have diplomatic relations. We like to help it out if at all possible since it shares so much with us."

"Aren't you afraid of the risks? What if foreign governments find out Canadian diplomats are working for the CIA? Nobody would trust us and our reputation would suffer."

"There are safeguards in place to keep that from happening and each request is considered on its merits."

"But why me," I said, putting off the time when I would have to make a decision. "I was in over my head in Colombia and a lot of people got hurt as a result. I wouldn't want that to happen again."

"They've done their homework and like what they've seen, that's why. As a matter of fact, you made a big impression on the CIA Station Chief over dinner in Bogota a few weeks ago. Don't you remember?"

Longshaft's question didn't call for an answer, and I asked him instead where the CIA wanted to use me. "In Cuba," he said. "The Americans closed their embassy in Havana shortly after Castro came to power and withdrew its staff, including the CIA component. Russia then sent troops, nuclear warheads, and missiles targeting the United States, as well as naval units to Cuba. That provoked the missile crisis of 1962. You might have been too young to remember it, but nuclear war between U.S.A. and Soviet Union almost broke out."

"I wasn't that young," I said. "I was in high school."

"What you couldn't have known — since it's one of Canada's most closely held secrets — is that the president of the United States appealed personally to the prime minister afterwards to send an officer to Cuba to carry out tasking requests for the CIA. He agreed since the reinsertion of the missiles could provoke nuclear war."

I was intrigued, but said nothing and waited for Longshaft to provide more details.

"If you accept, you'll be promoted from second to first secretary and go to Cuba on a two-year posting. The Havana embassy is small — smaller even than the one in Bogota — and you'd become deputy to the ambassador. Your day job would be to write political and economic reports, issue passports, and deal with consular cases that may arise. But your weekend and after-hours work would be monitoring Soviet army, naval, and air deployments for the CIA. Alfred Cook, Canada's ambassador in Havana, has been consulted and he's agreed to accept your nomination if you agree to go. What do you say?"

"Wouldn't you rather send me back to another embassy in South America to do the same sort of work I did in Bogota?"

"Helping the CIA in Havana is also a priority."

"Then I'll do it," I said. "But I'm planning to get married. Would I have time fit in a wedding?"

"The name of your fiancé is Heather Sinclair, I believe. O'Connor sent in a negative report, saying she was a hippie, a believer in free love, and soft on the left. He recommended you be denied permission to marry her."

"I'd leave the Department if we couldn't get married."

"Don't worry. The Department's given you permission just the same. You won't be leaving for Havana until September so you'll have plenty of time to get married and to become familiar with the files and talking to the experts on Cuba. The Department will pick up the tab for hotel accommodation until you leave."

Heather's mood improved dramatically when I told her the Department was posting us to Cuba, in her opinion, the most socially and politically advanced country in the Americas if not in the world. When I said we'd have to get married before leaving for Havana, she called her parents in Winnipeg and told them we'd be arriving within two weeks to get married. I could only hear her side of the conversation, but it didn't seem to go well, at least at the outset. "His name's Luc Cadotte," I heard her say. "I know that's a Métis name ... that's because he's a Métis from a town on Georgian Bay.... I know what you think about the Métis but I don't care.... I don't care if Granny and Granddad will be upset... I don't care if your friends talk ... you can ask him yourself what he does for a living ... you can ask him yourself what his father does for a living … I don't care … no I'm not pregnant … no I don't want a wedding at the United Church…. I want a public ceremony at the registrar's office … I don't care who you invite for drinks afterwards…. We're moving to Cuba where Luc has a job…. If that's the way you feel about it, we'll get married in Ottawa…. Okay, we'll see you at the airport."

In the end, the wedding was a great success. Heather's parents, who initially greeted me frostily, became quite friendly when they discovered I wasn't a long-haired hippie. The only potentially unpleasant moment occurred when granny, who had had too much to drink at the reception, came up to me and said, "I knew you were a Métis as soon as I saw you. There's something about your eyes that gives you away — something half Indian, half white, and half Devil." She then burst out laughing, hit me affectionately on the shoulder, and I forgave her for her ingrained racism.

Back in Ottawa, Mary gave me a temporary office on the ninth floor to use and I kept myself busy preparing for my new posting. But as winter gave way to spring and then to summer, Heather grew bored. Then one day in early July, when I returned to our hotel room after work, she wasn't there. She had however left me a note to say old CUSO friends from Colombia had dropped in and she was leaving with them to spend a few days at a cottage across the Gatineau River in Wakefield, Quebec. "You don't need me and I have to get out this apartment for a few days or else I'll go crazy. My friends don't have a phone and so you can't call me. Don't worry about me. I'm a big girl and can take care of myself."

I was suspicious. It was no secret that in the hills around Wakefield in those days there were a number of communes populated by American draft dodgers and deserters and their libertine Canadian friends, many of whom spent their time growing and smoking pot between forays into Ottawa to protest

American involvement in the Vietnam War. And, although I didn't want to think about it, in my imagination I saw her smoking pot and making love to each and every member of the commune, male and female — and each one had the face of Charles Bullock, her former boyfriend in Bogota.

The more I thought about it, the angrier I became. But as the days and then the weeks went by without hearing from her, my anger turned to resignation and a great sense of loss. I missed her so much that when I came home one evening in mid-August and she was there, I rejoiced. She offered no explanation and while friendly enough, she was distant. Something had happened to change her opinion of me during her absence, but we carried on planning for our departure for Cuba in September.

A week before we left, Harvey Lieberman came by to tell me what the CIA expected of me in Cuba, beginning with the context. "The communists are winning the war in Vietnam, the Warsaw Pact has crushed the Prague Spring, the Russians are pulling ahead of us in the arms race, and, for the last couple of years, they've been flying bombers carrying nuclear weapons out of Russia and down the east coast of the United States to Cuba. Recently, they've positioned submarines in the port of Cienfuegos. No one knows what they're up to and they've got people worried. Some of the folks in Langley even think they're planning to put missiles and nuclear warheads back into Cuba."

"What do you want me to do?"

"You're to snoop around Soviet bases, take pictures of weapons and electronic systems and observe troop movements. But first we want you to do a little job for us in Havana harbour. At this moment, a Soviet freighter, the SS *Kama*, is tied up at the Soviet Black Sea naval base at Sevastopol with a suspicious cargo of large cylindrical objects tied down under camouflage netting on its deck. It's scheduled to arrive in Havana this weekend, we need you to get to Cuba before then."

"How can you so sure," I said. "Have you seen the manifest?"

"Don't ask me how we know — we just do. Some of our people think missile launchers are under the netting, but others disagree. They say the Russians wouldn't be crazy enough to provoke another missile crisis."

"And you want me to find out what's really on the ship when it reaches Cuba."

"That's right. And to do the job, you'll need these," he said. He opened his briefcase and handed me an illustrated copy of *Jane's Weapons of the World* and a camera with a long telephoto lens. "You'll be able to identify the type of launchers on the deck — if indeed there are launchers — with the help of this book."

When I looked at his handouts doubtfully, he hastened to say, "*Jane's* is the best source on military hardware available anywhere. And they're proud of that camera at Langley. It's the latest Japanese model with a lens modified in our research laboratories to take photographs in dim light."

"I haven't done this sort of thing before," I said. "Any tips?"

"Your predecessor tried to blend in with the general population by dressing like a *campesino* — scruffy pants and a straw hat. MININT — that stands for Ministry of the Interior if you don't already know — never caught him, but the experts in Langley think he was taking a big risk. They suggest you dress like an off-duty Russian soldier in green military-style pants and in a green long-sleeve shirt."

For a moment I thought I was playing a role in Graham Greene's *Our Man in Havana*, a black comedy movie where Alec Guinness, the anti-hero star, is recruited by the SIS to spy on the Cubans and ends up making a laughing-stock of everybody. Or James Bond being outfitted by Q in the London SIS gadget lab to fight the KGB in *To Russia with Love*. After what I had been through in Colombia, my new mission to Cuba had a distinctly amateurish air. I had to resist asking Lieberman if he had been joking when he told me the CIA expected me to skulk about in green pants and green shirt with a copy of *Jane's Weapons of the World* in one hand and a James Bond–style camera in the other. Instead, I told him to thank his people for the special camera, but to send me a smaller one. "With something that size," I said, "MININT would catch me on my first day on the job and send me home."

"I've given you all you need to do your job," he sniffed. "But if you insist, I'll get you another camera, but it won't do as good a job. Just do your best and Langley will be happy.

"How about bringing me back from Havana for a formal training session at your headquarters?"

"That's completely out of the question. But if you ever happen to be in the Langley area, I'd be pleased to arrange a tour of our museum."

After Lieberman left, Longshaft came by to see how the meeting had gone. "I had the impression the CIA doesn't attach a lot of importance to my mission," I said. "Lieberman just handed me a camera and *Jane's Weapons of the World* and told me to do the best I could. His people aren't even inviting me to their headquarters before I go."

"I wouldn't read too much into that. Lieberman is always telling me how much Langley values the work of their Canadian spies — even if only to confirm what its U2 flights and its other people on the ground tell it. The president of the United States even thanks the prime minister whenever he visits Canada. But more important, our collaboration is good for Canada's intelligence program. Every year when we go to Cabinet to get approval for the security and Intelligence budget, we always bring up the work we do for the CIA in Havana."

"You tell Cabinet the CIA considers Canada's help to be of vital importance to the United States."

"We don't say it that crassly, but you're right."

"And as a result, Cabinet passes the budget as presented to it by officials."

"I like to think Cabinet passes the budget because all the items listed are needed to safeguard our national security, but it never hurts to remind the ministers of the good work we do for the Americans in Cuba."

"But surely the officer sent to spy for the CIA can also spy on Cuba for Canada?"

"He could if he wanted, but that's not necessary. Our strategic interests in Cuba coincide with those of the Americans, but our bilateral relations are different. We trade with the Cubans and the Americans don't. We maintain correct diplomatic ties and the Americans don't. We allow our citizens to travel and holiday in Cuba and the Americans don't."

"What about the FLQ?" I asked. "Rojas told me when I first met him in the church said they'd been to see the Cubans. Have we asked them what the FLQ wanted?"

"We have. We sent our ambassador in to speak to officials in the foreign ministry after we got your message. The Cubans confirmed the FLQ had been in the country but denied offering them any support."

"Do you believe them?"

"The Cubans, like everybody else, want to keep their options open. It could well be they were really saying they hadn't provided any support to date but might well do so in the future. Eventually we'll want to make sure the views of the foreign ministry coincide with the position of the communist party and Castro himself. So look around, and let me know if you run into the FLQ, but don't do anything to jeopardize your work for the CIA."

Before leaving for the airport, Longshaft called me into his office for a briefing on Ambassador Cook and MININT. "Before you left for Colombia," he said, "I told you there were three types of ambassadors in the Department: pragmatists, idealists, and do-nothings. I said O'Connor was a do-nothing and you wouldn't be able to turn to him for help if you were in a jam. Cook, on the other hand is a pragmatist, a hard-working officer who values a job well done and the respect of his peers more than ambition. If you get into trouble, don't hesitate to turn to him. Now what do you want to know about MININT?"

"Anything you can tell me."

"They're really good at what they do. They receive their training from the East Germans — one of the best spy and counterspy outfits in the world. They're almost in the same league as the CIA and the SIS, although that's something the Americans and the Brits would never admit. They've blocked dozens of assassination attempt on Castro's life, from defusing bombs hidden in lobsters to uncovering explosives in cigars and detecting poison in his Sunday dinner. Sounds farcical but they're the only reason the president is still alive. And they'll be keeping a close eye on you just as they do with every Western diplomat posted to Cuba."

"But why would MININT go after a Canadian?" I said. "Aren't we supposed to be Cuba's best friend in the capitalist world?"

"Friendship has nothing to do with it. MININT doesn't trust anyone — not their own people, the Russians, the Chinese, much less the Canadians. The locally hired Cuban secretaries, clerks, drivers, mechanics, handymen, maids, cooks, and cleaners at our embassy all work for MININT. You can take it as a given that the houses and apartments provided to the Canadian staff are bugged. So is the embassy building and the ambassador's residence. We used to send technicians from Ottawa to dig them out of the walls, but MININT just put them back in when weren't looking. Now we leave them in and assume the Cubans listen to everything we say."

"I suppose protesting or complaining to the government wouldn't help."

"We did that once but the Cubans showed us a basket full of microphones we'd planted in their embassy in Ottawa and said they'd stop listening to our conversations if we stopped listening to theirs. And so we dropped the subject. We provide guards to patrol the embassy but they're elderly commissionaires from Ottawa who can't stay awake at night. So be careful what you say, even in your own office. You'll probably be tempted to hold discussions in your garden or on one of the nearby beaches. Bear in mind the Cubans use directional microphones that pick up those conversations. They bug our vehicles, and we do the same to theirs. The only secure place to talk is in the safe room — that's a special room inside the embassy communications centre, custom built to keep out MININT's electronic ears. It's hot as hell inside, but you'll have to use it to discuss sensitive matters with Ambassador Cook — especially anything to do with the CIA."

"How about personal security? Would I be roughed up if I was caught taking pictures? Not that that would stop me from doing my job."

"More likely MININT would try to blackmail you into working for it. They wouldn't hesitate to slash your tires or run your car off the road in the dark if you kept on monitoring military movements and the like. But don't be surprised if a sexy woman approaches you on the street and tells you you're the most handsome person she's ever met and wants to know you better. If you turn her down, a man or boy will come along with the same offer. Sometimes they'll offer you Cuban pesos at a cut-rate exchange rate. These are all standard MININT seduction techniques, and if you fall for any of them, you'll soon find your tryst or money exchange has been filmed and a not-as- friendly MININT officer will be threatening to tell your ambassador on you if you don't co-operate. They do these things with all our new staff as a matter of course, and some even fall for them. But then again," he said, "we use the same tactics with the Cubans coming to work at their missions in Canada. Sometimes we get lucky."

"What about Heather? Do you think MININT will target her because she's such a free spirit?"

"I thought about that when I saw O'Connor's letter. I told the undersecretary the Department's old patriarchal ways were out of date and officers should marry whomever they wanted and he agreed."

"Even if their wives believe in free love?"

"Even if they believe in free love, smoke pot, and accompany their husbands to communist countries. It's up to you to be sure she behaves herself and doesn't jeopardize your mission. Just remember, what she doesn't know, she won't be able to tell MININT. "

10: The Workers' Paradise

On a hot September Monday afternoon, Heather and I left Ottawa for Havana on a Cubana charter filled with happy tourists downing the first of what would be many complementary rum drinks handed out by the smiling cabin staff during the flight. They had answered ads placed in the *Ottawa Journal* by the Cuban embassy offering package vacations at derisory prices on the pristine beaches of Varadaro, the playground of the American rich before the Cuban revolution. As soon as the plane was at cruising level, Heather joined the others in the aisle, laughing and drinking and sharing her enthusiasm for our coming posting.

"It'll be a chance to see the workers' paradise up close," I heard her say, her voice rising. "I'm going to be a volunteer in a worker's brigade cutting sugar cane and maybe teach English in a Cuban school. I'll get to hear Castro deliver a speech on Cuba's national day. I'll attend performances of the Cuban National Ballet and see the great prima ballerina Alicia Alonso dance in a performance of *Giselle*." I stuck to cups of heavy sweetened black Cuban coffee with an uneasy feeling that Cuba wouldn't live up to Heather's expectations.

"Welcome to George Orwell's *1984*," said Rolly Anderson, the embassy's administrative officer, as we disembarked at Havana's José Marti International Airport. Heather frowned, upset that he would criticize Cuba's socialist paradise. He then led the way to the VIP room, a brightly lit deserted room furnished with uncomfortable sofas and armchairs, took our passports and baggage tickets, and went off to clear us through customs and immigration. The official hostess, a sour-faced woman in a uniform several sizes too small for her, appeared and silently offered us mojitos, Cuba's favourite rum cocktail, from a selection on a tray.

I said no but Heather took one and asked the hostess to join us. Within a few minutes, the woman was smiling and telling Heather her troubles — about how hard it was to get to work in the mornings in the overcrowded buses, how the things she wanted to buy in state-owned stores were always sold out when she went shopping, how noisy it was in her apartment, how difficult it was to look after her old parents and her own family, how big the lineups were at the clinics when she took her daughter to see the doctor, and much more. Heather, fueled by three hours of drinking on the way down, recounted her life story and told her that her husband was the new deputy Canadian ambassador to Cuba.

As she spoke, Fidel Castro watched me from a framed picture on the wall. I got up and moved to another seat but his eyes followed me. I went to the washroom and his eyes accompanied me to the door and I was uncomfortable. Perhaps for that reason when I came back and joined Heather and her new friend, I worried the woman might get into trouble for speaking with such little restraint to outsiders. But I liked it even less when she gave Heather her telephone number and asked her to call her. "It would be an honour to show you how a typical Cuban lives."

Rolly returned with our passports and we went together to pick up our luggage and go the car park. "I gave the Cuban driver the evening off, I'll drive you to your house," he said. "That way we'll be able to speak freely."

On the ride in, I mentioned to Rolly my impression that the eyes of Castro in the VIP room picture had followed me around the room.

"That's an old illusionist trick that official artists and photographers in this country incorporate into posters and photographs of Castro. I wasn't kidding when I said welcome to *1984*. Thousands of MININT functionaries listen in to telephone conversations, and any hint of dissidence is met by a kangaroo court trial and imprisonment or death by firing squad. Having Castro watch them all the time helps maintain control."

"Don't the children receive free education and medical care?" asked Heather.

"They do," said Rolly. "And there are no gamines and homeless people in the streets like you see elsewhere in Latin America."

"Then how can you say Cuba is totalitarian?"

"Mussolini's Italy and Hitler's Germany provided free education and homes for orphans too."

"At least in Cuba everyone is equal."

"No they're not. The party elite shop in special stores for things not available to ordinary people."

The conversation was becoming heated. I intervened to calm things down by noting how friendly the woman in the VIP room had been. She had even complained about her troubles with the bureaucracy.

"The Cubans are like that," Rolly said. "They like human contact and will joke and gossip with you endlessly if given a chance. Just don't forget — they're required to account to MININT for every contact they make with diplomats. As we speak, that friendly woman is probably reporting on Canada's new deputy ambassador and his wife. I wouldn't be surprised if she was a member of MININT itself."

"I don't believe you," Heather said angrily. "I'm a good judge of character and know sincerity when I see it. She wants to show me Havana and I'm going to take her up on her offer."

"You might want to check with the embassy security officer before you do," Rolly said. "You'll save yourself some grief if she's not genuine."

"And who's the embassy security officer?"

"He's sitting beside you," he said. "The deputy ambassador is always the embassy security officer."

"Then it looks like I'll be able to do whatever I want," Heather said, but Rolly didn't find that funny.

Our house was in darkness when we arrived. "The power's out," Rolly explained as he led the way inside with a flashlight. "Fuel's expensive and the government shuts down the generating stations from six in the evening until six in the morning to save money. They do the same with the water supply, so there'll be no showers for you tonight."

Rolly lit a candle, set it on a table, and helped carry our luggage inside. He then provided us with the information we needed to get through the next twelve hours. "The master bedroom is upstairs on the right and your bathroom is next to it down the hall. Angelita — that's your maid — will have breakfast ready for you when you get up. The office opens at eight and the embassy is just a hundred yards down the street, so it's easy to walk to work."

After a difficult night trying to sleep in the heat, I woke up to hear water running in the adjacent bathroom and the window air conditioner humming. A few minutes later Heather came in wrapped in a towel, looking happier than I'd seen her for weeks. "I've been poking around this old house," she said. "It's a wonderful place filled with decaying furniture, mildewed paintings, and bookcases of mouldy old books. The cockroaches here have wings and are the size of sparrows. I even saw a scorpion, but they don't scare me. It's like a southern mansion after the Civil War in a Hollywood movie."

"The owners were probably well-off Cubans who opposed Castro in the war that brought him to power and left everything behind when they fled to Miami."

Heather's manic enthusiasm spilled over during breakfast in the kitchen where bacon and eggs, toast, orange juice, and Cuban coffee were on the menu. "I didn't know you could get food like this in Cuba," she told Angelita.

"If you are a diplomat, you can buy anything you want for dollars at the diplomatic duty-free shop."

"What do Cubans eat," Heather asked.

"We eat our own food," Angelita said with a forced smile.

But Heather continued to raise issues that embarrassed Angelita. "And this beautiful old house," she said, "Why would anyone abandon it to leave for Miami — even if they opposed Castro? I've read the Cuban constitution and Cubans today have more rights today than they did in the old days."

"Please, señora," Angelita said. "I'm just a maid. I don't have the education to answer such questions."

But Heather kept insisting that Angelita answer until I passed her a note saying there were microphones in the walls and to change the subject. But Heather read the note, shook her head in disagreement, and continued to press Angelita until the poor woman left the room. I went out the door, intending to escape to the embassy, but Heather ran after me and stopped me.

"Don't you ever tell me what to do like that again," she said. "You may be the deputy ambassador, but I know more than you do about Cuba. You and Rolly are anti-revolutionary fascists who don't accept that Cuba is the most democratic and socially just country in Latin America."

It was the first time I had heard her use boiler-plate Marxist jargon, and I didn't like it. She'd probably picked it up during her

Paris days from Jean-Paul Sartre, assuming her story that she'd slept with him was true. I also realized at that moment that she was naïve to the point of being dangerous.

Canada's embassy, at Calle 30, number 518, Miramar, was another former residence of a family that had fled Cuba to escape Castro. It was many times larger than our house and surrounded on all sides by a high fence of sharpened steel bars. Behind the building and visible from the street was a tennis court. On the sidewalk outside the entrance, a uniformed policeman wearing a steel helmet and with an AK-47 at the ready, stood in a hut, glowering at passersby. His job was to interrogate and take down the names of Cubans seeking to visit the embassy. He stopped me, holding up his hand and demanding I state my business. I showed him my diplomatic passport, he read it carefully, took out a pen, took copious notes, saluted, and handed it back with a polite "*Bienvenido a Cuba.*"

Inside, on the ground floor, Canadian and Cuban employees were processing visa requests, arranging for the repatriation of the body of a Canadian tourist who had suffered a fatal heart attack, selling bagged flour, spare parts, and wheat and toilet paper to Cuban state enterprises, and organizing cultural visits to Cuba of Canadian musicians and artists. Off to one side, Rolly handed out work orders to the dozen Cuban electricians, carpenters, and mechanics who kept the embassy and its vehicles in working order. Upstairs, behind locked doors, were the offices of Ambassador Cook, his private secretary, Louise Bourgeault, the deputy ambassador, and the security guards, as well as the communications centre, and inside it, the safe room.

"You've done well for yourself," the ambassador said, after Louise took me to his office. "You must be among the first members of your entrance class to be promoted."

"There were special circumstances," I said, not wanting to talk about my mission outside the safe room.

"Yes of course, I understand. But before we get into all that," he said, "let's have a cup of coffee and tell each other a bit about each other."

For the next hour, we traded stories about our hometowns (he was from Petrolia, a small place near Sarnia in southwestern Ontario), about our families (he was a bachelor), and about our postings (he had served abroad in Pretoria, Tel Aviv, and Moscow, and at headquarters as the director of the Middle Eastern division). With my sketchy career, I should have felt intimidated, but he made me feel comfortable by showing interest in Heather, my family back in Penetang, and my time in Colombia. He then motioned me to follow, and led me into the communications centre where the technician on duty unlocked the door of the safe room.

It was a five-foot by five-foot enclosure with an eight-foot ceiling, about the size of a small bathroom. But instead of a sink and toilet, it was furnished with two straight-backed chairs and a small table. Light came from a battery-powered sixty-watt bulb suspended by a wire fixed to the ceiling. Sheets of inch-thick lead lined the walls, floor, ceiling, and door to keep out electronic signals. A reinforced floor supported the structure's weight. Travel posters — one of Niagara Falls and others of the Bay of Fundy and the Old City of Quebec — were taped to the walls, presumably to make the interior look welcoming. Affixed to the inside door was a no-smoking sign in Canada's two official languages, with the words no-smoking underlined in red.

"These days, we have these things at our missions in all communist countries," the ambassador said. "They're not comfortable, but at least we can speak without outsiders listening to our conversations." He stepped inside, pulled the cord on the light to turn it on, and sat down on one of the chairs. I took the other one, and the technician closed the door and left us to talk.

"The air runs out in about fifteen minutes," he said, "so we got to be quick. Ask all the questions you want but make them short. Safe rooms don't come with air conditioning and there's a limit to how much heat we can take." Getting down to business, he said, "One of the challenges you're going to face is remaining undercover — to keep the Cubans from discovering your CIA connection."

"Don't you think the Cubans have their suspicions? For years Canadian diplomats have been prowling around the countryside equipped with big cameras. They must know what's going on."

"You might well be right, but I don't think so. And that's because you fellows come here with the rank of deputy ambassador and do the usual work of deputy ambassadors along with your espionage duties."

"How does that help?"

"The Cubans wouldn't believe anyone could do both jobs — at least that's the assumption we've gone on for years. Your normal embassy workload will be heavy: supervision of staff, preparation of economic and political reports, cultivation of contacts among Cuban officials and diplomats. And your work for the CIA is almost a full-time job. Every Friday morning, a courier from Ottawa comes in on the Cubana flight to deliver diplomatic bags with personal and official mail to the embassy. All instructions from the CIA and your outgoing replies are carried in the bags. No one else at the embassy can see your correspondence."

"Including you?"

"Including me. You report directly to Langley via the CIA Station Chief in Ottawa."

The atmosphere was glacial when I returned home for lunch. A morose Heather responded in monosyllables when I asked her how her morning had gone. Angelita scurried around anxiously as if she was afraid the mistress of the house would once again go berserk and subject her to another torrent of unanswerable questions. But Angelita's lunch of grilled marlin and french fries cheered her up, and when I asked her if she wanted to come along on a familiarization tour of the city that afternoon, she agreed.

Rolly pulled up in the embassy station wagon, Heather joined him in the front and I sat in the back. "Good news in this morning's mail," Rolly said. "Your car's arrived from Canada. It'll be cleared through customs today and you'll have it tomorrow morning. After that, you can do your own exploring. Meanwhile, I'll be your tour guide for the afternoon. Where do you want to go?"

"Why don't you take us to the old city and we can decide once we're there," I said. I had several objectives in mind for the car ride. Above all, I wanted to spend some time with Heather, whose outburst that morning had upset me. I also wanted to take a look at the port. The Soviet freighter was due to dock on the coming Saturday. When Lieberman had raised the matter, I thought the CIA must have been desperate to entrust someone like me with such an important mission. If my report turned out to be positive, what would the Americans do? Impose a maritime embargo as they did during the 1962 missile crisis? The responsibly the Americans were placing on my shoulders was enormous. I only hoped they had other ways to verify my findings.

When Rolly turned onto Fifth Avenue and began driving west toward the city centre, Heather's mood shifted once again. A church abandoned by its parishioners years before — doors off their hinges, grass and weeds smothering its gardens, windows broken and roof riddled with holes — was a beautiful memento of Cuba's spiritual soul. The heavily armed troops, who fingered their weapons and eyed suspiciously each passing car at the intersections, were centurions of a new glorious order. A massive, shoddily built building thrown together to house Eastern Bloc technical experts — more like a power plant than a hotel — was a noble example of Socialist realism architecture.

As we moved westward from Fifth Avenue onto the Malecón, the seaside drive into the city, Heather became ever more frantic — old men fishing from the seawall were images of a Rembrandt masterpiece; the waves, washing onto the sidewalk and roadway, were a sign of rebirth; the grimy abandoned former American embassy was a fine example of modernist architecture; a black youth facing the sea and playing a trumpet was a young Louis Armstrong; the pollution-spewing, rusted-and-held-together-with-baling-wire 1940s and 1950s model Chevrolets and Buicks were Maseratis, Lamborghinis, and Ferraris — and more of the same until we stopped for a coffee at the Plaza de San Francisco de Asis in the old city. Heather then closed her mouth and didn't open it again for the rest of the day.

On the return drive, Rolly drove by the port and I took note that it was unguarded. The way was open for me to sneak aboard SS *Kama*.

The next morning, Heather was again the person I had known in Colombia, funny, irreverent, and cheerful. Apparently unaware she had lost control of herself, she told me how much she had enjoyed our sight-seeing excursion. "Let's do it again, and soon," she said, and I agreed, but was wary, wanting to help her but not knowing how. When I arrived at the office just after it opened, I asked Louise to find time for me in the ambassador's schedule and went in to see him when he was free.

"Heather and I have only just arrived, and we've already got a problem," I said. Cook scribbled a note asking if we should move to the safe room but I shook my head to indicate it didn't matter. In retrospect it would've been better if we'd kept our ensuing discussion from the microphones in the walls.

"Heather began her day berating the maid for not being sufficiently supportive of the regime and yelling at me," I said.

"By noon she had calmed down and was her old self for a spell. Then when Rolly took us for a tour of the city she lost control and began speaking a lot of nonsense about the accomplishments of Cuba since the revolution before clamming up and remaining quiet all evening. This morning she acts as if nothing happened. I'm worried about her."

"Had she expressed similar views before leaving Canada?"

"No she hadn't. At least not to the same extent."

"Any psychiatric problems?"

"She's always had lots of friends and seemed normal to me."

"Then I wouldn't worry about it," he said. "It's probably just cultural shock. She needs to get out and meet people. Not Cubans for the obvious reasons, but members of other western embassies. If I had a wife, I'd suggest Heather call on her, but I never married."

"Maybe she should start by getting to know the families of the members of our embassy?"

"Of course, but she shouldn't fall into the rut of socializing only with members of her own mission. I should have mentioned it yesterday, but for years now, the deputy ambassadors and their wives get together to play tennis and socialize on Saturdays. Since they use our courts, the Canadian deputy ambassador is always included. They follow up tennis with a lunch hosted at one of their homes and go out for dinner and drinks in the evening in the old city. Some years ago someone christened the group, Club Hemingway, and the name stuck."

"I'd like that," I said, happy to have an excuse to be in the old city to carry out my mission for the CIA on Saturday night.

"We ambassadors have our own little group, but we don't have as much fun as the members of Club Hemingway."

"Anything about them I should know?"

"Only that they're an eccentric group of characters, like a lot of us who accept postings no one else wants in these isolated out-of-the-way places. You'll have to be careful they don't involve you in any of their shenanigans. The Italian is not a career diplomat — he's a former politician by the name of Paulo Verdi who's lying low in Havana until a major indiscretion involving sex and an underage girl has been forgotten in Rome. The Frenchman's name is Guillaume Monpetit. He's an alcoholic — poor man — whose exposure to scenes of massacre during a posting in Liberia led him to drink. Or so the story goes. The Belgian's from the old colonial service. He can't stop talking about how good life was for the people of the Belgian Congo before independence. His name's Damien Claes. Rens Bakker is the Dutchman, and he's the one you have to watch. He's been up to some foolish things since he got here and bullies his ambassador. The Englishman is the only level-headed one. His name's Adrian Caruthers. It's rumoured he participates in Club Hemingway to keep an eye on its members."

The group welcomed us when we showed up on Saturday morning and we were soon on a first- name basis. Although neither of us was a particularly good at tennis, we were a generation younger and made up in strength and endurance what we lacked in skill. It was hot and humid, the temperature rose into the mid-80s, but we played doubles, giving those not on the court a chance to cool off in the shade with glasses of lemonade — or in the case of Guillaume, with lemonade to which he added generous shots of gin from bottles in his tennis bag. As the morning went on and the matches became ever more contested — and as the temperature rose into the mid-90s — our new friends began going to Guillaume for shots of gin to add to their lemonade. The more they drank, the more they egged each other on, and there was ever louder laughing and shouting. Guillaume, with a drunken smile, waved a bottle of gin at Heather and me, inviting us to join in the fun. Heather accepted with alacrity and was soon celebrating along with the others. I declined Guillaume's offer, and sat in silence, ignored by the others, until it was time to return home to shower and go to lunch.

It was Paulo's and his wife Antonietta's turn to host Club Hemingway at lunch. I came dressed in crisply pressed and tailored green pants and shirt under the impression it looked smart if unconventional. Stupid me — I quickly discovered my outfit may have been suitable for weekend spying missions, but not for attending a lunch with a group of sophisticated Europeans.

"I didn't know a soldier was coming to lunch," Antonietta said when she saw me, provoking a torrent of unfriendly laughter from the others. Heather had put on the makeup and sexy outfit that had scandalized Mrs. O'Connor in Bogota and received an altogether different sort of welcome — everybody clapped when she made her entrance.

Otherwise, the lunch was a relaxed, elegant affair, organized by uniformed Neapolitan servants who had come with Paulo and Antonietta from Italy to take care of their household and entertaining needs. I would later learn that Antonietta was a wealthy woman who had supported the lavish lifestyle of her husband when he was a politician in Rome and now maintained him in Cuba. Although their house, like those of the other deputy ambassadors, was the former home of a Cuban family that had fled into exile in Miami, the Verdis had furnished it with rugs, drapes, tables, chairs, and the like, imported from Italy. A generator purred outside, ensuring the air conditioners never stopped working. A big tank sat on the roof providing a steady supply of water. An Italian gardener was at work outside cutting the lawn.

The dishes were laid out on the dining table for the guests to serve themselves before taking seats around small circular tables in the wide passageway leading to the conservatory. The wine and food choices were limited, but of the highest quality — glasses of excellent light white and red Italian wines, prosciutto with imported Parma ham, pâtés of various sorts, antipastos, a selection of cold cuts, mixed salad, imported Gorgonzola and Pecorino cheeses, *flan caramel, mousse au citron,* and fresh fruit salad. I shuffled along diffidently at the end of the queue as befitting my position as the most junior member of the club, served myself some salad and pâté, picked up a glass of red wine, and went to join Heather, who had saved a place for me at a table for four.

Rens Bakker — the colleague Ambassador Cook had told me was not to be trusted — was in the midst of a heated discussion with his wife when I sat down. "I get so tired of these Saturday get-togethers," his wife, Geraldine, was saying. "Every Saturday we do the same thing. We spend the mornings drinking too much and making spectacles of ourselves on the tennis court. Then we do our best to show the others we can put on a better lunch than anyone else. It's so false, such a flattering of egos. And at night we always go to the same places to eat and tell each other the same stories and jokes.

"Pay no attention to Geraldine," Bakker said turning to speak to us. "She always speaks her mind, even in the company of others. If you don't like it here," Bakker said resuming the quarrel with his wife, "why don't you go back to Holland and live with your mother. Nobody's forcing you to stay. She'd be happy. I'd be happy. You'd be happy."

Embarrassed, I looked at Heather to gauge her reaction to this airing of dirty laundry by the Bakkers. She was keeping her head down and continued eating as the quarrel progressed. "I should have left you years ago," Geraldine said. "But you promised it wouldn't be long before you became an ambassador and we'd live in a big residence and mix with the best people. Instead we're always sent to these awful places and are forced to associate with second-rate diplomats."

Heather smiled when Geraldine made the last remark. Then she sat up and took notice when Geraldine began accusing her husband of being unfaithful. "And every time I go away for a holiday, I come back to find another woman in my bed."

"So what?" Bakker said. "I told you I believed in open marriages when we met and that's still my view. How about you," he said, turning to Heather. "Do you think open marriages are good things? I believe in being frank about these matters. Sex is just sex after all. It's not love."

"I suppose I do," Heather said, looking at me as she provided her answer.

"There, you see," Bakker said, turning back to his wife. "Modern people like this young woman think like me."

The Dutch couple carried on quarreling but I was no longer listening. However, when Heather and I returned to the dining room to select our desserts, I said I wanted to sit somewhere else. But she took her *flan caramel* went back to join the Bakkers. "I like listening to other people arguing," she said.

Caruthers, who was also serving himself dessert, spoke to me as soon as Heather left.

"I couldn't help overhearing your conversation," he said. "Rens can be such a bore — always arguing with his wife and going on about free love. Why don't you join my table? My wife's not with me and I'm sitting with the Claes."

As we walked back to Caruthers' table, he said his wife rarely attended the lunches or evening drinks and dinner, but always showed up for tennis. "She has her own circle of friends outside the Hemingway Club."

I didn't learn much about Caruthers's background as we ate our desserts. He said he'd been a captain in the infantry during the war and later served at British missions in Berlin, Prague, and Moscow — or so he claimed.

"After serving in European posts like those," I asked, "why come to Havana?"

After thinking for a moment, he said, "I often ask myself the same question," and left it at that. On the other hand, he squeezed from me details about my early life in Penetang, my years at university, and my time in Colombia with an expertise in interrogation I hadn't encountered since my dinner with the CIA station chief in Bogota. He asked about Heather but he learned nothing about her from me. I think he already knew her background.

After Caruthers finished with me and began toying with his coffee cup and looking bored, Damien Claes took over. But instead of asking me questions, he talked non-stop, with frequent nervous glances at his wife, whose name was Kimberly, about their lives in the Belgian Congo. He said he'd met and married his wife at Ostend on the coast of Flanders in mid-1933, before joining the Belgian colonial service and being posted to Africa. They had loved the colonial way lifestyle — friendships with always respectful houseboys; a sense of pride in uplifting ignorant Africans from their state of savagery; the hospitals, schools, clean water, sanitation, roads, railways, and honest administration; the journeys back home by steamer; shuffleboard on the deck by day; formal dinners at the captain's table in the evening; bridge with like-minded partners late into night; summers among the dunes with family. He was deputy to the governor of Katanga province, he said, when Lumumba became president, and his world had collapsed.

During a pause in the monologue, I changed the subject. "Don't you ever get tired of life in Havana?" I asked.

"No we don't," Damien said, looking at Kimberly for confirmation. "And that's because we have Club Hemingway."

"What's so special about Club Hemingway?"

"Why, it's special because it's exclusive. Nobody but the deputy ambassadors of Italy, France, Britain, Belgium, the Netherlands, and of course Canada, can become members."

"Don't forget the wives can be members too," Kimberly said, mildly admonishing her husband.

"Your club doesn't seem very democratic."

"It might not be democratic, but that's the rule. From time to time, African colleagues — deputy ambassadors — ask to join, but we always say no. We want to maintain our exclusivity. We politely tell them they can establish their own club if they want — nobody would stop them. They go away angry, but rules are rules."

"What's the reason the group is called Club Hemingway?"

"'The name arose out of quite extraordinary circumstances. Just after the Cuban missile crisis, the atmosphere in Cuba was tense. MININT was up to all sorts of nasty things to make life difficult for the Western embassies left in Havana, and one of the only means of entertainment available to diplomats was to get together Saturday mornings to play tennis at your embassy...."

"This sounds like it's going to be a long story."

"Take pity. I can't go any faster. I'm not as young and quick-witted as you. And so to add some variety to their lives, someone came up with the idea of creating a club restricted to the deputy ambassadors from the Western embassies who had lived through the crisis. That's how Club Hemingway was born."

"You still haven't said why it's called Club Hemingway."

"The reason is self-evident. The founders wanted to name it after Hemingway because he was the most famous Western writer ever to live in Cuba, the embodiment of the western spirit, the winner of the Nobel Prize for literature, the author of *The Sun also Rises, A Farewell to Arms, The Old Man and the Sea*..."

"And 'Ten Little Indians' and 'The Indian Camp.'"

"What do you mean?

"Those are just two of his short stories about drunken squaws and morally bankrupt, suicidal Indians. He's an embodiment of nothing noble as far as I'm concerned."

"You're a Métis aren't you?" said Caruthers, intervening in the conversation.

"Yes I am. But so what?"

"It shows."

Before I could challenge him, Damien continued his story as if my tiff with Adrian hadn't occurred. "And that's why the founders named the group Club Hemingway and expanded its activities from tennis to include luncheons to discuss the Great Ideas of the Western World and social drinks and dinner at Hemingway's favourite restaurant and bars — the Bodeguita del Medio and the Floridita in the old city. Club members used to go Marlin fishing as well, but interest faded and that stopped along with the discussions on Great Ideas."

11: The Ministry of the Interior

That evening around nine, Heather and I took our newly arrived car to the old city to rendezvous with the others at the Bodeguita del Medio. The members of Club Hemingway were already drinking mojitos among a crowd of off-duty Russian soldiers at the bar. By that time, determined not to be an object of ridicule ever again in Cuba, I had shed my green pants and shirt forever in favour of beige cotton slacks and a silk *guayabera*. I was more preoccupied than usual, worried whether my plan to break away from the others to investigate the deck cargo of the SS *Kama* would go off without incident, and I wasn't good company.

Heather loved the place and went around pointing out signatures that authors such as Pablo Neruda, Gabriel Garcia Marquez, as well as, of course, Ernest Hemingway, and movie stars like Ava Gardiner and Errol Flynn, had scribbled on the walls. But where she saw art, I saw graffiti, and there was no meeting of minds. I thought the dinner of overcooked pork, beans in watery sauce, and fried bananas was awful, and she considered it authentic. By the time we left for the Floridita to drink daiquiris, she was at the Dutchman's side. I wasn't that surprised when I returned from my spying mission, when the others told me she'd left with him.

Heather made no apologies when she returned home the next morning. "I told you I'd sleep with anyone I wanted when we met," she said. "And sex is just sex — it scratches an itch but means nothing."

Unable to control myself, I went to Bakker's house, barged in like an aggrieved husband in a cheap romance novel, and would have hit him if his wife hadn't intervened and made me leave. The Dutch ambassador called my ambassador to complain. After Cook hung up on him, he summoned me to the safe room to deliver a reprimand, saying my behaviour was as bad as that of Heather's. "If you weren't working for the CIA," he said, "I'd send the both of you home."

Fortunately my first effort as a spy had been a success — I confirmed there were no missile launchers under the netting of SS *Kama* — as were my subsequent expeditions on behalf of the CIA — or so I thought at the time. My attempts to effect reconciliation with Heather were less fruitful. I did everything to make her see reason, eventually coming up with the idea of getting her a dog. But not just any old dog, I wanted to give her a loyal companion that would somehow make her believe that the affection it showed to her was really coming from me. Aware that diplomats at the ends of their postings often sought good homes for the pets they couldn't bring back to their home countries, I asked Rolly to pass the word to Western embassies to let them know that I wanted a dog. Before long, a diplomat at the Swiss embassy gave me a lovable, three-year-old chocolate Lab named Bella. But Heather didn't get the message and moved to a guest bedroom and left Bella with me. I even showed up for tennis one Saturday morning and went through the motions of shaking hands with Bakker, hoping Heather would appreciate the gesture. But she didn't, and neither did Bakker and the other members of Club Hemingway. Nobody, with the exception of Caruthers, would speak to me — and all he said was, "I told you so," before I gave up and went home.

It was only a matter of time before MININT, which was obviously monitoring what was going on, took action. They had already tried their standard means of enticement to see if I was bribable — attractive women approaching me on the street or at the diplomatic free shop to hand me their telephone numbers, telephone calls at home from unknown persons offering me gold for next to nothing. But I had the impression these approaches were perfunctory, as if MININT assumed I was unassailable. But a few weeks after the start of Heather's affair with Bakker, a Cuban official I hadn't seen before came up to me at a reception, asked to see me alone, and handed me photos of Heather and Bakker naked and making love in bed.

"These are the only copies, and we'll destroy them if you'll work for us," he said, lying brazenly. "If you don't cooperate, we'll send them to your ambassador." I just pocketed them and said nothing. I nevertheless told the ambassador what had happened, and he made no comment other than to tell me to warn Bakker MININT would probably try to blackmail him as well.

"They'll be after you next," I said to Bakker, who laughed and said someone from MININT had already shown the pictures to him and threatened to tell his wife and Dutch government if he didn't cooperate. "I told him the same thing I'm telling you. My wife knows and doesn't care, or at least she puts up with me. My ambassador knows and doesn't care. My authorities back home know and don't care. You know and I don't care. Nobody can blackmail me. Now go away and leave me alone."

Heather was just as dismissive when I tried to talk to her and went out of her way to spite me. When I came home one day for lunch, I found her chattering away with the sour-faced woman from the VIP room. "I've invited our friend for lunch since I knew you wouldn't mind," she said. "Afterwards, we're taking the car and she's going to show me around. And tomorrow I'm going for lunch at her place." I ate quickly and left for the office with a cold goodbye.

Heather even took another lover — apparently Bakker encouraged her to do so — a Cuban tennis coach who came from time to time to give lessons to Club Hemingway members. Caruthers, who knew from his own sources about the pictures with Bakker, told me the tennis coach was a member of MININT and dangerous. I spoke to her again, but she still wouldn't listen. We then got into a raging argument, dragging up every slight, real and imagined, that we had inflicted on each other since we had met. I crossed the line, however, when I told her I was sorry I'd ever met her. "You're not half as sorry as me," she said. "I know for a fact you betrayed Rojas to the Colombian army."

"Who told you that?" I said, hoping to be able to discredit her source.

"That's what my CUSO friends from Colombia said last summer at their place in the Gatineau Hills. They didn't know how I could live with a monster like you. I was going to leave you but I didn't want to give up my chance to taste life in the only true democracy in the Americas. Our marriage has been dead since that time."

Matters came to a head when I was away on a three-day trip for the CIA to Santiago de Cuba on the eastern side of the country. MININT sent photos of Heather in bed with the tennis coach to Ambassador Cook, but made no demands. They were passing some sort of message having to do with me. Whatever their reason, the ambassador didn't wait for me to come back and went straight to our house and told Heather she was behaving disgracefully and had to leave Cuba immediately.

Heather didn't want to go and told him she was a Canadian citizen and had no right to banish her. "If you don't go willingly, he apparently said, "I'll take away your diplomatic passport and change the locks on your house; after all, your passport is the property of the Canadian government and the rent is paid by the embassy." Ambassadors don't have authority over dependants, but Heather packed up her things and went back to Winnipeg anyway. She didn't even leave me a farewell note.

I returned home a day or two later with only Bella to greet me at the door. I had angry words with the ambassador, but he told me Longshaft should never have sent us to Cuba in the first place. I was immature and she was irresponsible. If I didn't like his decision, I could leave as well. I sent a message to Longshaft in which I provided all the ugly details of Heather's dual infidelity. In reply, he took my side. Husbands and wives were always getting into trouble in the Department, he said. No secrets had been passed to the Cubans because Heather didn't know any. I was better off without her. Give Cook time to calm down and all would be well. Above all, carry on with the good work for the CIA.

I stayed on, knowing full well her departure was for the best, but nurturing the hope we could get back together some day. In those days, telephone connections to Canada from Cuba were virtually non-existent, so I wrote her letters but she never answered. Thankfully Bella was there to keep me company as winter turned into spring, then summer. She sensed I was upset and followed me around the house, slept on the floor beside me and did her best to comfort me. I took her for long walks and started bringing her to the embassy as I carried out my deputy ambassador duties.

Carruthers was the only Club Hemingway member I continued to see. We met occasionally for drinks. By that time, I was convinced he worked for the SIS and I admired his professionalism. As usual, he left it to me to do most of the talking. He never probed for information on my work for the CIA but was always interested in my impressions of developments in the parts of the country I visited. I assumed he incorporated them into the reports he sent back to his headquarters. Then one day, he mentioned I might find a visit to the bar of the Havana Riviera Hotel useful, but didn't say why.

I knew the hotel well, and had been dropping in from time to time because I liked its 1950s Las Vegas gambling décor and strange history. Meyer Lansky, the notorious mafia boss, built it and opened its doors to the public in December 1957, and it became the best known hotel-casino in the Caribbean basin. Each year, tens of thousands of American tourists came to play roulette, craps, and blackjack under its giant crystal chandeliers and to take in shows starring headliners such as Frank Sinatra, Ginger Rogers, and Nate King Cole. It was also where, in 1970, the Cuban government lodged visiting delegations of Third World revolutionaries — Freedom Fighters, if you like. Occasionally, I came up with a tidbit the CIA found helpful at the Riviera. I even saw Caruthers there once, talking animatedly with a rough-looking, full-bearded character, but we pretended not to know each other.

Assuming Caruthers had given me a good tip, I went that night to the Riviera, ordered a beer at the bar, and looked around the room. Four unshaven men in their mid-thirties, dressed in creased work pants, rumpled T-shirts, and running shoes, were sitting by themselves at a corner table drinking rum and cokes, smoking cigars, and talking. From their accent and turns of phrase, they were Quebekers. Craving company, I picked up my beer and went to join them. They stopped speaking and eyed me warily as I approached, but they said yes when I asked them in French if I could sit down.

"Where you from in Quebec?" said the first questioner, greeting me with the special warmth and trust Quebeckers accord to anyone met abroad who speaks French the same way they do.

"I'm not from Quebec, but from Penetang — that's on Georgian Bay."

"I know where Penetang is. A lot of Métis live there."

"I'm a Métis, but I don't live there."

"You here on holiday?"

"No I live here. I work at the Canadian embassy."

"What's your job?"

"I'm a spy for the CIA. No I got that wrong. I'm really a spy for the Canadian government."

I burst out laughing when I said that, and they joined in, howling at the absurdity of my answer.

"And I bet you're here to spy on us," someone said.

"Only if you're dangerous terrorists."

That precipitated another eruption of laughter and someone raised his glass and proposed a toast to Canada's spy in Havana. I raised my glass but in honor of the Métis people of Canada. Someone else raised his glass and toasted Louis Riel, and I told them he was my hero.

"Now let's talk serious," one of them said. "Why don't your people get together with the Indians and revolt against the English colonizers. You'd soon bring the government to its knees."

"Because Canadians have always preferred peaceful change," I said, using a platitude to fend off a discussion that would lead nowhere.

"You're just repeating the stuff they tell you in English schools. Why don't you think for yourself?"

"I do my best."

"Your best isn't good enough! Look at the facts. Didn't the English conquer Quebec by force of arms? That's not peaceful change. Didn't the Canadians seize and colonize the lands of the Indians? That's not peaceful change. Didn't Sir John A. Macdonald send troops out west to take the land of your ancestors? That's not peaceful change. And look at what peaceful change brought Riel? He played the game and got himself elected to Parliament. But the colonialist-imperialist government refused to let him take his seat in Parliament and hanged him when he dared lead a revolt."

"Castro didn't make that mistake when he overthrew Batista — he took up arms, mobilized the oppressed, and set up a true communist society in this country," someone else said. "But we won't make that mistake when our turn comes."

As he spoke, I understood I was talking to members of the FLQ. It was important to keep the discussion going.

"At least we've never had colonies overseas," I said to provoke him.

"But Canada exploits the people of the Third World by bribing their leaders into allowing mining companies to pollute their lands and take their mineral wealth for the benefit of a few fat cats in Toronto and New York. We export our cigarettes around the world and pretend tobacco is good for your health. And you say Canada isn't a colonialist power?"

It was a damning indictment, but I remained silent.

"You haven't thought about these matters, Mr. Whoever-You-Are from the Canadian embassy, *n'est-ce pas?*"

"I have, but I still think Canada's the best place in the world to live, and is doing more for the people of the Third World than anybody else."

"That's the problem with Indians, Métis, and Quebeckers. They don't know they're both the oppressors and the oppressed. They've been brainwashed by the blood-sucking oligarchs, the boot-licking media, the Roman Capitalist Church, and their pussy-footed governments over the years. They need to shed their slave mentality before they can change society."

"How do you do that?"

"That, *mon ami,* is not so hard. You need to take dramatic revolutionary action to make the people the aware of their true condition and prepare them for the coming classless society."

"What do you mean?"

"Just wait and you'll see. Now if you don't mind leaving, we've got work to do."

They weren't smiling when I left their table, perhaps wondering if they had said too much to a stranger who had come out of the night to ask them questions they shouldn't have answered. Maybe they thought I really was an undercover agent. Maybe they thought I had lulled them into saying too much by claiming I was a Métis — a member of a downtrodden race they assumed would automatically share their views. I had some questions of my own. What was a FLQ delegation doing in Havana? Was it seeking Cuban help for the big operation it had been talking about for years? Was the Cuban government paying their hotel bills? If so, were Canada's relations with Cuba as good as we thought they were?

12: The Communist Central Committee

Ambassador Cook, whom I consulted, was as worried as I was, and I sent off a message to Longshaft with my account of my encounter at the Riviera. The following day, I received the following reply:

> I have discussed your report with the Task Force and would like to register four points.
>
> 1. We were most interested to receive yet another indication the FLQ may be planning a major operation "to prepare them for the coming classless society."
> 2. The consensus among members of the Task Force is that Cuba values its relations with Canada too highly to put them at risk by supporting the FLQ. Without access to cheap agricultural products, tourist dollars from Canadian visitors, and spare parts for American model cars, trucks, and tractors, its economy could collapse.
> 3. By separate message, the Latin American

Affairs bureau is sending instructions to Ambassador Cook to call on the vice minister of Foreign Affairs to seek assurances Cuba will not support the FLQ. We expect the vice minister will once again confirm that FLQ members sometimes visit Cuba but that Cuba does not provide them support.

4. The Task Force now believes assurances of this nature from the government of Cuba are not enough. We need to be certain that the Communist Party, the power behind the government, is aware of our concerns. Since, it is not appropriate for the ambassador to open up back channel contacts with the Party, the Task Force wants you, as deputy ambassador, to approach the Central Committee to pass a clear message that Canada will not tolerate any interference in its internal affairs. To that end, please meet at the earliest opportunity with Juan Carlos Rodriguez, head of the Americas Department of the Communist Party.

Longshaft

At noon two days later, a Soviet Zil limousine with darkened windows pulled up in front of the embassy. The policeman on duty saluted as the driver, who looked like a professional wrestler in a well-tailored black suit, got out and walked to the reception desk and asked for me. I had been waiting for the call, and came down the stairs where he greeted me with unsmiling courtesy and informed me he had been instructed to drive me to the headquarters of the Central Committee. At my destination, another black-suited giant accompanied me to meet Rodriquez, who shook hands and said with apparent sincerity that he'd been looking forward to meeting me ever since I arrived in Cuba.

"If your embassy hadn't phoned to set up this appointment," he said, "I would have called you myself. Now let's have some lunch. We've got a lot to talk about." He then led me down a corridor lined with black-framed photographs of members of the communist party who had fallen in combat in Cuba's wars abroad to a small dining room with a table set for two.

"This is where I like to receive special visitors," he said, smiling and motioning for me to take a seat. "There's nothing more pleasant than agreeable conversation with a good friend over an excellent meal of Cuban seafood washed down with a glass of chilled Crimean white wine. You agree, I assume." I agreed.

As the waiter entered with two glasses of wine and set them down before us, Rodriguez said, "I'm told you have an interesting background." I took that as a cue to tell him about my early years in Penetang, including my summers as a deckhand on the freighters.

"So the deputy ambassador has a proletarian background," he said.

"I understand the head of the Americas Department has a bourgeois background," I said, repeating what I had read in his official biography.

"Many of us who fought with Fidel in the struggle to overthrow capitalism come from middle-class backgrounds," he said, not amused by my attempt to be witty. "My father owned sugar plantations and ensured I went to a Jesuit private school."

"Just like the president," I said.

"That's right, but my brother and I went to Harvard to study law. Fidel studied law but did that here in Havana."

"Did you fight in the Sierra Maestra with the president?"

At that moment, the waiter arrived with the first course. "We're starting with fish," Rodriguez said. "It's snapper caught this morning in the Bay of Pigs, grilled to perfection and served with fresh lime juice. You won't find anything better in any of the great restaurants of downtown Penetang."

But when I picked up my fork and dug into the snapper, the fish released a horrible odour — like the smell of a bloated, long-dead bear I once came across in the weeds while fishing on Georgian Bay. I put my fork down and looked at Rodriguez who was already eating his fish with gusto and carrying on our conversation as if nothing was wrong.

"No, I wasn't in the Sierra with the commander-in-chief," he said as I took a tentative bite of the snapper, only to gag at the taste and spit it out. "Anything the matter with our proletarian food?" he asked me, sounding concerned. "There shouldn't be. Our portions are from the same fish."

"No," I said, "I was just getting rid of a bone." With a great effort of will I ate two or three forkfuls, forcing them down with a glass of what turned out to be vile, warm rotgut.

Rodriquez surveyed my struggle impassively as he carried on with his story as he ate his snapper and took sips of what appeared, from the condensation on the glass, to be cold white wine. "As I was saying," he said, "the struggle against Batista was conducted on two fronts — a rural one and one in Havana. I fought in Havana. My job was to organize the people, plant bombs, and eliminate enemies of the revolution."

"Were you supported by your family?"

"Sadly, that wasn't the case. My father even betrayed me to the secret police, but I managed to escape and go into hiding in Havana. He left with my mother and brother for Miami after the revolution. But the less said about that period in my life the better. Let's get back to you. Have you had an opportunity to get out of Havana to see some of the country?"

I was sure MININT had briefed Rodriguez on my travels and assumed he was making small talk. I made small talk in return, describing the museums, shrines, and sugar mills I had visited. He appeared interested and so I told him about a trip I made to a prison, now a museum, on the Isle of Youth where Castro had been imprisoned after the failed attack on the Moncada barracks in the mid-1950s.

As we chatted, the waiter cleared away the dishes and brought in new glasses of wine and the second course. "It's fresh Cuban lobster," Rodriguez said. "One of the things Canadian tourists love to eat when they visit Cuba."

Rodriguez proposed a toast to the health of Canada–Cuba relations. I raised my glass and reluctantly took a sip of my plonk, but he made a great show of sniffing the bouquet and examining its colour before downing his with a sigh of appreciation. And when I turned to my lobster, I once again could smell putrefaction. By this time my stomach was aching and I was certain the Cubans were deliberately serving me foul wine and spoiled food. I had no intention of playing their game and told Rodriguez I wasn't hungry. "Something the matter with the lobster?" he asked, smiling.

"I've just lost my appetite," I said, forcing myself to smile back. To change the subject, I asked him about Che Guevara.

"I knew him well," Rodriguez said, becoming animated. "I helped him hunt down war criminals and CIA agents after the revolution. I helped organize his trips to the Congo and to Bolivia to fight imperialism. I'm still mourning his death at the hands of the CIA. I mourn all the great revolutionary leaders, such as Diego Rojas, likewise murdered by the CIA."

Taken aback by his mention of Rojas, I said that I had heard that Cuba had been one of his biggest backers.

"It is Cuba's revolutionary duty to support national liberation movements like the ELN that are struggling to bring change to their countries."

That was my opening. "I hope Cuba doesn't think Canada is governed by a repressive government that needs revolutionary change. We're a social democracy that treats everybody equally."

"Including your people — the Métis and the Indians," he said, not smiling.

Dessert was served — vanilla ice cream covered in whipped cream smothered in hot chocolate fudge sauce and cherries. I declined and he ate. The waiter then came with coffee. It smelled wonderful but I said no and he picked up his cup and drank slowly. The time was approaching to speak frankly. Rodriguez made the first move.

"I know why you wanted to see me. And you know I know," he added, looking at me sharply.

"I'm listening."

"You met members of the FLQ in the bar of Riviera Hotel two days ago and your government wants to know if the Party supports their campaign to install a revolutionary government in Quebec."

"That's right."

"You can tell your government that Cuba has no intention of harming its friendly relations with Canada by supporting the FLQ — whether it takes its fight to another level or not. That's a promise from the commander-in-chief himself. All sorts of people who want to overthrow their governments come to Cuba for help. From time to time, individuals show up uninvited, like the people you met at the Riviera. We put them up for a few days, feed them well, give them boxes of cigars and bottles of rum, and send them on their way."

"That's good to hear," I said. "Canada wouldn't want to join the American blockade and cut its trade ties with Cuba."

"Now you probably want to know why I wanted to see you."

"Not really," I said, suddenly afraid he was about to give me bad news.

"We've known for a long time that you helped the CIA get Rojas. 'Why would the person responsible for the death of one of Cuba's best friends in the Americas accept a posting to Havana?' That was the question we debated when we received word you were coming."

"You've got your facts wrong," I said, a bit too defensively, "I assumed you knew Rojas was a friend of mine. I was devastated when I heard of his death, so soon after visiting him at his camp in the Llanos."

"And accompanying him on the raid on Sucio to gain his confidence to better betray him?"

"He insisted I go with him to make a report to the outside world."

"He was a trusting person and you took advantage of him. According to our sources in the ELN, you caused his death."

"Then why did you accept me as deputy ambassador?"

"We wanted to turn you away, but we had our relations with Canada to consider. We didn't want to create a diplomatic incident when your government appeared to think we were somehow supporting the FLQ in its plans to create a revolutionary government in Quebec. Would you like to hear more?"

"Do I have a choice?" I asked with false bravado.

"From the moment you and your wife set foot on Cuban soil, we've followed your every movement — your every activity. We were there when you played tennis. We were there when you went for drinks with Club Hemingway at the Bodeguita del Medio. We were there when you had drinks at the Floridita. We were with you when you boarded the SS *Kama*, like a common thief, to paw through its cargo. You obviously had come here on some sort of espionage mission — not for Canada — you don't have an offensive spy agency. You were probably working for the CIA. That made sense, given what you did for the Yankees in Colombia."

He paused to give me time to absorb his words, to take another sip of coffee, and to light a cigar. "Want one?" he said smiling, offering me the box.

I shook my head and he carried on with his indictment.

"Now where was I," he said. "I'm having so much fun I lost my train of thought. Ah, yes I remember. We then had to decide what to do with you. We couldn't just declare you *persona non grata* and expel you. Your people would retaliate and expel one of our people from Ottawa — someone a lot more valuable than you. The Canadian public wouldn't believe us if we said you were spying for the Americans, and our campaign to attract Canadian tourists would be damaged. And so we decided to let you stay and continued our close observation of your activities. In the interim, we would try to find out if you were a spy for hire. Someone who'd work for the CIA one day might work for us."

"Is that the reason you tried to blackmail me?" I said. "To threaten to show my ambassador pictures of my wife in bed with the Dutchman if I didn't cooperate?"

"That's right," he said, after taking another puff on his cigar — he was enjoying himself.

"Then why send the pictures with the tennis coach to my ambassador and ask for nothing?"

"For a spy you're not very smart. By that time, it was clear our approach to recruit you wouldn't work. We wanted you out of the country but didn't want to create a fuss with Ottawa. We calculated that your ambassador would order her home after he saw the pictures. We assumed you loved her — even if she's a tramp — we thought you'd go with her and never come back. That would have solved the problem, but you didn't go, and so we decided on a frontal approach – I'd host a lunch fit for a scum like you, and as we ate, to take measures at your house to force you out."

I got up and hurried to the waiting Zil. This time the driver let me open my door for myself and didn't respond when I said

I wanted to get back as soon as possible. Instead, he took me on a slow tour of the city, deliberately keeping me in suspense until dropping me off in front of the embassy. I ran home to a horror show. The door was open and Bella was dead in the hallway, her throat slit, chairs were overturned in the dining room, dishes were smashed in the kitchen, dresser drawers were open and clothes and books scattered on the floor upstairs in the bedroom. The telephone rang. I picked it up but there was no one there. I called for Angelita but she was gone.

I rushed to the embassy and sent a message to Longshaft, telling him the Cubans knew I was working for the CIA and had trashed my home to make it clear they wanted me out of the country. I also said, almost as an afterthought, that Rodriguez had provided assurances, coming from the president himself, that the Cubans would adopt a hands-off policy on the FLQ.

The next day, even before Longshaft's instructions to leave Havana arrived, Ambassador Cook was driving me to the airport. I watched the rear-view mirror, expecting to see the Zil, but nobody was following us. But as I boarded a Cubana plane filled with happy Canadian tourists returning to Ottawa from Varadero, I saw the sour-faced woman from the VIP room on the tarmac laughing at me.

Part Four

The FLQ

September 1970 to December 1970

13: The Kidnappings Begin

My first priority when my flight from Havana landed at the Ottawa airport was to get in touch with Heather. Our marriage was over but I wanted to say goodbye in person — to bring closure to a relationship that had never had a chance of succeeding. But when I went to a payphone and called her parent's number in Winnipeg, there was no answer. I remained at the phone stuffing dimes into it and calling again and again until someone picked it up and I heard her father say hello.

"It's me. It's Luc calling from the Ottawa airport," I said. "The posting to Cuba's over and I'm home to stay. I need to speak to Heather." But he hung up and I was left listening to the dial tone. I put in more dimes and called again and again, until I finally gave up and went to pass through customs and immigration, pick up my suitcase at the carousel, and take a bus downtown to the Daley building.

"You're not disappointed the Cubans caught me?" I said when I met Longshaft.

"More surprised than disappointed — but that was bound to happen one of these days. You did some good work in the time you were there, and we wanted you back anyway."

"What about their dirty tricks?"

"We'll get even. We always get even in the end. We'll start by expelling the resident MININT agent, but we won't be killing any dogs."

"I hope my new job has to do with the FLQ."

"It does. Frankly, we're all worried the threat is growing. The bombings and bank robberies are increasing. The RCMP has jailed twenty-three terrorists but has got nothing out of them.

"Where do I come in?"

"By default, you've become our expert on International Terrorism. Speaking frankly, we were looking for an older, more experienced officer for the job, but we couldn't find anyone who knew anything about the subject. Your messages out of Bogota and Havana are the only credible reports anyone has seen on FLQ activity abroad, and the only indication it's planning a big operation in the near future. For that reason, the Task Force wanted you back as soon as possible to fill in the blanks in our knowledge base. We don't know, for example, whether the FLQ is in any way affiliated with a network of Latin American terrorists."

"Or whether a network of Latin American terrorists in fact exists."

"Or whether they're smuggling arms, ammunition, and bomb-making equipment into Canada for the FLQ."

"At least we know Cuba won't be involved."

"I wouldn't be so sure about that. They're masters of ambiguity — saying one thing but doing something else when it suits their purpose."

I thus returned to my old ninth floor office to focus this time only on questions of international terrorism. A week after I started work, Harvey Lieberman knocked on my door and came in. I expected him to chew me out — to say I'd let the CIA down — but he didn't. "Don't feel bad," he said. "You weren't our only man in Havana." He went on to make some vague remarks about the members of Club Hemingway which made me think Paulo Verde and maybe Guillaume Montpetit were doing some freelance work for the CIA. He then let me know the real reason for his visit — he wanted back his camera and the copy of *Jane's Weapons of the World.*

"You don't need them anymore," he said, "and neither will the person who'll replace you as deputy ambassador. The folks at Langley have cancelled the program." I gave him his camera but had to tell him I'd left his copy of *Jane's* in Cuba.

Then at eight in the morning on October 5, 1970, a beautiful fall day in Montreal, four heavily armed individuals, disguised as deliverymen, kidnapped American consul-general Nicholas Peabody from his house in the English-speaking Montreal neighbourhood of Westmount. I was eating breakfast when I heard the news on the radio, and I raced from my central Ottawa apartment to the Daley Building to follow developments. Longshaft's door was open as I hurried by, and he waved me in to join him as he watched the television news.

"This is probably the big operation the FLQ has been promising to pull off," he said. "In a few minutes the Task Force will be meeting in the operations centre. I'll do the chairing and you'll be the note-taker."

A reporter covering the story came on the air to say the Che Guevara cell of the FLQ had issued a communique in which it took responsibility for the kidnapping. The document also contained a political manifesto and the following list of conditions and a warning.

1. The government must allow CBC television to read the political manifesto live on air.
2. The police must end its search for the kidnappers.
3. All imprisoned members of the FLQ must be freed and sent to Cuba.
4. Five hundred thousand dollars in gold bullion must be given to the freed prisoners.

5. Failure to read the communique live on air by midnight would lead to the execution of the consul general.

"That doesn't give us much time," Longshaft said, as he got up to leave for the operations centre. But before he could get out the door, Mary stopped him to say External Affairs Minister Hankey wanted to talk to him. He was on the line. When I tried to leave, Longshaft told me to stay. "Listen in to the conversation and take notes. You'll have to do the follow-up anyway."

I picked up an extension and listened as the agitated minister wanted to know what Longshaft was doing about the kidnapping. Longshaft said the Task Force would meet in a few minutes to decide what advice to give the government. "I can tell you now, however, that we'll be recommending the FLQ demands be rejected out of hand. Canada follows a long-standing policy of never giving in to the demands of hostage-takers. It's a policy we adopted at the urging of the Americans years ago."

"But this time the victim is an American consul general," the minister said.

"Yes, being American and a consul general turns it into another sort of problem. Our American friends will want us to bend the policy."

"What can I do that's useful while you bureaucrats deliberate?"

"Why don't you call in the American ambassador to say how sorry you are that Peabody's been kidnapped."

"I'll do that and tell him we're doing everything in our power to get him back unharmed."

"That would be reassuring."

"And I'll hold the line on giving in to the FLQ."

"That would make our lives easier. I'll send a Foreign Service officer by the name of Luc Cadotte to your office to take notes on your discussion. The Task Force will need them."

It was only a mile from the Daley Building to the East Block of Parliament where Hankey had his office. By walking fast, I made it to the entrance in fifteen minutes, in time to see the chauffeur-driven Cadillac of American Ambassador Thomas Swift IV pull up at the entrance to the East Block. The grandson of a businessman who made his fortune smuggling booze across the border from Canada during Prohibition, Swift lived on inherited wealth. In Washington, he was the man you went to if you needed someone with deep pockets to bankroll Republican candidates for congressional office. In due course, the President named him ambassador to Canada. In Ottawa, he was known as the great snob who spoke to nobody other than his wife, the prime minister, carefully chosen members of Cabinet, certain captains of industry, his Presbyterian minister, and Longshaft — whom he apparently met in Europe during the war.

On exiting the back door of his car, he brushed by me, ignoring my attempt to greet him, walked by the duty commissionaire who tried to stop him, and went up the stairs to the minister's office. The minister's private secretary knew who he was and opened the door to let him in. I followed close behind with notebook and pen in hand.

After the customary greetings, Hankey opened the discussion. "I want to assure you the police are doing everything in their power to find your consul general."

"I expected nothing less."

"Kidnappings of diplomats are rare in Canada. This is the first one I've heard of."

"I know that, but a host country is responsible for the safety of all foreign diplomats on its soil, Peabody included. Canada let us down."

"The RCMP is the finest police force in the world and always gets its man."

"Minister, those are just words. The United States wants action."

"I know that, but I called you here as a courtesy to let you know how sorry we are as the police go about their business."

"But surely you knew something like this could happen. The FLQ has been saying for years it's prepared to kill and kidnap to set up a Cuban-style government in Quebec. If you don't believe me, just look at the communiqués it issues after each terrorist attack."

"I don't think anyone could have imagined they'd target an American diplomat."

"Especially one who's a friend of the president."

"I didn't know that."

"He's not just any ordinary consul general. He comes from a prominent New England family and was a major financial supporter of the president at the last election. He thought he'd be sent to Ottawa as ambassador but lost out to me."

"I wasn't aware of that — never even met him."

"You should have made the effort. If you had, you'd be able to put a face to the person the FLQ is threatening to kill."

"Our Task Force looking into its list of demands as we speak."

"You've only got to midnight."

"I know, but it wants us to free its members in jail and send them to Cuba. It would set a bad precedent if we did that."

"Is it still Canadian policy never to give in to terrorists? Never to negotiate, never to make concessions."

"It is, and that's your policy too, isn't it? Are you suggesting we do otherwise with Peabody?"

"No, not at all. It's just that the United States is the leader of the free world. Speaking personally, I think we should be exempt from rules applied to others."

"Speaking personally, I'm convinced the kidnapping is a FLQ publicity stunt. It'll release your man safe and sound in a few days."

"Speaking officially, I hope you're right."

After Swift left, saying he would see himself out, Hankey told me to stay and asked me what position I held in Longshaft's bureau. After I said I was the resident intelligence analyst for inter-national terrorism, he asked if I thought the kidnapping was a publicity stunt. "Or do you think the FLQ will murder Peabody if we don't give in by midnight?"

"They'd kill him without hesitation, but they won't call it murder. They'd call it revolutionary justice."

"But that wouldn't be the Canadian way. Our way is elections, dialogue, compromise, things like that."

"The FLQ doesn't accept the Canadian way. The ideals of Fidel Castro, Che Guevara, and all the revolutionary leaders of Latin America going back to Bolivar are their way. They'll kill Peabody for sure if we don't give in. What we have to decide is whether we can accept the damage to our relations with the Americans if we stick to our principles."

"But they're the ones who pressured us into adopting this no-concessions policy."

"As Ambassador Swift indicated, they consider themselves exempt from the rule. They're the people on the hill. The chosen ones. The ones who have a God-given duty to save the world from rogue states and terrorists. The rules are different when applied to them."

"I think I already know the answer — but what will happen if we don't give in and Peabody is killed?"

"The Americans are our largest trading partner and the most important member of NATO."

"Okay, I get the point. Now a final question — you're not obliged to answer — how do we square the circle?"

"Authorize the CBC to read the manifesto. The people of Quebec won't rise up in rebellion when they hear it, but don't give in on the prisoners, at least not yet."

Nobody ever told me if my advice to Hankey influenced on the government's decision. But that evening, just before the midnight deadline, a CBC news anchor came on the air. "For humanitarian reasons," he said, "to save the life of United States Consul General Nicholas Peabody, the CBC is interrupting its regular programming to read the following political manifesto from the FLQ:"

The *Front de libération du Québec* is neither the Messiah nor a modern day Robin Hood. It is a group of Quebec workers who are determined to use every means possible to ensure that the people of Quebec take control of their own destiny.

The *Front de libération du Québec* wants total independence for Quebeckers, united in a free society and purged for the good of the clique of voracious sharks, the patronizing big bosses and their henchmen who have made Quebec their private hunting ground for "cheap labour" and unscrupulous exploitation.

We live in a society of terrorized slaves, terrorized by the big bosses. We are terrorized by the capitalist Roman Church, we are terrorized by the closed circles of science and culture which the universities and their monkey see, monkey do bosses.

Factory workers, miners, and loggers; service-industry workers, teachers, students, and the unemployed, take back what belongs to you, your jobs, your determination and your liberty.

Workers of Quebec, take back today what is yours, take back what belongs to you. Only you know your factories, your machines, your hotels, your universities, your unions. Don't wait for some miracle organization.

Make your own revolution in your neighbourhoods, in your places of work. If you don't do it yourselves, other technocratic usurpers and so on will replace the handful of cigar smokers we have now, and everything will have to be done over again. Only you are able to build a free society.

We are the workers of Quebec and we will fight to the bitter end. With the help of the entire population, we want to replace this slave society with a free society, operating by itself and for itself, a society open to the world.

Long live free Quebec!
Long live our imprisoned political comrades!
Long live the Quebec revolution!
Long live the *Front de libération du Québec* !

The next morning, the Che Guevara cell issued a statement saying it hadn't executed Peabody because the government had allowed the CBC to read its political manifesto. However, it kept up the pressure by vowing to kill its hostage if its other demands were not met by noon, Saturday, October 10. That brought Swift back to Hankey's office. I was there as the note-taker.

"This time I've come with instructions from the State Department," he said, pulling out a diplomatic note and reading it to the minister.

The Government of the United States presents its compliments to the Honorable Government of Canada and would like to express its concern that Consul General Peabody has not yet been freed from his captors. In this regard, it draws to the attention of the Honorable Government of Canada the provisions of Article 29 of the Vienna Convention on Diplomatic Relations to wit: "The receiving state shall treat him with due respect and shall take all appropriate steps to prevent any attack on his person."

It further advises that his Excellency, Thomas Swift IV, has been empowered to make certain proposals to the Honorable Government of Canada to bring to a speedy conclusion this unfortunate incident.

The Government of the United States of America avails itself of this opportunity to renew to the Honorable Government of Canada the assurances of its highest consideration.

"What's this about? Why a note? " Hankey said, placing it on his desk.

"Washington doesn't think Canada is taking its concerns seriously, and wants to remind you of your international obligations."

"And your proposals?"

"We want you to exchange Peabody for the FLQ prisoners. It's been done before. Brazil just did a deal with terrorists to exchange political prisoners for two kidnapped ambassadors."

"Is that right, Cadotte?" Hankey said, pulling me into the discussion.

"That's right, sir," I said. "One was a German and the other American."

"I thought you were opposed to negotiating with terrorists," Hankey said to Swift.

"We are, but we sometimes let other countries do the negotiating for us. In Brazil the initiative worked out well. We got our man back and the terrorist kidnapping of diplomats has ended."

"Is that right Cadotte? The kidnapping of diplomats in Brazil has ended?"

"You can take my word for it, Minister," Swift said. "You don't have to ask the note-taker."

"Mr. Cadotte is the government's expert on international terrorism, and I trust his knowledge and judgment."

"The ambassador is right sir," I said. "There's been no kidnapping of diplomats since the exchanges of prisoners for ambassadors last year. But that's because the Brazilians now kill the political prisoners they pick up and dump their bodies into the sea. There are no prisoners to exchange and the terrorists know that. Other Latin American governments do the same thing."

"That's barbaric," Hankey said. "We'd never condone such behaviour."

"It gets worse," I said. "The Brazilian secret police — and the other Latin American secret police services — torture their prisoners before they dump them into the sea. They then arrest the individuals identified under torture by the original group of terrorists, torture them and dump them into the sea — starting a new cycle of arrest, torture, dumping into sea, arrest, torture, dumping into sea ad infinitum. Don't forget the countries of Latin America don't care about human rights."

"That was very interesting but irrelevant," Swift said. "The United States wants you to free the FLQ prisoners in exchange for the life of Peabody — and to do it well before the new deadline. Naturally, if asked, we would say the decision was taken by Canada without consultation with the United States. We can maintain our public no-concessions policy that way. The Brazilians agreed when we suggested a similar cover story for the release of our man in Rio de Janeiro."

If Swift thought the Canadian government would change its no-concessions policy by putting pressure on the minister, he was to be disappointed. On October 9, on the eve of the dead-

line set by the FLQ, the minister of Justice of Quebec made the
following statement of principle.

> No society can accept that the decisions of its
> government and of its courts of law can be
> questioned or erased by the use of blackmail
> exercised by any group because this signifies the
> end of all social order.

The Task Force now expected the worst. To maintain its
credibility, the FLQ would have to kill Peabody or launch
another spectacular operation. On Saturday, October 10, on
another cool sunny fall morning in Montreal, three men and
a woman pulled up in front of the home of Hubert Jolicoeur,
Quebec's minister of tourism. They entered his house, dragged
him out, forced him into their car at gunpoint and drove away.
Within an hour, their communiqués began to arrive at radio
and television stations across the city. The kidnappers identified themselves as members of the Patriot cell. In language
even more hysterical and theatrical than that used by the Che
Guevara cell in its communiqués, they said Jolicoeur would
die if their imprisoned comrades were not put on a plane to
Cuba by October 15.

A week of frantic activity began. The Quebec government
fled to Montreal from Quebec City to take refuge, with its
senior officials, in a heavily guarded skyscraper. The Federal
government brought in the army to guard public buildings in
Quebec and Ottawa. Soldiers with rifles stood at the doors of
Parliament. There was even a guard posted at the entrance to
the Daley Building. Bodyguards were assigned to anyone in a
position of authority.

I spent most of my time going through intercepted messages
and writing assessments on terrorist actively around the world

to feed the appetite among senior official and ministers for anything that could help them understand terrorism as a phenomenon. At Longstaff's request, I sat in on the daily meetings of the Task Force, and generally made myself useful. One morning Longstaff told us the American president had called the prime minister but offered no insights on the conversation. On another, Longshaft was summoned to the minister's office to sit in on a visit by Swift. The meeting hadn't gone well, he said.

14: The Torture Directive

Then all hell broke loose. A policeman, checking out an illegally parked car on a road near Dorval Airport early in the morning of October 16, just hours after the expiry of the Patriot cell ultimatum, found Jolicoeur's body crammed into the trunk, lying on a dirty spare tire, with a rosary chain twisted around his neck. All Canada mourned his death. There were cries for the suspension of *habeas corpus* and the arrest and jailing of anyone who, guilty or innocent, had displayed the slightest sympathy for the FLQ. The prime minister called a meeting of Cabinet for next day to decide what to do. Hankey brought me along in case ministers asked questions only an expert could answer.

As we walked across the lawn from the minister's East Block office to the Centre Block, men and women emerged from a larger crowd to tell him it was high time the government got tough on the terrorists. Really tough. No pussy-footing around. Shoot them down like the dogs they were. We went in the West Entrance past saluting guards — there were no security checks in those days — to the staircase leading to the Cabinet room. Ministers were still arriving from their constituencies around the country. Longshaft, who had gone in ahead, was standing in a corner talking to the RCMP commissioner.

The mood among the Quebeckers was one of grief, anger, and worry. The ministers from the other provinces were concerned, but not as emotionally involved as the Quebeckers — a member of their cultural and political family had not been left to die in the trunk of a car. The Quebec ministers who had known Jolicoeur personally, there were many of them in the intimate world of Quebec politics, kept repeating they hadn't believed the FLQ would go so far as to murder a hostage. A common criminal, someone holding a rich man for ransom for example, might do such a thing — but not a group of people who claimed they stood for justice.

They probably also believed the FLQ members, for all their extremism and fits of political outrage, were also family. If you went back far enough, you'd probably find they were blood relations, perhaps distant cousins. But they were misguided family. They didn't seem to understand that the Quebec they were fighting against no longer existed. The province was already a decade into the Quiet Revolution — women had been liberated, the church had been put in its place, *pure laine* Quebeckers now occupied the seats of economic power. Violence was not needed to bring justice to the people. So why turn a wife into a widow and behave like desperate Third World freedom fighters when freedom had already been won?

Clustered around the coffee machine, the Quebec ministers shared accounts of developments in their ridings. One said rumours were spreading of other kidnappings and killings. Someone said he had heard the FLQ had enough dynamite to blow up downtown Montreal. Another said people in his constituency weren't going to work, schools were closing, and universities were cancelling classes. Another claimed people who had stopped going to mass were now flocking to church services to seek divine help. Yet another said the stock market was on a downward slide. The ministers who didn't speak French looked on with tight smiles, feeling excluded.

The prime minister came in, followed by the clerk of the Privy Council, and sat down. He was from a wealthy bilingual Francophone family, a man with a well-deserved reputation for intellectual rigor and honesty. He was also someone who wasn't afraid to take tough decisions. The day after he authorized the deployment of the army to help maintain order, journalists waylaid him entering his office and accused him of turning Canada into a police state. He stared them down, saying "there are a lot of bleeding hearts around who don't like to see people with helmets and guns. All I can say is go ahead and bleed. It's more important to keep law and order in society than to be worried about weak-kneed people who don't like the looks of a soldier with a helmet and a gun." When asked how far he was prepared to go — would he authorize wire-tapping and other restrictions on public liberties? — he replied, "Just watch me. Society must take every means at its disposal to defend itself against a parallel power which defies the authority of the elected representatives in this country."

The ministers took their places around the conference table, their assistants found theirs, and I sat behind Hankey. The prime minister started off by providing a briefing on the situation in Quebec as he saw it. "The premier and his Cabinet are in a state of panic," he said. "They're worried about their personal safety and that of that of their families. The top editorialists, the trade union and industrial leaders, the archbishops of Quebec and Montreal, the university presidents, and others of that ilk are saying the government has lost control of the situation. Incredible as it may be, these members of the elite are demanding the premier step aside in favour of a non-elected, self-appointed government of national emergency."

"And the stock market is falling, don't forget the stock market," a minister called out from the end of the table.

"Of course we must never forget the markets," the prime minister said. "But I'm mainly worried about public order and the confidence of the people in elected government. That's why I called you here today — to find a way to bring this to an end while keeping the public on side." He asked the RCMP commissioner to give a status report.

"I have bad and good news. The bad news is we have no leads in the hunt for the Che Guevara and Patriot cells. The murder of Minister Jolicoeur is an ominous signal. The Che Guevara cell can be expected to kill Peabody if their demands aren't met. The police can't control the crowds, hunt down the terrorist cells, and help the army protect politicians and public buildings at the same time. They're stretched too far. To make matters worse, thousands of separatists are out on the streets trying to profit from the public's fears by saying they are the only ones who can control the situation."

"And what's the good news?" asked the prime minister.

"The good news is the FLQ has the ability to cause a lot of fuss and bother but it in no way poses a threat to the democratic institutions of Quebec and Canada. It may take time, but we'll round them up and bring the crisis to an end."

Two of the Quebec ministers who had traded stories around the coffee machine before the meeting spoke up to dispute the commissioner's account. The minister who said he had heard rumours of more kidnappings and killings now said he knew for a fact such things were going on. The minister who just a few minutes before had said he "had heard the FLQ possessed enormous quantities of dynamite," now said someone "in a position to know" had told him the FLQ had placed cases of dynamite primed to explode at time of its choosing at strategic locations around the city.

"Is that true?" the prime minister asked the commissioner.

"With due respect to the ministers," the commissioner said, "those are unsubstantiated rumours."

"Then let's get back to business," the prime minister said. "I'd like to report that the American president called me to tell me to make an extra effort since Peabody was an old friend. I almost told him friendships should never be confused with national interests, but I didn't. He wouldn't have understood anyway, and I didn't want to make him even more agitated than he already was."

"What did you tell him?" Hankey asked.

"I said we were doing the best we could, but he didn't buy it. He even said we should just let the prisoners go to Cuba if that was all what it took. He didn't seem to understand how freeing prisoners could undermine law and order. He offered to send their hostage-rescue intervention team to Montreal to find Peabody. I didn't say no — although I wanted to — but thanked him for the offer and told him we'd let his people know in due course if it was needed."

Hankey provided his update. "The embassy in Washington has reported the American media are saying Canada isn't doing a good enough job in looking for Peabody. Apparently there was an editorial in the *Wall Street Journal* saying Canada was now an honorary member of the Third World, filled with anarchists and terrorists. It's even predicting our international credit rating will fall."

Several ministers said that if the stock market continued to fall, there would be factory closings, layoffs, and God knows what. The minister of defence proposed calling out more troops to help the police do their job. That was the cue for Garfield Whitcombe, the minister of public safety to say that sending in more troops wouldn't be good enough. "Cabinet should invoke the War Measures Act," he said. "My people have done some research and they tell me it hasn't been used since World War I. It's a draconian, martial law measure and bleeding hearts won't like it," he said, turning to look at the prime minister as he spoke. "But it would give the government the power to end the crisis once and for all."

"What powers are you talking about?" the prime minister asked.

"Under the act, we would have the authority to declare the FLQ a banned organization, to suspend *habeas corpus*, to arrest suspects without warrants, to deny them bail, to keep prisoners incommunicado, and so on. Interpreted liberally, it would let the police to conduct a massive roundup of separatists such as university students and their professors, and while they they're at it, poets, singers, and novelists. They're usually separatists anyway."

"There doesn't seem to be much balance in your proposal," the prime minister said.

"No there isn't. But there's nothing else on the books to deal with the unrest."

"In that case, let's go for it," the prime minister said. "It'll at least calm the public and make the Americans happy. And once the crisis is over, we'll restore democratic rights and freedoms and hopefully never have to treat the people that way again."

After Cabinet voted in favour of invoking the act, Whitcombe asked the ministers of defence, foreign affairs, and justice, their assistants, the RCMP commissioner, and Longstaff to remain behind to take part in a special meeting of the Cabinet Committee on Security and Intelligence.

"My advisers informed me a few days ago," Whitcombe said, after the others left the room, "that clearing the streets of demonstrators might not be enough. They told me we needed to able to compel FLQ members to talk, to tell us where Peabody is hidden. They said we couldn't allow them to hide behind the law. And I agree with them."

"I see where you are going with this," said the justice minister. "As a matter of fact, my advisers have mentioned to me you were thinking of bringing something like this forward. But I told them Canada isn't a Third World country that tortures detainees as a matter of course."

"I agree," Whitcombe said, "and we wouldn't do such a thing, even if we had the power to do so. But we need to close off all loopholes and take advantage of every opportunity that comes our way to hit back. For example, we have a list of FLQ members who are dual nationals — Canadian citizens born abroad and retaining the citizenship of their countries of origin. As we pick them up in the weeks ahead here in Montreal, we need to put them on planes and send them back to their homelands where the local police can question them on our behalf. They might unearth clues to help us in our search for Peabody."

"And will the War Measures Act authorize that?" Hankey asked.

"It will," said Whitcombe said. "Before the day is over, the FLQ will be declared a banned organization and the government will govern by fiat."

"I don't like it," said Hankey. Looking at me, he said, "I've been told me the security forces down there torture their prisoners."

"They probably do, but I'm told they get results. Would you rather we did the torturing ourselves?"

"Of course not," Hankey said. "But could RCMP use information derived from torture?"

"Now that's an interesting question. My legal people assure me that there's a loophole in the law. There's nothing in our jurisprudence to authorize it, but nothing to prevent us from doing so. My staff has prepared a draft directive from me to the law enforcement authorities which meets the letter, even if not the spirit of the law. I'd like to read out the relevant excerpt with you now. Please accept my apologies, Commissioner, for not showing it to you before this, but we've all been busy."

> In exceptional circumstances where there exists a threat to human life or public safety, urgent operational imperatives may require the Security Service to discharge its responsibility to share the most complete information available

at the time with relevant authorities, including information based on intelligence provided by foreign agencies that may have been derived from the use of torture or mistreatment. In such rare circumstances, it is understood that it may not always be possible to determine how a foreign agency obtained the information that may be relevant to the threat. It is also understood that ignoring such information solely because of its source would represent an unacceptable risk to public safety.

"I don't agree with this directive," Hankey said. "We need to think about the long-term implications. Claiming torture is acceptable because Canadians wouldn't be doing the torturing is pure expediency."

"Striking a blow against the FLQ and finding out where Peabody is hidden would be a win for the good guys," Whitcombe said.

"But accepting information derived from torture from a country that uses torture in its anti-terrorism programs means Canada's implicitly approves the practice and makes it legitimate. That would encourage countries to do more rather than less torturing. Wouldn't that be a win for the bad guys?"

"But haven't you just made the case that the good cancels out the bad? In circumstances like this, we should look at what serves our direct national interest."

"That's not true," Hankey said. "The bad far outweighs the good. I have it on good authority that South American countries are now torturing every suspected terrorist they pick up, innocent or guilty, and up and dumping their bodies into the sea. Canada should be putting pressure on them to stop such practices rather than sending them dual nationals to be tortured. "

"I have no problem with directive," said the commissioner.

"I bet you don't," said Hankey. "It gives you authority to do anything you want as long as the circumstances are exceptional, but then doesn't say what it means by exceptional circumstances other than mentioning that lives or property might be at risk. An action one person might consider legitimate protest in the view of the police might be considered a threat to lives and property and trigger the exceptional circumstances clause. But what do you think it means, commissioner? Jamaican Canadians protesting police brutality outside Toronto City Hall? Armenian Canadians upset with Turkey for the genocide of their people during World War I and disrupting traffic in downtown Toronto? Indians blocking a road to prevent clear-cut logging on their traditional hunting lands? A bomb in a mailbox? A bomb on a train, bus, or plane? Someone being held hostage? The threat to the life of one person? The RCMP makes its share of mistakes. Why should we put such power in your hands? You get to decide and you're not even an elected official."

Longshaft looked at me and smiled. We had had had the same discussion when I was interviewed in May 1966, and I wondered if it would turn out the same way.

"But my main problem with this draft directive lies elsewhere," Hankey said. "Approving it would mean Canada would have joined the torturers of the world. It would mean we have changed the Canadian way of life. It would mean we have decided to move from using the power of the state away from protecting rights and liberties of our people to becoming a threat to rights and liberties, and I want no part of it."

"We can trust the commissioner to do the right thing, Geoffrey," Whitcombe said. And when the others agreed, Hankey left the room and the motion was adopted.

I returned to the ninth floor to carry on with my responsibilities, ill at ease at how easy it had been for Canada to accept torture as a legitimate tool in the fight against international terrorism. The next morning, as soon as the War Measures Act and the torture directive went into effect, the police raided ten thousand homes without warrants, arrested five hundred separatists, threw them into jail but did not charge them with any crime, and imposed press censorship on the media. Calm returned to the streets. In short order, the police arrested the members of the Patriot cell — the three men and a woman who had kidnapped and murdered the minister of tourism. I knew what was coming when I learned the captured woman was a dual Canadian-Colombian citizen by the name of Gloria Sanchez — the government would send her to Colombia to be interrogated under torture. That had been the contingency Whitcombe had in mind when he obtained the approval of the Cabinet Committee on Security and Intelligence for his torture directive. What I hadn't expected was that I was to accompany her on the flight.

Longshaft didn't ask me to do it. He told me in a tone of voice indicating I had no choice. My role, he said, was to gain her confidence and persuade her to tell me where the consul general was hidden. If she complied, the pilot would abort the mission and return her to Montreal. If she didn't — too bad for her.

But I said, "She doesn't know where the Che Guevara cell and Peabody are holed up. You know that, and so does Whitcombe. She won't be able to tell me anything even if she wanted. Why don't you get someone else to do the job? It's just a public relations exercise to keep the Americans happy anyway."

Longshaft took his time before responding. "Everything you say is true … up to a point," he said in the soothing tone of voice of a father speaking to a rebellious teenage son. "But our decision to send Sanchez back to Colombia must be looked at in context. Don't you look at decision-making in context, Luc?"

"Of course I do," I muttered.

Longshaft's tone changed and he went after me with prosecutorial fervour. "And did you not tell the officers interviewing you for the position of Foreign Service officer in May 1966 that you put national security above human rights in the ordering of Canada's foreign policy priorities?"

"You were there, sir. I did."

"Do you still feel that way."

"I do, depending on the context."

"And what was your definition of national security at that time? Do you remember?"

"To safeguard the national territory of the state from foreign aggression and to defend its citizens against terrorism," I said, pulling the words from memory.

"And did you not tell that same interview board that that the use of torture to obtain information was acceptable if it would save a human life?"

"You're taking my words out of context. I said torture was acceptable if it saved a lot of lives."

"But you still support the use of torture in exceptional circumstances?"

"I did, but I'm no longer so sure after hearing Minister Hankey's views."

"The minister doesn't live in the real world. He hasn't woken up to the fact we live in a world where the existence of countries is threatened by international terrorism."

"That's not true," I said. The existence of countries is not at stake; their well-being is at stake."

"Don't quibble with me. Existence and well-being are almost the same thing."

"Maybe, but I still won't go."

"But when I hired you, I assumed you were a man of your word. I thought you were telling the truth when you said you put the fight against terrorism above human rights and accepted the use of torture to save lives in exceptional circumstances."

"With respect, sir, you're distorting my words."

"If you can find any errors in my description of your views, I invite you to do so."

Not wanting to prolong the inquisition, I said nothing.

"Now what I want you to understand," he said carrying on where he had left off, "is that you're not as smart as you think you are. It's quite possible Sanchez knows where Peabody is being held. The chances aren't high, but there's still a possibility. The only way we'll know for sure, to be 100 percent certain, is to let the Colombians question her. They'll torture her, of course, but we'll find out what she knows. What is not just a possibility, however, is that if we don't take this step, if we don't send her to Colombia, the Americans will make us pay. They are the big partner in the relationship and we are at their mercy."

In the end, I gave in and said I'd go. I did so partly because Longshaft had worn me down and I couldn't take any more of his hectoring. But I also wanted to meet Sanchez, to find what she was like as a person, to gain some insight into how someone who had come to Canada seeking a better life could turn against the country that had made her welcome.

"I thought you'd come around when I clarified the context," Longshaft said. "You push back and I like that. That's a sign of strong character, like the Métis soldiers in my battalion — the type of person with the mental toughness we need in our type of work. I was going to tell you later, but I'm sending you on a posting next summer to Washington as the bureau's representative to the CIA and the NSA. On your return, you'll work for me again on the ninth floor."

I should have been happy but I wasn't. Instead, I ignored his flattery and asked him to tell me how upright Canadian citizens could bring themselves to write a torture directive — something that ran contrary to all the principles Canada had defended so strongly at home and abroad since Confederation.

Longshaft didn't become angry and treated my question seriously.

"Have you ever heard of the Guardians?" he asked.

"I've heard rumours. It's a group of elite public servants who try to influence the politicians to adopt whatever consensus emerges from their discussions, isn't it?"

"The Guardians do more than try to influence the politicians, Luc. They almost always get their way, although the politicians don't realize it. What you must understand," he said, putting his arm around my shoulder and speaking in a conspiratorial tone, "is that there's always been a small coterie of people in Ottawa with the courage to break the moral code of the country to save the nation. And I'm proud to say I'm a member of that group. And if I have my way, you'll soon be invited to join. We need representation from the aboriginal world."

"I thought it was some sort of high-level lobby group."

"Nothing as vulgar as that. We deal with the really big and tough moral issues facing the country. If it wasn't for the Guardians, the regulations barring the entry of Jews into Canada before the war would never have come about, and the country would have been swamped with undesirables. The law expelling Japanese Canadians from their homes after Pearl Harbour would never have been passed, and Canada's war effort would have been exposed to sabotage. Going back a generation or two, the Guardians supported the head tax on Chinese migrants and the tough-love regulations directing the police to seize Indian children and send them to residential schools to educate them in the ways of the white man. "

Longshaft looked at me with a small cold smile after he made his last point, gauging what my reaction was to these outrageous revelations — especially on the residential school system — but I said nothing. I wanted to stick to the subject we were discussing.

"And so that's how the decision was taken to come up with the torture directive?"

"Exactly. Although the members prefer to call it the Exceptional Circumstances Directive. It emerged as an unspoken consensus as the politicians began to worry about the danger the FLQ posed to the country."

"Minister Hankey didn't seem to be part of your consensus."

"There's always someone who is out of step. I tried to talk sense to him ahead of time to let him know what was coming. But he didn't seem to understand what I was saying. He's in the wrong line of work."

"Maybe he reflects Canadian values better than his colleagues."

"I don't agree. Look at the enthusiastic reaction the directive has received by the press and public since it was announced. "

"Do you think the day will come when a Canadian minister of public safety will send a directive to the law enforcement authorities authorizing them to have the torturing done by Canadians in Canada rather than farming the job out to foreigners?"

"Not to handle crises like the current one. When the next really big terrorist attack occurs — and one will eventually come along, international terrorism is here to stay — the immigration minister will rush through legislation to strip dual national Canadians of their Canadian citizenship and expel them to their countries of origin on a massive scale. And Cabinet will direct the head of CSEC to launch a vast program of electronic spying on literally everyone. The know-how hasn't yet been developed, but the NSA, the CSEC, and their partners are working on it."

I had learned enough to become thoroughly frightened. I left and called the RCMP to get a plane to fly to Bogota. The officer in charge told me arrangements had already been made to fly Sanchez to Colombia that evening on a Canadian Forces transport. I was welcome to come along. The Colombian secret police, he said, had already confirmed their willingness "to process her" immediately on arrival. I thus sent a message to the Bogota embassy giving it my travel plans and asking it to reserve me a room close to the airport, and made ready to depart.

15: Return to Bogota

An unmarked car with an RCMP driver picked me up at the Daley Building that afternoon and drove me to Dorval Airport to wait for the arrival of Sanchez. It was already dark when we got there, and a dirty wind was blowing wet snow mixed with rain across the tarmac. Although I had seen shackled people before, it was still a shock to see her struggle out of the paddy wagon. With dark brown skin and pronounced Indian features, she looked more like a forlorn gamine, lost on a street in downtown Bogota, than a terrorist who had helped murder a hostage. I waited until the RCMP constable, who had come with her and who would hand her over to the Colombians, led her inside and removed her handcuffs. I took a seat beside her and the policeman sat at the back.

"You a cop?" she asked me in French, as the plane waited to take off.

Not wanting to explain why a Foreign Service officer was flying with her to Colombia and wanting to carry on in French, I said, "No, I'm not." and nothing else. I would tell her more about myself later if necessary.

"Where we going?"

"Didn't they tell you?"

"They said I was being sent to Colombia, but that makes no sense."

"You're being expelled to Colombia."

"And why's that?"

"Because you helped kill Minister Jolicoeur. Canada doesn't want you."

"I wasn't the only one. Besides, you can't do that. I know my rights. I'm a Canadian citizen."

"Not any more. The government has stripped you of your Canadian citizenship."

"That'd be illegal. It can't do things like that."

"The War Measures Act gives the government the authority to override normal laws to deal with people like you. It now rules by decree. The FLQ has been outlawed and its members are guilty of a crime."

"But I haven't been convicted of anything."

"You should've thought of that before you killed the minister."

"But the secret police will pick me up. I know what happens to people like me over there."

"So does the Canadian government. That's why it asked the Colombians to question you — to get you to say where Peabody is located before your friends in the Che Guevara cell kill him."

"But the secret police will torture me."

"The Canadian government is counting on that. The minister of public safety has even issued a directive to the commissioner of the RCMP to let it use any information the Colombians can force out of you."

"But I don't know where Peabody is held. I told the police that. The FLQ is divided into cells. Each cell is autonomous. The members know only the location of their own cell. That's for security reasons. Everybody knows that. It's to prevent the capture of one cell from rolling up the whole network. It's classic urban warfare technique. I thought I was being sent to a woman's prison somewhere in Canada. Now I find I'm being sent to my death. You believe me, don't you?"

"My opinion doesn't count. I just know that if you don't tell me where Peabody is, the policeman sitting over there will hand you over to the Colombians."

"This is a nightmare!"

"I'm sorry. It wasn't my decision."

Sanchez stopped talking and turned her face to the window and stared out. She was telling the truth but there was nothing I could do.

"Want a cigarette?" I said, holding one out to her.

"You're offering a condemned prisoner her last cigarette," she said and laughed. I laughed back and told her I believed her — that she didn't know where Peabody was hidden.

"Then why don't you tell the pilot turn this thing around and take me back to Montreal?"

"I could only do that if you told me where Peabody is hidden, but you don't know."

"Do you know *Waiting for Godot*?"

"You mean the absurdist play by Samuel Beckett — where no one shows up?"

"That's one way of looking at it?"

"What's your way?"

"It's about waiting for death."

"You sound like my wife."

"She sounds interesting. Where is she tonight?"

"I don't know. She left me."

"Why."

"Because I was a pain in the ass."

"There must be more to it than that."

"She was a nymphomaniac."

"Better than being a boring housewife."

"Not to me."

"Anyway, I'm waiting for Godot on this flight, even if I don't believe you when you say we're going to Bogota."

"We're really going to Bogota."

"I still don't believe you. You're just trying to scare me into talking when I haven't anything to tell you. You're going to fly me around in the dark even if I can't tell you anything. That's it, isn't it?"

"I wish that were the case."

"I still don't believe you. Why not turn back and let me go back to my cell?"

"I'm sorry."

After a while, she asked me where I picked up my accent.

"I'm a Métis from Ontario."

"Ah, a member of an oppressed people. You should be on our side."

"Why did you join the FLQ?"

"Can you give me another cigarette?"

"Sure. Now tell me why you started kidnapping people? Didn't you know the government would never surrender to your demands? That would just encourage terrorists to carry out more kidnappings."

"That's not what we thought. Brazil, Guatemala, and Paraguay let hostages go in exchange for political prisoners."

"Those governments now kill their prisoners, to discourage future kidnappings."

"How come you know that?"

"It's my job to know things like that."

"Oh, I see…"

"What led you to help kill another human being, someone who had a family?"

"It was hard not to like him. I had to keep reminding myself he was the enemy, and not a real person."

"Don't you feel guilty?"

"No."

"Why not?"

"Because I wasn't guilty of a crime. I was obeying a higher moral code — a code that allows me to kill for the greater good, permits me to ignore the moral limits ordinary people must follow, and compels me to kill to eradicate the evil in society and change the political consciousness of the people."

"That was a speech, not an answer."

"I know. It's what I had to tell myself before we killed him."

"Did you have time to get to know him? Did you eat with him?"

"I did. I had time to share meals with him, to get to know him. But our struggle is a war, and in a war, the rules of civilized behaviour don't apply," she said, beginning to cry.

"How could you help kill someone you broke bread with?"

She kept on sobbing and later, speaking softly, said, "On a human level, taking a life can never be justified. He was a family man, even if he was a representative of a repressive government. I can explain why we did it on a political and logical level, but reasons never equal justifications."

"What were your reasons?"

"We did it to make the English respect the Quebeckers. It was a question of pride and dignity."

"Surely you didn't kill someone just to be respected?"

"No, there was more to it than that. We wanted to provoke an uprising among the Quebec people, an uprising in the streets so huge it'd be like the French revolution, the Paris commune, and the 1917 revolution in Russia all rolled into one. It'd be so overwhelmingly mind-altering, the consciousness the people would forever change and an independent communist state of Quebec would emerge from the mix. There'd be another Cuba in the Americas."

"Do you really believe that? Sounds to me like a lot of unrealistic doctrinaire banalities."

"I truly do. Why else would I take such risks?"

"What about your parents? Do they want the same things?"

"No, they're self-satisfied bourgeois who bought into the phoney Canadian dream of multicultural bliss. They're deluded. Happy with their new lives in Canada."

"What made your family decide to come to Canada?"

"The usual — my parents were *campesinos* in the Llanos. Paramilitaries drove them out during the civil war and they ended up in a barrio in Bogota. My father worked at odd jobs but couldn't support the family and my mother had to do things on the streets I don't want to talk about. They wanted out and one of my mother's clients told her about Canada. All you had to do was buy a one-way ticket to Montreal and claim status as a political refugee fleeing persecution and they'd let you stay."

"What sort of job does your dad have?"

"He drives a taxi and my mother cleans offices. They live in Saint-Henri and watch the Montreal Canadians play the Toronto Maple Leafs on CBC on Saturday nights."

"Do you remember Colombia?"

"Of course. I was ten we came. I hated the barrio."

"Don't you feel Canadian?"

"No, I'm a Quebecker. My first language is French."

"Do you speak Spanish?"

"Yes, but only with my family, and we haven't seen each other for a long time — too many quarrels."

"Aren't you worried there'll be a backlash against all new Canadians for what you did? That people will think you can't be trusted — that you'd turn your backs on the country that gave you their citizenship?"

"Canada didn't give us citizenship because it loved us. That's the version of history they teach in school, but it's the capitalist version. The business oligarchs needed cheap labour to build the railroads, open the West, dig the mines, and fuel the capitalist industrial machine — to make them a lot of money. That's the way it was in the past, that's the way it's today, and that's the way it'll be until the people rise up in revolt and install a Cuban-style government. New Canadians don't owe anything to Canada."

"I don't think many new Canadians would agree."

"Why don't you ask them? Their answers might surprise you."

"Did you ask to see your parents after you were arrested?"

"No I didn't. I don't ever want to see them."

"Not even if you knew you were going to be handed over to the Colombians who will torture and kill you?"

"There you go again, trying to scare me. I know we're not on our way to Colombia. Where do they find guys like you? But for the sake of argument, to answer your real question, even if I knew I would be captured and sent to Colombia, I still would have participated in our revolutionary action. It's my way of sacrificing my life for oppressed people everywhere, not just in Quebec, but in Colombia and everywhere else in Latin America and Africa. And if you want to talk about values, what's worse? Killing one man, like that Quebec minister, to free a whole society, or sending someone to a country like Colombia to be tortured to save the life of a hostage?"

"I don't accept your premise that killing a minister will bring about a free society," I said. "Quebec and Canada are already free."

"You're just avoiding my question. You don't want to admit that freeing a whole society is a noble goal and sending someone off to be tortured reflects the workings of sick minds."

"I didn't make the decision to send you to Colombia."

"You mean like the Nazi death camp guards who said they were only obeying orders?"

"But I didn't kill Minister Jolicoeur. You're the one who has to accept the consequences for your actions."

"And so do you, if we're really going to Bogota."

"Would you like something to eat?" the steward asked her, interrupting our conversation.

"Do you have any red wine to go with the main course?"

"There's only one course and there's no wine. This is a military flight."

After dinner, Sanchez fell asleep, waking up six hours later. "You're not a cop are you?" she said.

"No, I'm a Foreign Service officer."

"What's that?"

"I work for the Department of External Affairs —in other countries they'd call it the foreign ministry."

"Why is a Foreign Service officer doing this and not a cop?"

"Because I wanted to give you a last chance to say where Peabody was before you're turned over to the Colombians."

"Are you a priest on the side?"

"No I told you. I'm a Foreign Service officer."

"What do Foreign Service officers do?"

"We staff embassies and high commissions abroad and work at pretty much everything when we're back in Ottawa."

"Where've you been?"

"A few months in Colombia and a few months in Cuba."

"Did you learn Spanish?"

"Yes I did."

"Why are you doing this to me?"

"I'm trying to save your life."

"I don't believe you. You're really just a cop disguised as a Foreign Service officer — and your plan isn't working. You can tell the pilot to turn this plane around and take me back to Montreal."

"But I'm a civilian. I didn't have to come on this trip. I could have left you in the hands of the police. But I wanted to talk sense to you."

"'I think you're lying."

"You're probably right. Maybe just a little. But I'm glad I came anyway."

"Why's that?"

"I've had the chance to meet you. I like you."

"Even if I've just killed someone?"

"Even if you'd just killed someone."

"You think you're funny."

"You think you have all the answers."

There was nothing more to say and I drifted off to sleep, to wake up with a start to the roar of the crowd chasing the gamine through the streets of downtown Bogota. It took a few seconds to realise it was just the noise of the plane's engines. I looked out the window to see the sun rising over the Andes. I thought of the dirty war being fought in the jungles below the clouds. I thought of Rojas and the discussion we had in the church and missed opportunities. I thought of the time, the week before, when I walked home late at night from the ninth floor, past the Parliament Buildings lit up in the full moon. Military helicopters were flying up the Ottawa River, bringing fresh troops into the besieged city. Soldiers stepped out of the shadows, rifles at the ready, demanding that I identify myself and explain what I am doing out alone so late at night. I could have been in Bogota … or Havana. I thought of what the future held in store for Sanchez.

The prime minister told Cabinet that once the crisis was over, the government would restore democratic rights and freedoms, and hopefully never have to treat its citizens in such an arbitrary way again. But he should have qualified his remarks by adding "until the next terrorist crisis comes along." When that crisis occurred, we would once again chase dehumanized enemies like gamines down the streets and embrace the suspension of rights and freedoms. A population under threat couldn't care less about torture directives. After all, people are as innately cruel as kind and loving, and history shows it doesn't take much to cut through the veneer of civilization to reach the depths below. But maybe Canadians would care if they knew why people became torturers.

There's no shortage of literature on the subject. Great writers like André Malraux, George Orwell, and Arthur Koestler saw torture through the eyes of torturer and victim. Some people use torture to extract information to save lives and protect property … as in Canada's own torture directive. Some do it to defend the nation and preserve family values. Some do it because other democratic counties like the United States, France, and Israel resort to it in their wars. Some do it because they think it's a short term expedient — a means to an end — the end being to safeguard a way of life, a way of life in which there'll be no need for future torture directives. That's what Garfield Whitcombe and his advisers think it's all about, but sometimes the end never comes and the means become the end.

The police say torture acts as a deterrent to terrorism. Psychologists say torturers are usually ordinary people who start by slapping around their victims, are rewarded by their peers for their actions, and eventually commit more acts of abuse. Torturers are also ordinary people who get a chance to play God, to dominate, to humiliate, to make suffer, to possess physically, to break spirits, to destroy identities, to look deep into souls, to search for the buried self, to rape, to make scream, to hear cries for mercy but to hit again and again until the tortured says anything, anything at all, incriminating friends, enemies, the local butcher, the priest, anyone at all to make the pain stop if only for a while as the police round up the incriminated to torture them until they give up useless information. Or maybe they just do it to have fun, to have some laughs.

I am certain the Canadian public would care if they knew these things. That's why the drafters of the torture directive took pains to say Canadians would not do the torturing themselves, nor would they encourage others to torture — although occasionally they might submit well considered questions to the foreign torturers to be sure they didn't waste time flogging some poor sod with a half-inch-thick flayed electrical cord for nothing. Or perhaps, if no one noticed — or if they noticed but didn't mind — they would watch the torturers at work from behind a one-way mirror as "interested observers," divorcing themselves from the screams and blood and guts in the best Canadian moralistic tradition as they waited for the answers.

Minister Hankey was right when he said adopting the torture directive would mean Canada had legitimized its practice and increased the sum total of evil in the world. I wondered if the minister of Public Safety and his advisers had given these considerations any thought. But if they had, I wonder if they really believed it was possible to separate using information from a torture victim, in vaguely defined exceptional circumstances, from the horror inflicted on another human being — guilty or innocent. I wonder if they knew that in making torture legitimate, they were introducing corrosive rot into the fabric of good old Canada, eroding its moral core and turning it into a country absent of honour, decency, and compassion.

I looked at Sanchez sleeping peacefully, a small smile on her lips, convinced that when she woke up the plane would be approaching Dorval Airport, the attempt to trick her into revealing Peabody's hidden locale abandoned. I now regretted cultivating such close relations with her. I had sullied the memory of Minister Jolicoeur. She had, after all, helped murder him. No, it was worse than murder. She had helped execute him. Murders were acts of emotion, revenge, greed, hatred, jealously, anger. But executions are carried out for cold, impersonal reasons of state or to serve ideological goals. They occupy a different and lower category of abomination.

At dawn, Sanchez woke up, smiled, and said good morning, still under the spell of our human contact. I said good morning, but in such a way she knew something had come between us while she slept. She told the steward she was hungry, but after he brought her breakfast, she saw the Andes from her window, and set her tray aside. The plane came down and circled Bogota in preparation for landing at El Dorado Airport. The skies were clear with scattered clouds. The Tequendama River, its waters black and filthy, flowed westward to the Tequendama Falls where it dumped the raw sewage of five million people into the pristine jungles below. Vast barrios spread like giant metastatic cancers into the forested slopes stretching off into the distance. On sidewalks in downtown Bogota good people beat gamines. In prisons and military caserns throughout the city owned by the devil, good family men tortured the guilty and innocent alike. Afterwards, they went home, ate their dinners and played with their children.

Sanchez was crying but I didn't offer her comfort. I had never believed she knew where Peabody was hidden. She would be tortured and killed for nothing. But Jolicoeur was also killed for nothing. The plane landed and taxied to an isolated part of runway where an unmarked van and the embassy car with Alfonso at the wheel was waiting. The secret police were outside when the steward opened door. They came in without comment and dragged her out, clubbing her with their open hands as a sign of what was to come. The RCMP constable looked shaken, out of his league, but he followed them outside. I waited until everyone was gone, then took my bag and greeted Alfonso, who neither said hello nor smiled. He drove me to a hotel and departed, still silent. The next morning, before I boarded the plane, I extended my hand to Alfonso, but he didn't take it.

The following day, I reported for work on the ninth floor and Longshaft came to see me. He asked me no questions about the flight, but glanced at my face and told me to take a few days off. I was at home watching television when a political commentator came on the air. As the national anthem played in the background, he said the Che Guevara cell had been located and Peabody was alive. A police negotiator was talking to the kidnappers. The kidnappers insisted they be flown to Cuba as a condition for freeing their prisoner. An hour later, I saw the cell members, their faces covered with red scarves, hustling Peabody to a car that sped off down the road escorted by police cruisers to Doral Airport.

I was elated. Sanchez had told the Colombians where Peabody was to be found! I was wrong when I thought she didn't know where he was hidden! She would live! I watched the car with the terrorists and their prisoner drive up to a Cubana plane on the tarmac and come to a halt. I saw Peabody emerge from the car, walk to a police car, and be driven away. The terrorists went up the ramp stairs to the top, turned around, held their right arms aloft with clenched fist Black Power salutes, and tore their masks off with their left hands. I recognized the FLQ members I met at the Riviera hotel in Havana.

I hurried to ninth floor to join the celebration in progress. Longshaft, his face ashen, came in and motioned for me to follow him to an adjoining office. Before he could speak, I said Sanchez had obviously told the Colombians where to find Peabody and would not die. Longshaft handed me a sheaf of intercepted messages from the headquarters of the Colombian secret police to its outlying stations, and walked out of the room. I read them with mounting revulsion and horror. They described the interrogation of Sanchez over a three-day period — beatings, rapes, electric shocks, and the disposal of her body over the sea. They would send a report to the RCMP and expected their Canadian friends to thank them for their fraternal collaboration. I broke down in tears because they also said Sanchez had never known where Peabody was being held. She had been telling the truth all along.

Epilogue

I went home to spend Christmas in Penetang and to think about what I wanted to do with the rest of my life. Although I didn't talk about my time on the Task Force, my family guessed that something had gone badly wrong and didn't bother me. Eventually, Grandpapa got me alone to find out what had happened. I said I had done unethical things in carrying out my duties and was ashamed of myself. Grandpapa didn't ask for the details but shook his head in disgust. "You've never been at ease in that diplomat job of yours in Ottawa," he said. "Maybe you were trying too hard to prove you were just as good as a white man. Just remember, no one appointed you spokesman for the Métis people. Just be yourself. That's all you need to be happy."

He didn't say anything else, but I understood what he meant. Corinne, who was working as a nurse in Midland, came for lunch on New Year's Day, and we were married as soon as my divorce from Heather came through. With Burump's help, I became an aid officer, and she accompanied me on my next posting to Dhaka, Bangladesh, where I worked in the development assistance section of the high commission. Although she took time off every time a baby came along, she always found work as nurse in our subsequent assignments in the newly independent countries of sub-Sahara Africa.

I never returned to the ninth floor, never found out if Longshaft continued sending junior diplomats to Canada's embassies in Latin America to report back to him on international terrorism, and, thankfully, was never invited to join the Guardians. I never got another promotion, but was rewarded in other ways. Helping street kids was one cause I adopted, and there were others. If it hadn't been for the nightmares, life would have been good.

As for Heather, I ran into her once in the Rideau Mall, on the other side of the street from where the Daley Building used to be before they tore it down to make room for a tower of condominium apartments. It was in the summer of 2001, not long after I had retired, and I was back in Ottawa getting ready to attend the annual get-together of the officers who had joined the Department in 1966. It was the first time I'd seen her since Cuba. We sat down over coffee and talked about the matters old friends, and people who aren't old friends and who haven't seen each other for years, are apt to discuss. She didn't comment on my bald head and I didn't tell her she looked years younger than she should have for someone her age. Neither of us referred to our time together in Colombia and Cuba.

"How's the family?" I asked, assuming she had one. She told me her family was well. She and her husband — they were both teachers — had retired and spent their summers at the lake and their winters at their condo in Florida, just like her parents used to do. Their children had grown up and left home, and, as a special treat, she had brought her grandchildren from Winnipeg to show them the sights in Canada's national capital.

"And how's your family?" she asked in return, assuming I had one since she had one. From the friendly but indifferent tone of her voice, I gathered she really didn't care. She just wanted to be polite. I told her I had been married for years and our kids had grown up and moved away. "Grandpapa and my parents passed away a long time ago," I added, "and my wife and I moved back to live in their house in Penetang after I retired."

We both got up to leave, exchanging addresses, saying we had to get together some day, we had to stay in touch, time went by so fast — all the empty formalities people say and do when they don't want to see each other again. She didn't ask about Bella before she left ... but that didn't surprise me. I then went off to the reunion, looking forward to seeing Dan O'Shea and Gregoire Harding again, and to hang out with individuals who had meant so much to me in that first wonderful summer in the Department before everything went wrong.

A Conversation with the Author

Tell me about your novel.

Exceptional Circumstances is primarily a tale of love, espionage, and intrigue. Luc Cadotte, the protagonist from Penetang, a small town on Georgian Bay, is at heart a decent person. He feels compassion for the poor and marginalized, but he is anxious to prove a Métis can do as well in the world of diplomacy as any white person and allows ambition get the better of him. He leaves his home to attend the University of Ottawa, and on graduation joins the prestigious Department of External Affairs. He serves in Colombia and Cuba from 1968 to 1970 and in Ottawa as a member of the Task Force on International Terrorism managing the FLQ crisis of October 1970. He makes friends with one of Latin America's most charismatic guerrilla leaders, a defrocked Colombian priest, but inadvertently betrays him to the CIA. He befriends a FLQ terrorist involved in the kidnapping and murder of a Quebec government minister, but delivers her into the hands of the Colombian secret police to be tortured and questioned. In the end, he seeks and finds redemption.

But my novel is more than a stand-alone adventure story. For those who wish to dig deeper — using this section as a guide

— it also represents the post 9/11 world of diminished civil liberties. Luc becomes Everyman in a mediaeval morality play — a mixture of good and bad striving to affirm his identity, to advance his career, and to find the right wife. In his professional life, he interacts with characters that see no evil or see no good, are cold war warriors, are out to save the world, are tormented politicians, are fanatical ideologues, or are crass egoists with bloody hands. In his social life, he meets three women, the first is sweet and lovable, the second is a social-climber, and the third is a nymphomaniac. Throughout, he discusses with his fellow characters the pros and cons of some of the great ethical questions of the post-9/11 world as they affect all Canadians.

Why did you make the October Crisis the centre of action of the novel? The crisis occurred more than forty-five years ago.

The action builds up through parts one to three to the climax in part four that focuses on the Crisis of 1970. I then use my prerogative as a novelist to alter the actual October Crisis with two key fictional changes (and several inconsequential ones such as changing the names of the FLQ cells and the murdered minister) to look at how that crisis would have turned out if the Canadian government had had at its disposal the powers it acquired in the post-9/11 world. In the first fictional change, the terrorists kidnap the American consul general in Montreal rather than the British trade commissioner; in the second change, the police possess the authority to use information, *in exceptional circumstances,* obtained through torture to help its investigation as long as the torture is not carried out in Canada — an authority the director of CSIS now possesses.

I move on to address the following questions as the story unfolds. What if the American government insisted that Canada accede to a demand to exchange FLQ prisoners in jail for the life of the American consul general? What if the police captured a FLQ militant who was a dual citizen? What if the RCMP, either through malice, incompetence, or design, sent that citizen back to the country of her birth to be tortured and questioned?

In the fictional version of the October Crisis, the United States puts pressure on Canada to send Sanchez back to Colombia to be interrogated under pressure to reveal the location of the kidnapped American consul general. To many people, this scenario is simply too incredible to be believed, even in a novel. In their view, the United States is the champion of liberty and democracy around the world and would never ask a close ally to do such thing.

Perhaps the United States of the 1970s would not have, but post-9/11, the United States lost its moral compass. Remember Abu Ghraib prison in Iraq where prisoners were tortured and murdered? The secret black sites around the world where prisoners were taken to be tortured and to be "disappeared"? The secret renditions and the ongoing blight of Guantanamo? This egregious behavior has been documented in the 600-page summary of an exhaustive report by the Senate Intelligence Committee on the counterterrorism activities of the CIA. Even President Obama has admitted the CIA tortured prisoners post-9/11.

The CIA has maintained that its use of "enhanced interrogation techniques" were needed to deal with the threat to the United States by terrorists in the post-9/11 world. What is the truth?

The Senate Intelligence Committee concluded that the use of torture failed to provide any significant information to the CIA.

Why did you pick a dual-national Canadian, someone who immigrated to Canada with her parents at the age of ten, to play the role of international terrorist?

The Canada of today is multicultural with growing numbers of new Canadians coming from areas of instability and conflict. The first generation are dual nationals like the fictional Sanchez. Others are second-generation, born in Canada unhyphenated Canadians. The overwhelming majority of first- and second-generation Canadians are model citizens, but well over a hundred have left Canada to join terrorist organizations like Al-Qaeda and the Tamil Tigers and travel abroad to fight in places like Syria, Algeria, Somalia, and Afghanistan. There is nothing unusual per se about Canadians volunteering to fight in foreign wars. Thousands signed up on the Union side in the American Civil War, a battalion was raised in Canada to fight on the government's side in the Spanish Civil War and an unknown number enlisted in the American armed forces during the Vietnam war.

The concern today is that Canadians going abroad to fight with Jihadists might come home to attack targets in Canada. To deal with the problem, in June 2014, Parliament approved Bill C-24 (Amendments to the Citizenship Act) authorizing the government to strip Canadian citizenship of dual citizens (naturalized or by birth) for specified terrorist/security/treason grounds. And it isn't just deportation to countries of birth. It also applies to Canadian-born dual nationals who have a second nationality for some reason other than birth: i.e. parent's nationality, spouse, etc. It is the first time ever in Canadian law that there is a possibility for a Canadian-born citizen to lose Canadian citizenship. And the first time ever that any Canadian citizen can lose citizenship on grounds other than fraud.

The issues are among the most difficult faced by Canada since it became a country and merit more debate than they have received. I thus wanted Luc to sit beside Sanchez on the long ride to Bogota and ask her how it was possible for someone to seek to destroy the country which had welcomed her and given her a Canadian passport. I also wanted Luc to explore the moral implications of sending someone back to their home country when it is reasonable to believe that person would be tortured. What does that do to the moral compass of a country and its citizens?

Gloria Sanchez is a fictional Canadian-Colombian national sent back in a fictional account to her home country to be questioned under torture. In real life, has anything similar been done by Canadian law enforcement authorities?

Yes. In September 2002, the U.S. Border Service detained a dual Canadian citizen born in Syria, Maher Arar, between flights at John F. Kennedy Airport in New York. Acting on erroneous information supplied to it by the RCMP — whether by design, malice, or incompetence is not known — the Americans sent him to his country of birth to be interrogated under torture to determine if he was a member of Al-Qaeda. Following a public outcry, the Canadian government made representations to the Syrian government seeking his release. Almost a year after his imprisonment, and ongoing torture, he was allowed to return to Canada.

Have there been cases of other dual-national Canadians tortured abroad by their countries of birth on the basis of information provided by Canadian officials?

Yes. According to Amnesty International, Abdullah Almalki, a Canadian citizen born in Syria, was arrested, jailed, and tortured on the basis of erroneous information provided by Canadian officials. Abdullah's case was examined in a judicial inquiry along with two other cases of Canadian citizens tortured abroad with Canadian complicity: Ahmad Abou El-Maati (tortured in Syria and Egypt) and Muayyed Nureddin (tortured in Syria). The inquiry was headed by former Supreme Court Justice Frank Iacobucci. His report, in October 2008, enumerated numerous ways that Canadian action and inaction had contributed to their torture and other human rights violations. The government neither apologized nor offered redress as they did for Maher Arar.

Could such a thing happen again?

In my view, it could. The government has even provided a fig leaf of legitimacy to such practices. For example, on June 25, 2010, the government circulated to interested departments and agencies a "Framework for Addressing Risks of Mistreatment in Sharing Information with Foreign Entities." Mistreatment is defined in the document as "torture or cruel, inhumane or degrading treatment or punishment." It condemns the use of torture "by any foreign entity for any purpose," spells out Canada's binding international obligations to prevent the use of torture in any circumstance *but then authorizes deputy ministers and agency heads to violate these principles in exceptional circumstances.* Finally, it directs ministers "to operationalize," i.e. draw up their own individual torture directives to suit the specific needs and mandates of their departments and agencies.

The following is the relevant excerpt from the directive sent to the director of CSIS by the minister of public safety on December 10, 2010. Note: The ministerial guidance works in both directions. In addition to being allowed to use information obtained through torture from foreign agencies, CSIS is also authorized to share information with foreign agencies, in exceptional circumstances, even if likely to lead to torture abroad.

The first and foremost responsibility of the state and its government is protecting its citizens. The current threat environment and the number one national security priority of the government of Canada has been, and will remain for the foreseeable future, the fight against international terrorism. In this context, it is critical that information be shared quickly and widely among those with the mandate and responsibility to disrupt serious threats before they materialize.

The government of Canada relies on CSIS to provide security intelligence to various federal partners, and other key stakeholders such as provincial and municipal authorities, in order to assist with protecting national security and public safety. The service is expected to work in unique circumstances, and occasionally with international agencies that do not respect Canada's commitment to human rights. The CSIS must nevertheless always ensure that its actions do not appear to condone the torture or mistreatment of any individual, and that its interactions with foreign agencies accord with this principle.

In exceptional circumstances where there exists a threat to human life or public safety, urgent operational imperatives may require the Service to discharge its responsibility to share the most complete information available at the time with relevant authorities, including information based on intelligence provided by foreign agencies that may have been derived from the use of torture or mistreatment. In such rare circumstances, it is understood that it may not always be possible to determine how a foreign agency obtained the information that may be relevant to the threat. It is also understood that ignoring such information solely because of its source would represent an unacceptable risk to public safety [emphasis added].

Therefore, in situations where a serious risk to public safety exists, I expect and thus direct the Service to make the protection of life and property its overriding priority, and share the information, properly described and qualified, with appropriate authorities.

The RCMP, CSEC and the Canadian Forces among others, have either drawn up or are in the process of drawing up similar directives to share information tainted by torture.

In your opinion, does the government's decision to traffic in information derived through torture affect the balance between national security and personal liberties?

I leave it the readers to make up their own minds. The United Nations, Amnesty International, and the press have made up theirs. The United Nations Committee against Torture writes: "The committee expresses its serious concern about the ministerial direction to the Canadian Security Intelligence Service (CSIS) which could result in violations of article 15 of the Convention against Torture in the sense that it allows intelligence information that may have been derived through mistreatment by foreign states to be used within Canada; and allows CSIS to share information with foreign agencies even when doing so poses a serious risk of torture, in exceptional cases involving threats to public safety...."

The *Toronto Star* says, "As the notorious case of Maher Arar demonstrated, Canada's police and spy services have been burnt before when they red-flagged our citizens as persons of concern to other countries' security agencies. Arar was detained in the United States on the basis of inaccurate information from Canadian police linking him to terrorists and was bundled off to Syria where he was tortured."

And Amnesty International Canada has written to the government to make the following points: Under international human rights law, torture is never permitted; the ministerial direction violates Canada's obligations as a signatory to the Convention Against Torture; article 15 of the UN Convention Against Torture specifically prohibits the use of information derived through torture as evidence in any proceeding; the government's actions "disregard and undermine the findings and recommendations" of the inquiries into the Arar, Almalki, Nureddin, and El-Maati cases.

Does Canada really intercept and collect military and diplomatic communications of other countries?

Yes it does — as do most technologically advanced countries. Canada avowed for the first time the existence of the Communications Security Establishment Canada (CSEC) in testimony given to a Senate Committee examining Canada's security and intelligence community in testimony on September 22, 1983, by minister of State for External Relations, the late Jean-Luc Pepin. Pepin told the senate that the mandate of the CSEC was "to provide to the government ... in support of Canada's foreign and defence policies ... information gathered about foreign countries by intercepting and studying their radio, radar and other electronic transmissions." He also revealed that CSEC worked closely with the NSA, the giant American National Security Agency based in Fort Meade, Maryland; the GCHQ, the British Communications Headquarters in England; and the smaller intercept agencies of Australia and New Zealand. He confirmed that the partnership dated back to the post–World War II era and was commonly known as "The Five Eyes." This information is now publicly available. In the intervening years, much more information on the operations of CSEC has become available on the internet.

Longshaft mentions to Luc that following the next major terrorist incident, the prime minister would authorize CSEC to launch a vast program of electronic spying on literally everyone in the country. Please comment.

That has happened. In the wake of 9/11, the NSA launched a program of mass surveillance of people, sweeping up the emails, telephone calls, and Skype conversations of millions of people every day around the world that in some respects went beyond the excesses depicted in Orwell's *1984*. As confirmed by Edward Snowdon, the American whistleblower, CSEC (and the other Five Eyes partners) enthusiastically joined in the effort. CSEC has admitted that it collects metadata on randomly selected Canadians. The spy agency insists that its actions are lawful. The question is, however, whether the law itself violates the rights and freedoms of Canadians. In some quarters, such as among younger Canadians, digitally active Canadians and civil liberties groups, there has been strong outrage leading to court challenges.

In your novel you refer only to the RCMP and not to the Canadian Security Intelligence or CSIS. Why is that?

In the period 1966 to 1970, when the major developments in the novel take place, the RCMP Security Service, a top-secret branch of the RCMP, was responsible for dealing with threats to national security, including terrorism. In the aftermath of the October Crisis, the RCMP Security Service was involved in a number of scandals in which the rights and liberties of Canadians were violated. Accordingly, in 1994, the government disbanded the RCMP Security Service and transferred its responsibilities to a newly created civilian agency called CSIS. The counter-terrorism approaches of the two organizations, however, continued to overlap with the RCMP viewing the phenomenon from a law-enforcement perspective and CSIS from a preventative viewpoint. Rivalry and friction between the two agencies has impeded the fight against terrorism over the years.

You were the analyst for International Terrorism in the bureau of Security and Intelligence in the Department of External Affairs in the fall of 1970. Did you participate in the Interdepartmental Task Force managing the October Crisis?

Yes, in a junior capacity. The background is as follows. During my posting to Colombia in the late 1960s, a NGO with Canadian connections, called Miles for Millions, asked me officiate at the opening of one of its feeding stations providing food to poor rural *campesinos* in a remote region. Because the feeding stations were located deep inside rebel-held territory, I travelled by Colombian army helicopter, protected by a soldier who cradled a machine gun in his arms while his legs dangled from an open door as he scanned the terrain below, to a small hilltop landing strip. Unsmiling, heavily armed soldiers greeted me as I scrambled out, and marched me to the kitchen. A crowd of former rebels who had turned themselves in under an amnesty program waited patiently with their families for me to cut a ribbon and make a speech before they could eat their meal of roast pork and black beans.

The visit piqued my interest in Third World revolutionary movements. When I was posted back to headquarters in February 1970, I became the analyst for international terrorism in the Department's Intelligence Analysis Division. As such, I prepared the assessments for the Task Force managing the October Crisis and filled in as a staff officer backing up the senior officers making the decisions. Later on, I was a member of the interdepartmental committee managing the creation of CSIS out of the RCMP Security Service.

Did you encounter gamines during your posting to Bogota?

Yes, almost every day. I would see them wandering the streets at all hours of the day and night, hungry and ragged with no place to go for help. It was heartbreaking to see them sleeping under old newspapers on the steps to the embassy and nearby office buildings in the cold and drizzle of Bogota's mornings. Some of the little boys and girls were as young as four or five. Some were children put on a bus in some remote part of Colombia and told a relative would be waiting for them when they reached Bogota. All too often there was nobody at the bus terminal to meet them. Others were children from the barrios, abandoned by parents who couldn't feed them. Another wretched scene, one I included in the novel, was the sight of mobs of people chasing and beating gamines along the sidewalk outside the embassy for snatching watches or picking pockets.

Is Diego Rojas an actual historical figure? Was he a defrocked Colombian priest who took up arms, and joined the ELN? Was he killed in a battle with government soldiers?

Diego Rojas is loosely based on Camilo Torres, a charismatic, defrocked Colombian priest and exponent of Liberation Theology who joined the ELN and was killed during an attack on an army patrol in February 1966. I first heard of Torres when I was posted to Canada's embassy in Bogota as a junior officer in February 1968. Many of my friends were Colombian university students and young professionals. They mourned the loss of someone they believed could have brought justice to their country.

Is Rosario Lopez an actual historical figure?

No she isn't. I based her character on a middle-aged, soberly dressed woman wearing small silver cross who called on me at the embassy. She was a former nun who had left the church to devote her life to running a shelter for gamines. "Did the embassy have aid funds I could give her?" she asked. Although, I couldn't help her, I visited the shelter several times to talk to her about conditions in the barrios. It turned out she had been a friend of Torres and provided some of the information I used in the novel.

Do the Guardians exist? Are they a figment of your imagination?

The Guardians never existed as an organization. In the novel they represent the public service elite, in the small world of Ottawa, far from the major population centres elsewhere in Canada, who for generations, socialized together and met together in interdepartmental committees to prepare advice to governments, to prepare legislation, and to draft enacting regulations.

The elite of the elite were often called the Mandarins. Altogether, they provided a quality of selfless, non-partisan service to governments and to the people of Canada that was the envy of the world. But did any of the Mandarins ever say no when asked to prepare laws, orders-in-council and regulations to direct the RCMP to take by force if necessary the children of Indians and send them to residential schools, to impose a head tax on Chinese immigrants, to bar Jewish children fleeing Nazi Germany from entering Canada, to herd the entire Japanese-Canadian population of British Columbia into concentration camps after Pearl Harbour, or to draft torture directives authorizing CSIS, the RCMP and CSEC to use information derived from torture in Canada's anti-terrorism efforts post 9/11?

With rare exceptions, that would not appear to have been the case. It could be argued that the responsibility for these actions should be borne only by the elected representatives of the people. But we should ask ourselves whether the politicians could have devised and these abhorrent policies by themselves?

Did CUSO run a program in Colombia when you were posted in Colombia?

Yes. There was no Heather, but I became friends with a number of CUSO volunteers as well as with others from Sweden and elsewhere. The farewell party for the fictional Charles Bullock in Chapter 7 is based on a party I attended as a guest of a Swedish volunteer. I'll never forget the bitterness of a member of the Peace Corps who said his tour in Colombia was ending and he now faced the prospect of fighting in Vietnam or going into exile in Canada. He wasn't happy with either option and I felt sorry for him.

Did Canada send a diplomat to spy for the CIA at its embassy in Havana?

Yes, as strange as that might appear. The request was made by the American government with the knowledge of President Kennedy. In the context of the missile crisis, which came perilously close to igniting a nuclear war, the Canadian government's decision to support CIA monitoring of Soviet military equipment and movements in Cuba made a great deal of sense. John Graham, a retired Foreign Service officer, describes in his memoirs his adventures as a spy for the CIA in Cuba in the 1960s. (His book, *Whose man in Havana? Adventures from the Far Side* will be published soon.)

In my novel, Luc is not based on John and the incidents described never took place. By the time the Canadian government appointed me ambassador to Cuba in August 1981, Canada was no longer sending officers to Cuba with an Intelligence gathering mission.

Did MININT try to blackmail you when you were ambassador in Havana?

Yes indeed. I received three separate telephone calls in the first week in Cuba trying to suborn me. The first was from a woman who said she had seen me at some function or other and she thought I was ever-so-handsome. She wanted to meet me, she said. She would make sure no one would tell my wife. I hung up. The second was from someone who said he had a large quantity of gold left behind by a rich Cuban family that had fled the country after Castro took over. He had no way of taking the gold out of the country. Would I like to buy his gold? If so, he would give me an address where I could meet him to carry out the transaction. I hung up the telephone. The third attempt was from a man. He had seen me somewhere and thought I was ever-so-handsome as well. I hung up before he could finish his pitch and asked the maid to filter all subsequent calls. If I had responded positively to any of these propositions, MININT would have taken pictures and tried to force me to work for them.

Did MININT play dirty tricks on you — tricks similar to the ones dealt out to Luc?

They did and it was a devastating experience for my entire family. One day, my wife and I woke up to discover that someone had poisoned, Zaka, our beloved dog who had accompanied us from Canada. We rushed her to a nearby veterinarian who pumped out her stomach and gave us medicine to bring her back to health. However, to the great distress of all members of our family, she began to deteriorate and we had to ship her back to Canada to live with my parents and receive care from a local veterinarian. She never recovered and died six months later.

We returned home from the veterinarian to find telephone call after telephone call coming in, each with a message of hate and filth. My deputy came rushing in to say someone had poisoned his dog and it was now dead. The head of the commercial office came to say someone had nailed a dead rat to his door. The senior clerk came to report that all members of the Canadian staff were receiving threatening phone calls and that the Cubans working for the embassy had walked off the jobs. I went to the Foreign Ministry to protest. By the time I got home, the telephone calls had stopped, the Cuban employees had returned to work and a veterinarian sent by the Foreign Ministry was inside examining Zaka. We never found out why the Cubans targeted us. A week later, Fidel Castro came to dinner, but neither of us mentioned the incident. And in the time remaining in my posting, I could hardly wait to leave Cuba for good.

Did you personally witness the elaborate security measures MININT took to protect the life of President Castro?

President Castro often came to dinner at the official residence when I was ambassador to Cuba. His office rarely confirmed his acceptance of invitations before he appeared at our door, but several hours before his arrival, MININT troops would seal off the neighbourhood, plainclothes guards would take up positions in the garden, technicians would install new telephone lines, a doctor would set up shop in a bedroom and a MININT food taster would take up a position in the kitchen to watch the preparation of dinner and to sample all dishes destined for the president. Then exactly on time, the president would roll up to the front door in his big, black, bullet-proof Soviet Zil limousine, leave his personal Uzi pistol machine gun on the back seat, and come in to dinner wearing a bullet-proof vest under his well-pressed shirt.

In your novel you mention a Chinese Head Tax. What was that?

Responding to public pressure to control the entry of Chinese people to Canada, Parliament in 1875 imposed a tax on most Chinese immigrants that was so high it discouraged wives and children from accompanying their men to Canada. The tax remained in force until 1947. On June 22, 2006, the Canadian government apologized and offered compensation to survivors.

Did influential public servants really play a key role in the Canadian government's decision to turn Jews fleeing the Nazis away from its borders?

In *None is Too Many: Canada and the Jews of Europe 1933–1948*, Irving Abella and Harold Tropes describe how anti-Semitic senior officials of key departments including External Affairs and Immigration, and even members of the clergy, played a role in devising and executing policies that systematically excluded Jews as immigrants and refugees to Canada.

James Bartleman

Will your novel, other books of a similar nature, press reports, editorial comment, and parliamentary debate hinder the ability of Canada's security agencies to safeguard the safety of Canadians in a period of ongoing international terrorism?

Anything that promotes greater public understanding of issues affecting the rights and freedoms of Canadians is in the public interest, and ultimately in the interest of Canada's security agencies.

Acknowledgements

I should like to thank those who provided advice and encouragement, first of all to my wife Marie-Jeanne, and son, Alain Bartleman, for their critique of the first draft. Thanks as well to Patrick Boyer of Blue Butterfly press and Kirk Howard of Dundurn who accepted the concept and manuscript. Thanks to the staff at Dundurn especially to Michael Melgaard, my editor. Thanks in particular to Alex Neve, Secretary General of Amnesty International (English branch), who read the manuscript on the long flight to Juba, South Sudan, and offered authoritative comments on the Conversation with the Author section. Thanks to Penny Collenette from the University of Ottawa law faculty and to Dr. Brian Osbourne, Professor Emeritus Queens University, for their encouragement, and to John Graham, Pierre Beemans, and Ed Gorn, who made helpful suggestions. John served in the Department in many countries, including the Dominican Republic, Cuba, London, and Venezuela. I met him when he was high commissioner to Guyana in the early 1980s and I was director for the Central American and Commonwealth division. Pierre and I became friends when he was CUSO coordinator in Bogota and I was second secretary at the Canadian embassy in the late 1960s. Ed and I met when we joined the Department in the mid-1960s and have stayed in touch over the years.

Finally, any resemblance the characters may have to individuals, living or dead is entirely coincidental as are the incidents described in the book to real events, unless otherwise identified and qualified in the Conversation with the Author section.

Also by James Bartleman

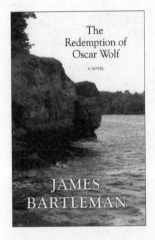

The Redemption of Oscar Wolf

In the early 1930s, Oscar Wolf, a 13-year-old Native from the Chippewas of Rama Indian Reserve, sets fire to the business section of his village north of Toronto in a fit of misguided rage against white society, inadvertently killing his grandfather and a young maid. Tortured by guilt and fearful of divine retribution, Oscar sets out on a lifetime quest for redemption.

His journey takes him to California where he works as a fruit picker and prizefighter during the Great Depression, to the Second World War where he becomes a decorated soldier, to university where he excels as a student and athlete, and to the diplomatic service in the postwar era where he causes a stir at the United Nations in New York and in Colombia and Australia.

Beset by an all-too-human knack for making doubtful choices, Oscar discovers that peace of mind is indeed hard to find in this saga of mid-20th-century aboriginal life in Canada and abroad that will appeal to readers of all backgrounds and ages.

Also Available from Dundurn

The Fire Thief
by Stephen Guppy

Set in the 1960s, *The Fire Thief* is the story of Sonny Wheeler, who grew up in a time of '50s conformity that exploded into revolution, protest, and days of rage for many of his generation. When his mother remarries, teenaged Sonny moves with his new family to Danforth, Washington, a city that exists solely because of the nuclear power plant humming at its core.

This is the Cold War at its height: his stepfather is a nuclear engineer, his home is visited every month by FBI agents looking for Soviet spies, and the daughter of high school science teacher is named Marie Curie. Sonny's only connection to the world outside this stifling city is his wild Aunt Alice, a lounge club singer who rejects all of the social norms of the age. Having fallen in love with the angst-ridden Karen, Sonny follows her descent into radicalism and joins the Weathermen, a revolutionary group dedicated to the overthrow of the state and the atomic utopia their parents had created. After staging the theft of plutonium from the nuclear plant, Sonny is forced to go on the run and seeks refuge in Las Vegas with his dying Aunt Alice. Having accidentally fathered a child, Sonny is torn between caring for his son and coming to terms with his own fatherless childhood. As he hides from the authorities and the effects of his drug use begin to catch up with him, Sonny Wheeler becomes a man searching for his moment of redemption.

Amidst startling imagery of a landscape littered with the effects of a nuclear age, Stephen Guppy presents us with the lonely ballad of a man trying to find his place in an increasingly confusing world. *The Fire Thief* is a thought-provoking novel of redemption about the bonds of family, the perils of radical politics, and the price of love.

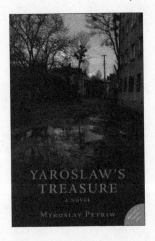

Yaroslaw's Treasure
by Myroslav Petriw

On a visit to Ukraine to retrieve a family heirloom secretly buried by his grandfather during the Second World War, Yaroslaw, a Ukrainian-Canadian university student, stumbles into a world full of spies and secret organizations, peril and political intrigue.

His discovery of the hidden cache yields clues to the location of a fabled lost treasure-the greatest in all Europe. Working against time, Yaroslaw and a small band of accomplices struggle to uncover and save a nation's heritage, operating in secret to prevent the corrupt leaders of the government and the Russians-from stealing it.

Yaroslaw's Treasure is a thrilling suspense story set against the gripping drama of the Orange Revolution, the 2004 popular uprising that saw hundreds of thousands of people take to the streets in Ukraine to overthrow a corrupt government and reinforce democracy in a land long occupied by repressive and foreign regimes.

Rich with history, romance, politics, and danger, *Yaroslaw's Treasure* superbly captures the wonders and horrors of Ukraine's past, swirls through the treacherous currents of its present politics, all the while providing entertainment as a first-rate thriller.

Available at your favourite bookseller

DUNDURN

VISIT US AT
Dundurn.com
@dundurnpress
Facebook.com/dundurnpress
Pinterest.com/dundurnpress